What the critics are saying

"The three writers have created stories that arouse, excite, and satisfy the desire for wishes to come true. I look forward to the next collection of tales." - *Sharon Bressen, Sensual Romance Reviews*

"Ms. Burke, Ms. Chance, and Ms. Wylde create stories that are deliciously erotic. Their heroes are gorgeous, sexy men who desire only their heroines. I thoroughly enjoyed each story in the WICKED WISHES anthology and would like to see another trio of stories from these very talented, naughty ladies." - *Michelle Gann, The Word On Romance*

D0971084

Discover for yourself why readers can't get enough of the multiple-award-winning publisher Ellora's Cave. Whether you prefer e-books or paperbacks, be sure to visit EC on the web at www.ellorascave.com for an erotic reading experience that will leave you breathless.

www.ellorascave.com

Ellora's Cave Publishing, Inc.
PO Box 787
Hudson, OH 44236-0787

ISBN # 184360406X

Wicked Wishes, 2002.
ALL RIGHTS RESERVED
Ellora's Cave Publishing, Inc.
© Craven's Downfall, Stephanie Burke, 2002.
© A Wish Away, Marly Chance, 2002.
© Serendipity, Joanna Wylde, 2002.

This book may not be reproduced in whole or in part
without author and publisher permission.

Wicked Wishes edited by Martha Punches.
Cover art by Scott Carpenter.

Warning: The following material contains strong sexual
content meant for mature readers. *WICKED WISHES* has
been rated Hard R and NC17, erotic, by a minimum of
three independent reviewers. We strongly suggest storing
this book in a place where young readers not meant to
view it are unlikely to happen upon it. That said, enjoy…

WICKED WISHES

CRAVEN'S DOWNFALL

Written by

STEPHANIE BURKE

This one is for my Middle Eastern Scottish Princess, a beautiful person, a brilliant soon to be doctor, a wonderful daughter, a sincere friend, and a total woman. Heads up, Gul Afroze! When you weren't looking, someone went and dumped perfection on you! Remember that when you take your exams, when you wade through the marriage proposals, and when your take your place in the world, complete, whole, triumphant, woman.

Chapter One

He looked over the mass of writhing bodies that surrounded his chair and sighed with boredom. There was nothing new going on. Same old sucking, same old fucking. No matter how you looked at it, the beings here were just going through the motions. Was there any pure lust left in the world?

He looked out over the toys scattered around the chamber, and felt, well, jaded.

The leather whips looked like so much show; the dildos of varying sizes were just large doorstops. The people were...well, they were kind of fun to look at, but they lacked something.

Tapping one long black nail against his right fang, he contemplated the group before him.

Orgies had become rather boring of late.

He looked down at the naked female, lips wrapped around the head of his penis, and sighed. This was *not* good. If her suction of a mouth, a suction that was so strong she could probably suck the brass off of a doorknob, couldn't get a rise out of him, he needed help.

"Thank you, lover," he purred as he tangled his hands in her long red hair. "But this just isn't working. I think I am...bored with you." He made a shooing motion with both hands, ignoring her shocked and hurt face. "Run along now. I'm sure someone will appreciate your obvious talents, but that person isn't me."

Turning his back on her stricken face, he stumbled over a few bodies engaged in a threesome, stepped over a heaving woman being taken in the animal position, and side-stepped over a pair doing interesting things with a silk scarf, a willow branch, and some honey. But even that sight didn't make him feel anything.

Taking one long last look over the great hall, he turned his back on the ribald entertainment and made his way to his personal quarters.

Naked and unconcerned, he moved with a grace usually reserved for felines. His long ankle-length hair nearly dragged the floor, and it floated around his bare feet as he delicately navigated the deep rose floors and walls of the hallway. Maybe it was time to change that color? As carnal as it was, it was giving him a headache.

Tucking a few loose strands behind his delicately pointed ears, he ran his hands over his chest, stopping to check to see if his nipple bar was still in place. During his last orgy, some minor fairy managed to dislodge the fastening ball as she suckled upon the nipple. A choking land sprite was not his idea of a fun time, so he replaced the ring with the sturdy bar. It felt better and damn if it didn't make his chest look more powerful.

He continued at an unhurried pace until he stopped in front of a large wooden door. He paused there, placed his palms laden with silver rings against the door, and rested them against the leather-covered surface.

Ah, he loved the feel of leather against his skin. The material felt so full of vibrancy and life. It seemed to absorb a bit of the life force of those who wore it, and offered a special comfort. What could be more comforting than one's own arms?

Shaking his head at his whimsy, he brushed more of his hair behind his ears, gently untangling errant strands from the many-jeweled studs that lined up to the delicate point at the tip, and reached out to grasp the doorknob.

With a flick of his wrist, the lock gave, and he entered his personal domain. No one would enter this room, even if the lock was not present. It was a special place, designed by one who believed in honesty to oneself above all else. For who could stand to see their innermost desires reflected back at them a million times over?

Only someone who had a deep, strong connection to Craven could open the lock when he was not present. And no one he knew of had that connection.

A cool wash of air caressed his bare skin. He absently thought of the carnal pleasure he took as the cold caressed his vital parts, contrasting with the natural heat of his body, before he stepped further in to the room.

He smiled as he saw a million reflections of his own turquoise eyes staring back at him.

From every crystal-faceted wall, ceiling, and floor, he saw the cool diamonds reflect his image at him. The curved and bent walls distorted some images so much that he looked fey — glowing eyes and otherworldly aura — while others made him look almost human. Though all the images were of him, the different images were of his personality, of his inner self, and they all had one thing in common. The frank sexual nature of each image would be startling to one who did not know themselves so well. He knew who he was. His name said it all.

Craven. Lord of Carnality, Master of Fleshly Desires, Prince of Pleasurable Pain, Dark Master of Desire.

He paid scant attention to the many leering faces that surrounded him, that showed his inner sexuality and love of the flesh. His facets were known to him. But it was the heart of the chamber that he sought.

In the center of this crystalline chamber sat his mirror.

But it wasn't just any mirror; it was his looking glass into the souls of men.

The *S* shaped mirror was purest glass, rough-edged and incomplete. To complete it would have taken away from its power, made it a thing completely of man, and destroying its connection to the earth.

The almost liquid surface of the glass showed none of the reflections that bounced off of the walls in this room. It waited, its glassy sheen unbroken, ready to be filled with the magic of its owner.

It levitated above a large rock of crystal, suspended and beckoning to him, daring him to peer into its depths and discover what he sought.

He slowly crossed to its stand, relishing the cool feel of the slick, icy surface of the diamond floor under his feet. In this place, his hair almost became an annoyance, as it detracted from the feelings of pure lust that began to fill the chamber.

Pushing that mild annoyance aside, he bracketed the small shard of glass between his hands, feeling the energy that surrounded this magical object. The small hairs on the lower part of his arms stood on end as he began to fill the mirror with his presence, with his personal power.

"My old friend," he purred as the mirror slowly began to spin between his cupped palms. "I fear I have become rather jaded of late and I seek a new experience. Show her to me."

The mirror began to spin faster and faster. Sparks of pure energy crackled around it as an unknown force began to make the air shift and blow. His hair flew wildly around his body, covering his flesh with the dark silk, flowing around the spinning glass but never actually touching it.

Small sparks of energy began to shoot bolts around the room as his eyes began to glow eerily in the illumination of the room.

"Yes, that's it," he breathed as a face began to appear in the whirling dervish that was his mirror.

Bringing his hands together around the spinning glass, he barely flinched as the sharp edges tore at his fingers, making his blood run red, and stabilizing the face that had begun to appear. The small blood sacrifice was enough, and now he could clearly see the face of the one who would end this tedious existence for a time.

He leaned in closer for a better look, and saw the woman with long dark hair and dressed in strange purple robes.

She sat on a hillside; the wind was blowing through her newly freed hair, and an odd look was on her face. On her hands and bare feet were strange reddish tattoos, but they only added to her beauty. Her eyes were a light shade of gold, her cheekbones high, and her nose straight and true. Her lips were full and lush, just right for sucking or nibbling or sucking or kissing or sucking.

Damn, there was life here, he thought as he felt his manhood quicken a bit at the thought of that perfectly sensual mouth lapping at the head of his cock, surrounding him with her heat.

His little flower seemed almost out of place on the rolling green hills which she sat upon, but he knew that this was to be to his advantage. She looked a little sad, but that just made his job a bit easier.

"What has you so down, my little beauty," he murmured as he peered closer at her image. "Tell me so that I may devise a way to bring you to me."

Nola sat alone on the hill behind her parents' house. The last thing that she wanted to do was to depress herself all over again. But she felt compelled to come here and sit on the hill where she had devised so many childhood fairy tales in her youth.

She closed her eyes and remembered the fairy ring at the bottom of the hill, and how as a child she and Gregor would sit and pretend to be lady and Prince of the fairy keep and her faithful prince.

She remembered tumbling down this hill through the summer heather and clover, and the laughter, always the laughter.

No one was laughing now.

"Why wouldn't you leave well enough alone," she sighed as she looked down across her old playground and remembered the good things about the past.

She never wanted to be trapped in the middle of this argument.

But Gregor had forced the issue of their long engagement, and her parents had put their proverbial foot down.

So here she was, just hours away from her wedding, and all she wanted to do was escape.

Not that Gregor wasn't a good man, he was one of the best men that she knew, but she didn't really love him as a woman should. Gregor was her best friend and confidant, but she could never picture him as a lover.

"So then why are there about a hundred guests waiting in that house for today's ceremony?" she asked herself. "Why can't I just tell my parents and Gregor I am not ready to be married yet? I want to travel and explore, and see what is there to be found. I want true passion before I find myself tied to a man for the rest of my life who is more like a brother that a lover or husband."

She had no idea why she wanted to say these words out loud, but she did and suddenly she felt lots better.

"So that is the problem," Craven chuckled. "I think that your wish can be arranged." He peered intently at the image, and uttered one word. "Come."

"I need to walk," Nola decided suddenly, feeling as if she had to move or go insane.

She stood up, the purple and lavender robe she wore tangling about her feet as a sudden wind blew around her, urging her to go in a certain direction.

Paying no attention to the sudden breeze, still lost in the urge to move her body, Nola took one step and then another, the tension slowly leaving her body as she walked.

"Yes," she sighed. "This feels better."

She tossed her head back as her feet sank into the rich earthen carpet of green, as the damp dew caressed her toes. She felt free, free as a bird.

And then she was flying, soaring above the ground.

Okay, falling would be more accurate.

Nola shrieked as her foot slipped and she found the grass suddenly above her head and the sky below her as her body began a graceless and headlong tumble down the hill.

Her robes flew around her, giving the appearance of a demented purple tumbleweed as she rolled head over heels down the hill.

Blue and green flashed erratically before her eyes as her chest tightened with the urge to scream, but a hard thump against the hillside forced the air from her lungs. She grew dizzy and disorientated as she continued to plunge downward, bumping painfully along the ground. Soon she couldn't determine up from down as she seemed to swirl faster and faster, until her eyes caught the familiar outline of the fairy ring.

Then suddenly she wasn't moving anymore. She wasn't doing much of anything, actually.

Nola had finally crash-landed in the center of her mystical childhood play arena, flat on her back.

What little air remaining in her, left her lungs with an audible *whoosh*, as the stars began to perform a tango behind her eyes just for her.

"Dead," she managed to gasp. "I am dead."

"With an attitude like that, no wonder you are so depressed," a deep masculine voice purred in her ear.

"Insane," she breathed, quickly changing her diagnosis. "Insane people hear voices, dead people hear nothing."

"Nice try," the silk-on-velvet voice chuckled. "But if you were insane, that would make me a figment. And as much as I love the sound of that word, I refuse to be imaginary."

Groaning, Nola tried to lift her head, but the world had gone crazy, the sky on the ground and the ground was where the sky should be.

Then she realized she had such a great view of her old fairy ring because she was suspended over it.

"What the hell?" she gasped as she suddenly stiffened, afraid that she would fall and lose whatever touch was keeping her afloat.

"No, not hell," the voice chuckled. "But some people call me the very devil himself."

"This is not real," Nola began to chant, her arms and legs stiff and extended far away from her body. If she fell, she didn't have far to fall, but any landing would have been painful and the preference was to avoid that pain. "This is not real. People don't float."

"You aren't floating, my purple passion flower. I am holding on to you. Wouldn't do to have you break your neck."

"Who are you?" she gasped, fighting the urge to curl up into a ball and scream. Today was not her day.

"You may call me Craven,"

"Craven? My mental breakdown has a name," she managed as she slowly turned her head to see if someone was holding the lines to some kind of net or platform. People just don't fly or float without some type of aid.

"I am here because you have allowed me to be here," he replied.

"Okay, you are here, so put me down," she responded instantly wondering if she would be dropped or placed gently on the ground. She preferred gentle.

"I will, after you agree to have your wish granted."

She stopped her mental struggles and sucked in a deep breath.

"I made no wishes."

"Passion? Wanting to travel, do exciting things? Those sound like wishes to me."

"Wait, you heard that? What are you, a fairy?"

"Yes," he replied quickly.

"No," she gasped in disbelief, but she *was* suspended far above the ground. "Fey? Really?"

"Really."

"If you are, then show yourself to me."

There was a parting of the air — not a shimmer of an appearance — the air actually parted and then she was struck by the most sensually perfect turquoise eyes that she had ever seen. The longest, thickest lashes that she had ever seen framed them.

"Where is the rest of you," she managed as she stared at the eyes peeking out at her from a tear in the air.

"You'll have to come here to see it all," he purred.

"Do you have six arms and seven legs or something?" she asked, still in some sort of shock to be talking and seeing something that clearly couldn't exist.

"I am human in form, Beauty," he laughed. "But you have to come to me."

"Why should I?" she thought aloud.

She must have a concussion, which would explain this. So why not have fun with this concussion before she got pulled back into the real world? She would bet that she was unconscious right now, just lying there waiting for her parents to come looking for her.

While a trip to the hospital might not be her idea of a postponement excuse for her wedding, she would take what she could get.

"Because you want excitement. Your crave action and adventure before you settle down and become the good little wife for the rest of your life," the voice purred,

Well, the voice was kind of right on that point. Smart figment. It had a point, really.

"Well, this has been an interesting flight of fancy," she returned, "But maybe I should be waking up now."

"You are awake, Beauty," the voice chuckled. "In the old days, this was so very much easier."

"Ha. So you can't prove what you are saying. Therefore I must be in an unconscious heap at the bottom of this hill and you are a concussion-induced fantasy."

"What have you got to lose?" the voice asked, striking a nerve.

"You are right, I really don't have anything to lose," she mused.

"So you spend some time with me in my kingdom. You'll learn a few things about yourself, and get some excitement. Maybe we can work on that passion thing, and then you'll know what it feels like to have your fantasies made flesh."

"Fantasies made flesh," she breathed as she considered this.

Hell, since this was a trauma-induced dream, she should take advantage of this now. She never knew that she had such a good imagination.

"Okay, Craven, is it? Then make my fantasies flesh."

"You must ask," he returned.

"I already did," she cried out. Floating like this was beginning to give her a headache, and she wanted her unconscious feet back on the ground.

"You must ask to journey to my kingdom in between the realms and to experience your deepest, wildest fantasies."

"Everything has a procedure now," she sighed, but repeated the words. "I wish…"

"State your name," he interrupted.

"Okay," she snapped. Floating like this was definitely making her headache worse. "I, Nola Jacobs, wish to be taken to Craven's kingdom between the realms for wildest fantasies and such."

"Very good," he replied, sounding very amused and pleased. "Now take my hand."

Before she could blink, a long tanned arm reached out throughout that gap in space and time, and reached for her.

It was a strong looking hand, though she was hesitant about grasping it, but it at least looked human. She didn't think that she could imagine the fey any other way.

That hand also had some interesting jewelry on it. Several rings covered the dark skin, proving that her imagination had good taste as well as fashion sense.

"Come now," that voice urged. "We haven't got all day."

With a laugh, Nola placed her palm in the hand that reached for her. What was the harm? It was her imagination, after all.

"Gotcha," the voice laughed, and suddenly she was falling again.

But strangely, instead of falling to the ground, she seemed to be falling up. Was that possible?

Then there was a klaxon-like rush of sound and the world began to swirl before her eyes. Maybe she was passing out in her unconscious state, she thought, before the color silver surrounded her, flashed and floated around her. Then the world went black.

Craven stood, the woman lying limp and unmoving in his arms, and for the first time in a long time, he smiled.

Chapter Two

"Nola," the hypnotic voice seemed to flow over the air and stir the very space around her.

"Nola," it called again, deep and rich and mellow.

"Wake up," it yelled, and Nola found herself snapping her eyes open and trying to leap to her feet all in the same moment.

"What…where…who?"

"That's three questions, my dear," the voice replied, "And you have to earn the answers."

Nola's head snapped around, her loose hair flying wildly about her face as she desperately tried to spot the owner of that hypnotic voice.

And there he was.

In all of his glory, there he was.

The man stood about six feet tall, maybe an inch or more, and stood in the corner, arms crossed and foot tapping.

His long dark hair covered him like a cloak, silky and shiny. It alternately hid and exposed his bronzed body to her view. His eyes, a shining unnatural turquoise, gleamed wickedly at her as his red tongue slipped from between full lips to lightly wet their surface. But the most surprising thing was, he was totally and completely naked.

He stood there, penis hanging low, chest pushed out, arms crossed, and he wore not a stitch of clothing. Who was this guy?

"So glad to see that you decided to join us," he said as he took a step towards her. "So very glad, indeed."

"Who are you?" Nola asked. The last thing she remembered was some wild dream about floating and a pair of turquoise…

"Make yourself at home, take off your clothes, stay a while."

"Who are you?" she repeated, the gasped as he seemed to float over to her, walking on air, his hair moved by mysterious unseen winds as it flowed around him.

"I am the Master of Dark Desire, the Lord of the Flesh, the Ruler of the Kingdom of Lust. I am Craven."

He stopped a scant inch before her, his eyes shining wickedly, the gleam of silver from his nipple bar making his body seem all the more masculine and strong.

"I should say so," she breathed as she watched his nakedness put on display for her visual enjoyment. She looked around, expecting a director to yell cut and wake her from this dream, but there he was, standing naked and unabashed before her. "You have to be craven to roam around in a get-up like that. Where is your shame, man?"

"I'm fresh out," he replied as his hair settled around him like a cloak, hiding the important bits from her view.

"Didn't that hurt?" she asked, looking direct at the flash of silver on his chest. "The piercing I mean," she added when she saw him smile.

"Pleasure is pain, pain is pleasure," he retorted, chuckling a bit as her face screwed up in confusion.

"I never found any pleasure in being hurt," she finally said, wondering if she were really having this conversation.

"How about when the pain stopped?" he asked raising one eyebrow. "Did you take pleasure in that?"

"Ass," she snorted, to which he promptly turned, parted his hair and presented.

"Oh my," she gasped as his perfect globes of muscular male flesh were exposed.

"Anything else you care to see?" he asked.

"Dic...uh, never mind," she said, a blush heating her cheeks.

"Coward," he laughed as he returned to face her. "I am also Lord of Painful Pleasures," he added as he rearranged his hair to his liking.

"But why am I here?"

"To face your greatest fantasies, Nola. That is something simple to one such as I."

"And what are you?" she asked as she began to relax a bit.

If he were out to kill her, she would be dead, and if he wanted to harm her, he would have done so by now. She found herself curious, though. She wanted to know more about him and his claims. If what she uttered in her dream were real... The possibilities were endless.

"I am Master of Dark Desire, Lord of..."

"Yes, thank you for the lesson in your lineage," she sighed interrupting him. "What I want to know is how you can do all that you claim."

"Easily, my dear girl," he replied. "I am a fairy. I live for this kind of thing."

Nola blinked, then blinked again for good measure.

"Okay," she finally said after a moment of silence. "If you are a Fairy, make my wish come true."

What is your wish?"

"I want a bath."

"That's it?" he asked and she nodded.

"Okay, knowing that a wish comes with a cost..."

"Cost?"

"I shall grant your request."

"Cost? Wait. What cost? You never mentioned *cost*."

Nola looked disgruntled as she glared at the man, uh, Fairy that stood nude before her. What kind of cost would she have to pay for that stupid wish?

"Done deal," he crowed as he turned and walked toward a far wall.

As he approached, it parted for him, like some great hand had opened it, and he disappeared inside.

"Follow me," his voice echoed as he disappeared into the blinding white light.

Loath to be left alone in this strange place, even if her only company was the man, Craven, she quickly wrapped her robes around her body and followed him inside.

As soon as she stepped through, there was a great rush of sound and that blinding flash of light.

As she blinked to clear the almost painful spots from her sight, the feel of the room grabbed her.

It was wet and hot. Maybe humid would be a better word she thought, as she stepped inside.

Then she gasped in pleasure.

Large pillars made of soft pink marble surrounded the room. Through the white haze of steam, she could just make out a set of stairs.

Taking a step, she looked down as her feet sank into something lush and soft.

The floor was carpeted by white rose petals. Inches of petals cushioned her every step, releasing their heady fragrance with each movement of her feet.

She wiggled her toes in appreciation, before curiously taking another step forward.

She saw the set of stairs, made of the same pale marble, which led down.

Stepping over, she drew in a deep cleansing breath, and ran her fingers through her long hair, letting the feel of the steam penetrate her through the skin.

Once she reached the steps, she dropped to her knees at the edge, headless of her robes, and peered over the side.

There, in the midst of all of this fantasy, was the greatest fantasy of them all.

A real, deep, sunken bath.

The heated water rippled gently, a smattering of rose petals and other flowers floated on top.

The smells were wonderfully floral and teased her senses, relaxing her and at the same time bringing her great joy.

"Oh my," she gasped as she let one hand trail in the soft water.

As she bent over, phantom hands began to tug and pull at her robes.

She turned quickly, ready to swat away the pervert who dared undress her, but saw nothing,

But again the hands tugged and pulled, harder this time, and before she knew it, her robes were rent into many pieces, and floated around her to be lost in the plush floor of flowers.

"Eip," she squeaked, so quickly was she stripped. She slapped her arms across her bare bosom, and hunched over to hide her most feminine places.

"Your bath," Craven's deep voice filled the room, and with a gasp, she dove for the water.

If he was in there, being covered by anything was better than standing there buck-naked.

But as the water caressed her, sank into her pores, a flashing heat began to fill her.

She sighed in delight as her pores opened and welcomed the moist wetness, refreshing her skin and relaxing her muscles.

"There is a bench there," his voice said, and absently she reached back until she could feel it.

Yup. Running the length of the small pool, there was a ledge, a marble ledge that held the head at a relaxed angle and was perfectly for sitting or reclining.

"How wonderful," she whispered as she placed herself upon the inclined ledge.

She was already in there, so she may as well enjoy it.

Arms still crossed over her chest, she eased back into the pool and let the water wash away her fears and worries.

She moaned as the heat increased a bit, making her body tingle.

Wait, that wasn't her whole body that was tingling, just certain parts of it.

What the hell?

Even as she sought to sit up, an incredible wave of pleasure shook her body.

She gasped as the heated water entered her cunt, surer than any man. Something tugged and pulled at her nipples, caressed her erogenous spots, and prickled excitement all around her skin.

This was not the bath that she expected.

"Craven," she called. "Where are you?"

"Right here," came the voice, from everywhere and nowhere.

She fought to answer, but was caught off guard but the loud moan that spilled from her throat.

Her senses were now pumping, her flesh tingling as wave after wave of orgasmic delight was teasingly promised and fulfilled.

Her clitoris began to burn and her nipples ached as if someone was tugging at them, laving them with a rough tongue, suckling upon them.

"What is happening to me?" she breathed as her body began to rock with the rippling of the water. She moaned and cried out as the ripples became waves and her head was forced backwards by the rolling waves of desire pulsing through her.

Never had she ever felt anything like this before. The water—the same water that she lay in—was making love to her, and doing a damn fine job of it too.

"Oh," she moaned as she felt something expanding her feminine walls. It was warm and wet, but it filled her completely, touching odd spaces that no man had ever touched that brought an intense, almost crippling, pleasure.

"Let go," a voice whispered into her ear, teasing the delicate nerve endings there, adding another element to the love play. "Enjoy this. You deserve this. You want this, you crave this."

"Yes," she breathed, almost mindless with pleasure. "I crave this.

"Then have it," Craven answered as the heat of the water spiked, and the tugging and pulling became intense. Her body arched off of the ledge.

"Yes!" she screamed as she flung her head backwards, her long dark locks floating around her, as her body became wracked with tremors. "Oh, yes!"

Then she exploded, her body clenching mindlessly at the water that filled her, that increased the pleasure wracking her body. Her breath gasped from her mouth, as her eyes dropped shut to savor each clenching convulsion.

The water heated up a bit, held the climax, and increased the pleasure, before it slowly lowered in temperature, just a bit, bringing her back to earth.

"Craven," she breathed, for all throughout her orgasm, she heard his voice whispering to her, whispering dark and delicious and naughty things. "Where are you?"

"Right here," replied the voice answered as she managed to pull her eyes open long enough to look around her.

"Where?" she breathed, as she realized that the arms were flung outward in a submissive manner, a welcoming manner, and hid nothing from his eyes.

"Isn't it obvious, my sweet, sweet Nola?" he asked as he chuckled.

"Where?" she asked again, finally believing all that he said was true.

"Why, I am the water in your bath, love."

Nola's eyes widened for a moment as comprehension sank in.

She was sitting in a pool of Craven? *She was sitting in a pool of Craven.*

"Uh," she gasped, looking at the water that surrounded her, her mind going to mush. "Uh."

"Say something," he laughed. "Or I shall begin to doubt you intelligence."

She blinked again, her mind coming back into focus.

The she said the only thing that she could say.

"Can I get you bottled?"

Chapter Three

"Now I suppose you want me to dry you off?" the voice chuckled as the water around her, that delightfully sensuous water, began to pull away from her like some thick gel. It slid from all corners of the pool and began to mound up before her, a clear liquid mass that rapidly began to take on human form.

"Craven?" Nola said warily as the form began to take on a familiar countenance.

"In the flesh," he answered with a chuckle as his shape began to solidify and grow opaque. Within in seconds, the water glowed gold and almost anticlimactically, the Fairy lord known as Craven stood before her.

"Impressive," she breathed as she stared at his naked form. That had been all around her, inside her, touching her? She needed to take more baths than her accustomed showers.

"Yes, I am," he said as she began to shiver. "Cold?"

"Damp," she replied.

"Yes, I know," he said with a leer.

"Damp," she said more forcefully, ignoring his quip, "And sitting here naked. Of course I am a bit cold. The heat is gone."

"Just banked," he mused. "But eager to get stoked into full strength again."

Nola blushed at his words, and tried her best not to look down to see if he actually was building up again.

"I am a bit chilly," she said quietly.

"Of course you are," he replied. "You are female, and according to the female rule book, you will be cold at bedtimes, in the middle of the night, when you are angry at your lover, and when you need an excuse to cuddle."

"Fuck you," Nola growled, turning her nose up at him.

"I thought you would never ask."

In a flash, the walls around them began to heat up, almost glowing with their warmth.

"Craven," Nola gasped, still a bit unsure of this magical creature.

"You wanted heat? I am bringing the fire," he said with a leer as he watched her naked body. She was trying to cover herself with her hands. Wasn't that...cute?

In a flash, the room began to heat and a warm, dry air began to circle her, lifting her hair, dancing along her nerve endings.

"Oh," Nola gasped as the naked form of Craven stood before her once more, in all of his glory. Suddenly, she was feeling a lot more heat internally.

"Burn baby, burn?" he asked as he stepped towards her.

Before she could speak, that familiar feeling of weightlessness took over.

Nola found herself being levitated, cradled gently, and carried out of the room.

"Craven?" she called, worry in her voice.

"Oh I love how you say my name," he purred. "Such need, such wanting, such uncertainty. Say it again."

"Craven," she yelped. But found herself back in the room where she started, lying on a plush padded table.

"Time to pay the cost," he whispered as he sauntered in behind.

Again, his hair was doing that reveal and conceal act, driving her mad even as she worried about what cost he would extract for a few moments of pleasure...well, extreme pleasure.

"What cost?"

"Why, all I want are your screams," he purred as she felt herself being rolled to her stomach by the phantom hands that earlier had rent the clothes from her body.

"What do you..." But her words were cut off as her arms and legs were pulled out to the side.

"What are you doing?" she hissed, a frisson of fear working its way up her spine. What would this creature do to her? All of the stories about watching what you said around the fey came rushing back t her.

"Extracting screams," he said as the table began to slowly rise to hold her up vertically.

The table began to part swiftly and silently, making padded supports for her arms and legs, holding her spread-eagled and firmly in place. She wiggled to try to break free, but she could not budge.

"Shake it, baby," he sighed. "I do love the sight of a well-rounded ass moving and gyrating."

"Let me out."

"Grinding if you will."

"Let me out."

"Humping the table."

"*Craven.*"

"Waiting for the fire whip."

"Craven, you... Fire whip?"

Nola's voice rose in pitch as the words *fire* and *whip* crossed her ears.

"Fire whip. Relax. You will enjoy this. Almost as much as I will enjoy administering each stroke."

Nola gulped. What was this depraved person going to do to her? Suddenly marriage didn't look all that bad.

"Look at it. Can you feel its seductive power? It just sings with lust."

"You are crazy," Nola whispered as he walked into her view. In his hands he held a small, thin wire.

"No, I am the Lord of Painful Pleasures. You are about to experience some."

As he spoke, the room began to heat and the wire he held began to glow. It thickened and suddenly almost looked alive in his hands, the gold sensuously wrapping around his hand and arm, as if begging to be caressed.

"It's moving," she gasped as she tried to squirm away.

"It is readying itself," he answered as the wire began to take on an almost blinding glow even as it wrapped itself around his body.

Suddenly, it burst into flames, making Craven appear to be trapped within the coils of some living fire snake that wound its way across his naked flesh, highlighting his perfection while burning with an intensity that matched his inner heat.

"Prepare yourself, Nola," he whispered as he held out one hand and the whip slithered into his grasp. "The whip is ready."

"No. Craven, please don't."

Visions of lashed flesh and sliced skin filled her mind. Would he flay the skin off of her body? Was this the cost of a foolish wish?

With a swishing sound, the first lash fell.

But instead of screaming pain, she felt as if her back was on fire, but not a painful one.

Her nerves came alive under the lash, sending messages of intense explosive pleasure straight to her woman's center.

She moaned as her body began to tingle again.

"The lash feeds desire, Nola. It finds the inner heat in its victim and magnifies it a thousand times. I will have your screams, Human, but they will be screams of pleasure."

Crack.

Again the lash fell and Nola moaned as the whip wrapped itself around her torso, licking at her nipples even through the padded table, making them harden and tingle.

Crack.

It flicked against her inner thigh, gently caressing her feminine lips, making them glisten with the dew of her arousal.

"I can feel your heat rising, Nola," he purred. "I want to feel more. You have yet to give me the screams that I crave."

Crack.

This time, the lash went higher, licking at her clit, causing a gasp of stinging pleasure to explode from her mouth.

"Not quite," he purred. "But close."

Again and again the fire whip kissed her body, singeing her flesh and made her writhe in ecstasy, pulling emotions from her that she had never felt before.

Dark, hard emotions that made her want to scream for fulfillment took her out of herself and morphed her into some animalistic creature that hungered for more.

"Yes," she hissed as the whip licked at her tender flesh. "Yes. Again. Harder."

"Damn." Craven gasped, sweat forming on his brow as he went about his work, his erection beginning to rise. "Damn." He looked down again.

Yup, it was on the rise. It had kind of hit half-mast before while he had lost himself inside and around Nola, but now it was definitely hitting way past the halfway mark.

It was something that had not happened in months.

It was puzzling that in the entire fairy realm, this one Human had that affect on him.

It was…cool.

"Fuck, yes," she hissed as the whip again lashed at her now dripping femininity. "Whip that clit. Hit me harder. Heat me up."

Groaning, Craven exploded into full erection as he plied his whip with skill, taking the time to strike a less sensitive area, to build up the anticipation.

Nola was lost in a sea of motion, all of it bubbling and erotic.

Her head swam with disbelief, but her body raged with an inner heat of its own.

The whip, something that she had always feared, now became an instrument of divine torture.

Each strike of its heated coils made her squirm on the table, her thighs quivered as her nerves sent signals of deep arousal and demands for fulfillment to her woman's center.

"Ask me for more." Craven demanded. "Tell me you want this."

"*I want this.*"

"Tell me you need this."

"I need this. Please."

"Then scream for me."

"Please!" she wailed, as she felt the tension within build to a fever pitch. Her body was on fire and growing hotter. Her nipples dug into the padded table, arousing them to the point of pain. Her clitoris was on fire, begging for another stinging kiss of the whip. She felt empty inside, empty and yearning to be filled. "*Please.*"

"Your wish is granted, but at a price."

That said, he tripled the speed of the whip, drawing her need to its highest point. The air was filled with her sobs of longing and the sound of the lash striking flesh.

He moved closer to her heat, as if drawn by invisible hands. Closer he stepped. Until inches separated them.

"I feel you," he crooned in her ears as the whip lay still in his hands. "I can feel you, smell you, *taste you.*"

"Please," she whimpered, a slave to her body and its cravings.

"Your wish is granted."

That said, he lifted the handle of the whip, a solid ebony shaft, and lifted it to her lips.

"Kiss it."

Desperately she placed kisses along the length and tip of the hilt.

Stephanie Burke

"I can almost feel that," Craven breathed as he watched intently as she peppered the head of the whip her small desperate kisses that told of her need.

Smiling, he pulled it away from her and ran it down the overly sensitized skin of her back, eliciting more moans and shivers.

Slowly he ran the hilt past the cleft in her bottom, making her quiver in nervous fear; then her wet inner lips were being caressed with the hot ebony.

"Your body kisses it so well," he purred then plunged.

As if struck by lightening, Nola's body arched backwards, her hands clenched into fists, and all hell broke loose within her.

"Yes!" she roared as she tried to draw air into her lungs. "*Yes!*"

The smooth shaft penetrated her, eased within her hungry cavern and fed the fuel to the fire that was taking over her mind.

"So very hot," he breathed as he slid the handle within, watching as pearly drops of her essence glistened on the thrusting hilt. "Oh, I love doing this."

"More," she begged as she tugged on her bottom lip with her teeth. "Please."

"With pleasure," he crooned and began to increase the speed of his lunges.

Craven felt his heart hammer in his chest as he watched the erotic display his little Nola put on. She was writhing and humping the table, grinding backwards on the ebony hilt, crying her need with her lower body.

To be inside her, he thought as sweat beaded on his forehead and his hair brushed against her, sending waves of heat through them both.

"Harder."

"Who am I to deny you," he breathed as he braced one hand above her and began to thrust in earnest.

"Craven," Nola gasped as he twisted the shaft, striking her clitoris in just the right area, stroking her inner button with just the right speed.

She felt the tension within her double, then triple, then reach a breaking point.

"I'm going to… *Here it comes!*" she roared.

Incredibly intense waves of climatic release exploded throughout her body. Her inner walls tried to grab and hold the ebony phallus, but Craven moved it, keeping her riding the waves of her release, keeping the orgasm going.

"Yes." Craven breathed in her ear as he felt her body wrap around the hilt of the whip, felt the incredible heat roar off of her, felt her climax as it rushed over her.

Slowly, he eased off his grinding, letting her come down from the climatic high, pulling the shaft from her body.

"Nola," he breathed, trying to keep from exploding across her back and losing the control that he had held perfectly for years. His cock was a throbbing instrument at its full arousal, hard as steel and getting harder. "I am going to enjoy you."

But here was no answer.

"Nola?"

He looked down into her face, and held in a bark of laughter.

Nola had fallen asleep.

"Just like a man," he snorted as he backed off from the table and allowed it to go back to its normal position. "But much sweeter," he sighed as he placed the hilt of the whip in his mouth, sucking and lapping her juices from its hot surface.

Now, he asked himself as he licked Nola from one if his favorite toys, *what do I ask for now?*

"You owe me another favor, Human. And I am going to have so much fun when I collect."

Chapter Four

Nola groaned as her attempts to roll over were stopped by a most remarkable throbbing in her lower regions.

Her thighs ached, her back ached…hell, her *hair* ached.

What had she been doing?

Then in a flash, she remembered what had happened to her, what he had done to her, and how she had reacted.

"I'm a slut," she sighed faintly, accepting what her mind was telling her. "I loved everything that he did to me, damn it." Her body rejoiced.

Peeling her eyes open, she closed out the images of herself writhing on that damn table, the feel of the lash like a fire in her veins… Cautiously she looked around.

Then she wished she had kept them closed.

"I am in leather hell," she groaned as she took in the walls, the ceiling, even the damn floor, all lined with black leather. Well, it looked like leather.

"You are in a play room, nothing more."

"Who said that?"

Her nude state caused her to forget about the aches and pains that came with vigorous bed-play as she balled up in a knot, trying to cover as much skin as she could. Being naked with Craven, well, that was something that felt natural. He had been the water in her bath. But being naked in front of strangers…other strangers, that was too much.

Looking around to catch the voyeuristic culprit, Nola saw nothing.

"Where…" Her voice trailed off as she still could not find the owner of that voice.

It was a sweet voice, though.

But Nola had enough of listening to the voices in her head. See where they got her?

"Down here."

"Eik." Nola squeaked as she again heard that voice and looked around, pulling her hair around her like a silken cloak.

Flipping over on her stomach, she inched her body to the edge of the platform she was laying on, noting that the leather material took on her body heat and almost felt alive.

"Yeah, come closer."

Slowly her peered over the edge and saw that it was a table. Only her eyes and a few strands of hair were hanging over the side. She gawked at what she saw.

It was a troll.

She didn't know that there were trolls under the hill.

This one was only about three feet high and was some odd purple color. In place of normal human ears, there was a set of fuzzy bunny…antenna.

It also had three eyes, but the one in the center of his forehead was closed. Besides the furry bunny ears, it was bald as an egg. She thanked God that it was wearing some sort of pants, because a look at the genitalia would have probably left her screaming and dysfunctional. Not that she was functioning normally these days.

"Uh," she gulped as she stared at the creature. "Hi?"

It grinned, showing razor-sharp teeth, making Nola grunt and back away in a hurry.

"Ungh," she groaned as she sat up and pulled her knees to her chest. Would he chew off her toes if she made a break for it?

"What?" the voice floated up to her. "Was it something I said?"

Before she could move, a tiny, clawed hand reached up and got a lock on the table. Nola watched in mounting horror as the little purple guy easily pulled himself up. First the fuzzy ears then the closed eye cleared the table. Then with a grunt, he flung his body up and in a flash was standing before her.

Nola's eyes opened in horror as the little beastie again grinned at her.

Before she could control herself, a piercing shriek filled the air. Her foot lashed out faster than a fire whip and the little...it went flying.

"*Ouch*," he bellowed as he flew across the room. Nola jerked her hands over her mouth, not sure if she was more horrified at her actions or at the little purple man.

He landed in a pitiful heap at on the floor; a shuddering gasp let her know that the air had been knocked out of its lungs.

"Why did you do that?" he whimpered. "I only wanted to talk."

"Sure," Nola shot back, trembling as a small sliver of guilt penetrated her mind. "That's what the spider said to the fly, right before he pulled out his juicer."

A muffled groan was her only answer.

"Um. Creature? I mean...little guy?"

No answer.

She wanted to lean over the table and see what had happened to him, but one too many horror movies, and the memory of monstrous creatures springing through the air to latch onto some helpless woman's face held her in her place.

"Creature?"

"Love," he snapped.

"Um, gee, this is so sudden," she hedged as she looked around for an avenue of escape. "I don't even think we have been introduced."

"I am Love, you idiot."

"Okay, Mr. Love. If you would be so kind as to direct me to my host, Craven, I am sure he can find a chicken or something for you to gnaw on."

"*I am a vegetarian,*" the indignant voice bellowed before he again leapt to the tabletop.

Nola was going to run and kick again, but the poor thing looked so...pitiful.

"Um, you are Love?"

"That's right," he snapped as he stood there, rubbing his back, eyes narrowed in her direction. "I am Love, Giver of Divine Pleasure, Balm to Lonely Hearts, Sanctuary for True Believers, Deliverer of..."

"Oh," Nola interrupted. "You are one of these fairy people."

He stopped mid-introduction.

"Fairy people?" he said softly.

"Yeah, the fey."

"The Fey?" He narrowed his eyes until they were tiny slits glinting menacingly at her.

Nola blinked, and then thought she had better start making amends...fast.

"Well, I am new here."

"Fairy people. I am the protector of all that is pure and true. I am also the scourge of the lovelorn."

"I am a doctor in training," Nola returned tentatively offering up her hand, then thinking better of it and pulling back. His teeth looked sharp and he looked pissed enough to want to change his diet.

"I am *Love*," he bellowed, both arms akimbo. "And I just wanted to meet you."

"Um, Love, why?"

"Because he thinks he is going to win this bet," said a new voice from across the room.

The new voice caused Nola to again shriek and ball up in a knot, protecting her nudity.

But his voice was silky smooth, almost as velvety in texture as Craven's.

Nola looked beyond Love and saw what fantasies was made of, at least what they would be made of if she had not met Craven first.

He had red hair, long blood-red curly hair that hung in ringlets down to his knees. His eyes were a twinkling green. His body was...*woof.*

He had no piercing, but what he lacked in adornment he more that made up for in endowment.

His cock hung about a foot long... flaccid.

Nice to look at, Nola quickly decided, but not to take home and play with.

He wore leather chaps that seemed to emphasize his girth, being that they only covered his legs. His feet were bare, but beautiful. His body was so pale it almost glowed.

"Now that I have seen the whole show, so to speak, you can cover up now."

Nola had been taken off guard, but not really impressed. *I mean*, she thought, *there was no fire whip strapped to his side.*

The little purple guy exploded in laughter, his fuzzy ears twitching.

The tall stud glared at the creature and Nola stared at them both like they were crazy.

"Geez. You would think that there would be a dress code around here." She again eyed the redhead's display while the bunny dude huffed with giggles.

"You are naked," the redhead pointed out, striking a pretty-man pose, flexing his muscles and making his cock jump.

"But I have some humility. Shame on you," she hissed at the flirting man. "And would you hush," she said, turning to the purple guy.

The redhead began to pout and crossed his arms over his chest defensively, as if Nola actually hurt his feelings.

"Who are you?"

Somehow the naked cowboy wannabe seemed more threatening than that purple bunny antenna.

"He's my twin," the purple guy chuckled as his laughter eased.

"Your twin?" Nola sneered, looking at the six-foot red-haired Adonis and then at the tiny purple man.

"Yes." Love chuckled his last chuckle and stood up, mirth swimming in his two open eyes.

"Well, who is he?"

Still in a pout, he answered her.

"I am Hate."

Nola blinked at the two of them.

"I am in deep trouble," she sighed.

Chapter Five

Craven chuckled as he looked around his throne room. Again, there were bodies writhing on the floor, slippery spots staining the carpets, and the sounds of moans and cries filling the air. Life was good.

"What has you in such a good mood?" one three-breasted beauty asked as Craven approached the fairy equivalent of a muse of this event. Lust was hot in her eyes.

"I have been challenged, my dear," he replied as he removed one exploring hand from his erection.

"And who will be the lucky recipient? You know, Vegras is still talking about the last time you tupped her."

"That was three years ago," he snorted and dismissed her words with a wave of his hand.

"Yes, but she said that no one else had ever filled her like you did. She even remembers how you held back for hours."

As she spoke, the woman licked full red lips and shuddered as she stared into the unique turquoise eyes of Craven.

Chuckling, he began to tap his front tooth with a long fingernail as he observed the woman.

"You're in heat now, aren't you?"

She whimpered and smirked at him.

"I bet the skin of your thighs are starting to get slippery with your want."

She nodded slowly, her lips parting as she gazed adoringly at him.

"I bet," he murmured softly, "that your nipples just got hard, like I have been sucking them, making them pop with pleasure. Then I would make you lick my fingers, lick them one by one so that they would be moist when I rammed them..."

"*Craven,*" a low and angry female voice shouted from the opposite side of the hall.

For a moment, all movement, all moaning, and thrusting ceased, then returned with renewed vigor. But Craven's attention was caught and he turned away from the heaving, panting woman, to face that one who looked ready to commit murder.

"Tatiana," Craven said as he walked towards her, stepping over the writhing bodies that littered the floor. "What brings you, of all people, here?"

"The Human."

Tatiana was a raging beauty, and in her fury, she was even more…just more.

Her eyes flashed lavender and her long silver hair flowed freely around her as she tapped one foot impatiently.

She was dressed in the finest gossamer gown; the nearly clear panels draped and caressed her body like shadows, and seemed to make her larger than life in the dim light of the room.

Tatiana, Queen of the Fey, mate and master of Oberon, was in a fine temper.

"Human?" Craven asked as he stopped before her, flashing his trademark wicked smile.

"Don't play games with me, Pain-boy. You know who I am talking about."

"But you used to like the games we played, Tatiana," he purred, his eyes dropping to half-mast as he recalled the delights to be had in the Queen's bed. For she wasn't always the Queen. Often, before she committed to Oberon (or 'forced Oberon to see things her way'), she was just another fey princess—beautiful and deadly in her own way.

"Craven," she hissed as he looked towards the heavens for help.

"So, what of it?" he asked quietly. "Humans often make wishes that we choose to grant. And this one was ripe and on the hill."

"Humans are never allowed here, Craven. They disrupt the order."

"Right now, Craven," Tatiana said slowly, "she is entertaining both Love and Hate. Who knows what those two will do to her, but more importantly, Craven, Human's don't belong here."

"It was her wish."

"And you had nothing to do with it? You didn't coach her just a little? *Craven?*"

"Maybe a little."

"And when does she leave, Craven."

He stopped at that.

"Let me recall…"

"When?"

"Well…"

"They are placing bets, Craven. Bets that the mighty Craven has fallen for a Human. A *Human*, Craven. They are…savages."

"I have fallen for no one, Tatiana. You should know this," he said with a significant look in her direction. "Some of the most beautiful women in the realm have tried, and they received only heartache for their attempts."

Tatiana blushed a bit at his comment, for she knew that she was one of the few that had fallen for the Master's charms. But then she met Oberon. And then…

"Humans are nothing but trouble, Craven," she insisted, shaking off her past feelings with a bit of effort. "Remember that Shakespeare character? Do you remember what harm he did with that silly tale of his? Imagine Puck playing a prank on us. Imagine."

That was one of the main reasons Tatiana had a hatred, well, deep dislike, for Humans. She helped one man out, *one man* mind you, who had been crying his eyes out, babbling about writers block, and for centuries she is branded a victim and a spiteful woman.

"I like this Human, Tatiana," Craven continued. "She has something that I have never experienced before."

"Virginity?" she asked, curious. "Because if it's a hymen you wish, I know potions that can turn any woman you choose…"

"No, woman." Craven sighed, then at her angered glance, remembered his manners. "No, My Queen. It is not that. There is something about her. She is…different."

After a moment of being scrutinized by the Queen of all Fairies, Craven shrugged his shoulders, at a loss for words.

"There is just something different about her."

"Well, you had better discover that difference and get over it soon, Craven. I don't want her here. We don't need the exposure."

"Yes, My Queen," Craven agreed, but not out of some deep need to please royalty. He had to figure out what it was about Nola that made him so susceptible to her. He had not even made well and proper love to her and already he was scared of how that made him feel.

Scared.

He froze for a moment as what he was thinking registered in his brain.

He felt something.

Something other than boredom and a need to sow his seeds.

Concern.

It was a novel experience.

Grinning to himself, he bowed shortly to the Queen and made his way back to the leather room where he had left Nola.

"What about this orgy?" Tatiana stopped him with her words.

"You preside."

"What?"

"Tell them to put tab A into slot B and to get the hell out of your way. I am going to handle...other matters. If you get stuck, call Oberon. I taught him some things that year when we were together and I am sure that they stuck."

"You and...and Oberon? My Oberon?" Tatiana stuttered, disbelief spread across her face.

"Well hell, woman. Someone had to teach him a thing or two to get you into his bed. That vibrating tongue trick is something, isn't it? He was always such an ardent student."

"Craven," Tatiana yelled, stamping her foot as she glared at him.

"Carry on with the orgy, My Queen."

He snapped his fingers and a spot in the center of the floor began to tremble and then opened.

The tangled bodies occupying that spot rolled over and to their delight, a shelving unit rose from the ground.

A shelving unit stocked with the most obscene sex toys and dildos ever imagined.

There were foot-long butt plugs, leather masks, vibrating eggs, floggers and whips, paddles, lotions and lubricants of all types.

"Spread the sexual joy, My Queen," he chuckled over the loud receptive roar as the toys were seized and used with rigorous abandon. "Learn a thing or two to take back to Oberon."

With that parting shot, he made his way back to the leather room...and to Nola.

He would experience a bit more of the range of emotions that he could feel.

After all, per their contract, they had a long time to experiment.

Chapter Six

Love now sat in Nola's lap, nearly purring as she stroked the fur on his belly. He had never had this much fun with a Human before. He almost felt bad that she was connected to...Craven.

That fairy had ruined so many of his schemes. He didn't deserve Nola with the lovely tan skin and the soft liquid eyes.

"If you are finished getting your rocks off..."

Hate was still miffed that Nola paid him scant attention.

Now he was leaning on the wall across from them, his eyes narrowed as he watched his twin receive what was rightly due to him.

"And why is it due to you, Hate?" Nola asked.

Hate flushed as he realized that he spoke out loud, but his eyes never left the bent-over figure of Nola.

She was still sitting, her legs crossed in a way that hid her breasts and her cunny from his sight, but she freed one arm to stroke Love's furry little belly.

"Because I am beautiful." He looked at her as if she was blind. Could she not see that he was worthy of praises too?

All Love did was tell her a few stories about Craven and the next thing he knew, Nola was rubbing his belly and murmuring in sympathy with him.

"You have an ego problem," Nola stated as she rubbed Love's belly again. "You need to be more of a gentleman, like your brother. He has manners."

"What do I need with manners when I have the total package?" Hate spat, glaring at the two of them.

"The total package?" Nola looked ready to laugh and Love quirked one smug look in his brother's direction.

"The total package," Hate reiterated, as if they hadn't heard him the first time.

"The ass." He turned and presented his bare rump, pointing out the dimples in the muscled flesh.

"Very nice," Nola said, deadpan.

"The cock. Have you ever seen such a magnificent dick?"

He swung the member in question in her direction, making sure to point to the neatly circumcised head that had absolutely no scar from the removal of the foreskin. It was red, thick, and arrow shaped, the way most women preferred, he assured her. Not to mention the thickness and the length.

Nola held back a yawn. If she hadn't seen Craven in all of his glory, and not even fully erect, she may have been impressed. Now she was faintly amused by Hate's loss of...control.

"The chest is broad and muscled, the legs are thick, unlike most human males who concentrated on the upper body and have pipe-cleaner legs. My hands are large and sensual and the face is one to break hearts. Not to mention my red hair. *Red*, Nola. *Red* hair. The total package."

"Er, um, very nice, Hate."

During his tirade, Nola ceased stroking Love's belly, and now the little creature whined pitifully.

He was beginning to grow on her, she thought. Almost like a Cabbage Patch Kid, who she always thought were so ugly they were cute.

"Nice. *Nice?* I show you the total package, what women and men have died to possess, and you say nice. Nice?"

"Um, Cute?"

"*Argh.*"

Hate exploded as he closed his eyes and yelled to the mortal world above.

"He's having a fit," Love added unnecessarily as he and Nola watched the screaming redhead.

"No shit, Sherlock," Nola said through her teeth. "Tell me something that I didn't know."

"You...you Human." Hate glared at her as he finished his vocal exercises.

"Yes," Nola said as a hint of fear penetrated her shock.

She could always use Love as a human shield, she thought as she looked down at his small furry body. Not that he would provide much of a barrier between her and his brother, but Hate wouldn't strike out at family, would he?

"Human. Prepare to have you nightmares become reality," Hate began, but was interrupted when the room began to pulse, to almost breathe.

"That is my woman, Hate," a low menacing voice grumbled as Nola began to smile.

"Craven," Hate hissed, his eyes glowing an eerie red.

"You want to give her nightmares? That is *my* job."

Nola's smile turned into a frown.

"You left her alone, Craven," Hate defended, his eyes losing their glow.

"So the minute I turn my back you come here and try to take away what I have done to her? Do you know how greasy that is, Hate? Kind of bastardly of you."

As he spoke, the walls at the far side of the room began to glimmer and stretch.

As they watched, slowly the form of a head and hands pushed, forced their way out.

Then the walls were parting smoothly, and the naked from of Craven stepped slowly into the room, the wall closing around as his body slipped through and he stepped free.

"Bully of you to show up," Hate snorted. "And I could have made that grand entrance, but I save my powers for useful things."

"Like trying to sell the total package," Love snorted, then chortled with delight as a flush suffused his brother's face.

"Nola, did they scare you?" Craven asked, as he seemed to flow deeper into the room, the others forgotten.

"Love can be pretty frightening and dangerous," she said, her eyes trained on his body as he stepped close enough to cup her cheek in his hand. "But Hate is…"

She paused, thinking pointless comments, but decided that it would not bode well to insult a creature that could make your nightmares a reality.

She looked over at him and noticed how he leaned in to hear what she would say.

"Hate just is."

"Is what?" Hate demanded, curious in spite of himself. "Not that I care what a Human thinks of me."

"Despite the fact that you tried to sell her the total package and failed woefully," Love added, *a just trying to be helpful* look on his face.

"Silence, brother," Hate snarled. "Or I will remove one of your ears. Then your eyes will look lopsided and you really will be blind."

"What does his ears have to do with his eyes?" Nola asked, then groaned as she brought Hate's attention back to her person.

"Well?" Hate demanded, tapping his foot and setting his enormous cock swinging. "I am waiting."

"For underwear, no doubt," Nola muttered under her breath only loud enough for Craven to hear.

He snickered and she shot him an evil look.

"What was that?" Hare was getting inpatient.

"I said that you are not the opposite of your brother. Love is not the opposite of hate. There is great passion in you, and that is not the opposite of Love. I believe the opposite of Love in indifference, and you are anything but indifferent, Hate."

"And that makes me?"

"Nice."

Chapter Seven

Craven was still laughing as he lay beside Nola on the hard stone table.

"Oh, shut up." she hissed, still annoyed with the fairy for laughing the way he did. "How was I supposed to know that calling Hate nice was a high insult? Now he's angry with me and who knows what he will do?"

After she pronounced Hate to be nice, the red-haired fairy let out a stream of expletives worthy of a Dublin dockhand and stormed from the room, dragging his giggling brother with him.

"He-can't-touch-you," Craven managed between guffaws of laugher. "You are mine."

Tears rolled down his cheeks as he lay beside his Human, hilarity still plastered across his face.

"It is not that funny," Nola hissed. "You try having an emotion upset with you."

His laughter tapering off, Craven lifted his eyes to Nola, slowly letting them roam up her body to her face, hot with indignation.

"He is a fairy. No more, no less. He cannot harm you, Nola. He can only influence what you believe. And a minor influence at that."

"And what is it that you have done to me, Craven? Is it influence, or is it something much worse?"

"Oh, definitely much worse."

"And what is that?"

As she spoke, her eyes traveled along his body. Her breathing increased as her nipples started to go hard.

"I have merely awakened a desire in you, Nola."

"And that is worse than influence?"

"Yes, Nola," he breathed as he pulled his body over to her, laying her back as his fingers began to caress that body that held him in rapt attention. "Because you can deny any outside influence, make excuses for those who attempt to coerce you, ignore that they do. You cannot lie to yourself, Nola. Your body, your mind, your soul will know the truth. And you will desire all your body craves all the more."

The truth of his words hit her as he spoke directly over her lips, his lips grazing hers at each word. More than anything, she wanted to open her lips, press her mouth against his, breathe in the air he breathed out.

It was scary, but it was the truth. Her body would not allow her to hide her arousal from him or from herself.

"Damn you, Craven," she breathed as her hands tangled in his hair, spreading it around her like a cloak, feeling the vitality of it caress her body.

"Damn yourself, Nola. This is what you wished for, what you wanted. It was always inside you. I just showed you to the door to set it free."

Then there was no more talking as his head dipped low to lick the flesh between her breasts.

She arched up into him as he lapped small circles around her nipple, not touching, but getting so very close.

Nola moaned and tugged on his hair, trying to force his lips where she needed them the most, but he resisted.

Trailing from one aching breast to the other, Craven left a pattern of small licks and bites on her flesh, the bites stimulating and awakening her nerves, the licks soothing the fire he inflicted with his mouth.

He ignored her moaning and the little gasps that escaped her throat and continued downward, nibbling at her ribs and licking straight down to her navel.

She giggled as he lapped at the small sexy divot, bringing his hands down to hold her hips still. His intentions were not to amuse but to arouse, and he knew that laughter could kill desire if overdone.

Holding her hips firmly, he slid to the end of the table, sliding to his knees as he pulled her to the edge, parting her legs and placing them on his shoulders.

Her laughter stopped as he slowly spread her legs and lifted them. It was such a submissive act, allowing him this control, but she realized it was something she desired.

Craven looked down at her slick flesh, the pouting lips of her opening glistening with her arousal, and almost lost control.

Nola was a quivering feast for his eyes, a perfect rosebud waiting to be plucked.

He lowered his head, his eyes catching hers, and he stuck out his tongue and got his first pure taste of Nola.

Nola's head thrust back at the first rough touch of his tongue against her sensitive flesh, but she tried to keep eye contact. His damn eyes staring into hers was the most personally erotic thing she had ever experienced. She felt as if her soul was open to his gaze.

Craven first lapped at the flesh to the right of her clit, then the left, feeling the smoothly shaved skin against his tongue. It felt new and fresh. But his main purpose was to determine which side was more sensitive.

She pulled back a bit when he ticked the fleshy lip to the right, but pushed against him when he stroked the left. The right was more sensitive and needed a finer touch.

Using his thumbs to part her, he stared at the rosy skin of her exposed sexuality.

"Beautiful," he breathed as he slowly teased the tip of her clit with his tongue.

"Oh!" Nola gasped as the sensations of him slightly manipulating her clit sent waves of heat through her body. They spread out through her stomach, down her thighs and up her chest until her whole body was vibrating.

He breathed over her parted flesh, feeling her tremble as his warm breath washed over her, then unable to resist, leaned in and took a long drink.

Nola moaned and tightened her thighs around his head, pulling him closer as she writhed on the tabletop.

His eyes still held hers, but now they were filled with a passionate fire, intent on making her his conquest again.

Craven felt himself harden as the flavor of Nola filled his mouth. He buried himself deeper, making his tongue into a fleshy spear he used to plunge into her depths.

Her near-screams of pleasure, her passionate whimpers, made his seed roil within his balls, and his shaft straightened to its fullest. One of his hands left her to grasp and stroke his own meat, his thumb circling the sensitive head.

He pumped his cock as he lapped at the silky smooth flesh, becoming more excited as he tasted more and more of her sweet dew.

But he had to slow down.

He felt his erection swell and his balls pull up against the base of his cock. He was much too close and he didn't want to explode. Not just yet anyway.

Giving his shaft one last rub, he brought his fingers again into play on the sensual torture Nola was gladly receiving.

"Want more?" he whispered against her, smiling as her head nodded vigorously and she pulled his head deeper into her heat. "Good."

Two fingers thrust deeply into her, curving slightly to stroke her 'G' spot, sending electricity stuttering through her body.

Nola screamed as her body tensed up as if struck by lightning.

"Craven," she wailed. "Please! More!"

Murmuring soothingly into her flesh, Craven eased back the hood of her clit, exposing the milky-white pearl to his ministrations.

"As you wish," he whispered, before he latched on and began to run his tongue over and over her exposed bud.

Tears filled Nola's eyes as tension built in her body. Her fingers fisted, then left his hair all together to pound on the table.

She was dying; she was flying. She was being reborn.

One of her hands went to her throbbing nipple, tugging and stroking, while the other returned to Craven's head, desperate for him to make the tension rise, to make it explode, to grant her relief.

"Cum for me," Craven purred as he felt her body tighten like a bowstring ready to fire. "Drench me, Nola."

And then he added another finger, the thickness stretching her, giving her the nudge she desperately needed to find her release.

"Oh, fuck!" Nola screamed as her body lifted off of the table. "I'm... Oh!"

Then rapture!

Her body trembled and tightened. For a moment, she felt nothing, then everything. Her eyes locked onto Craven's. That one contact kept her soul intact as her body exploded across the universe and into a higher plane.

Then her body was clenching around his fingers, each contact sending a deeper sensation through her body.

Her nose tingled, her toes curled, her thighs burned. This explosive release filled her, then her eyes slammed shut, forcing her to experience the final waves of release on her own.

Finally gasping for breath, her body eased and she felt the table beneath her back once more.

Craven, not leaving her alone, continued to gently caress and pet her, not stimulating her overly sensitive parts, but a calm gentle stroke until she began to return to her body.

Finally easing his fingers out of her still dripping cunt, he raised his fingers to his nose and inhaled deeply.

"Precious Nola," he breathed. "Smells sweet as a rose."

Her eyes eased open at his words and when he saw he had her attention, he continued.

"And sweet as honey."

Before her gaze, he hungrily lapped each finger, sucking in each knuckle, licking the flesh between them, until all traces of Nola were gone.

"And there's still more," he purred as her eyes smoldered in returning sensuality. "Make your body lie about that, Nola. And if you find you can, you are more depraved then I will ever be."

Chapter Eight

Her toes were numb.

Nola tried to move and realized that her toes wouldn't move. But that was okay because her face was numb as well. And her knees ached. And certain parts of her burned.

"You liked that, didn't you?" Craven purred as he winked at her and wiped his mouth with one hand. The other drummed on the still-tingling flesh of her upper thigh.

"Water," Nola gasped, swallowing hard to return some moisture to her parched throat.

"No. But if you are really that thirsty, I'll give you something to drink."

That said, he slowly climbed up her body, dragging his hot flesh and his hard erection up and over her swollen clit, trailing through the moisture that still flowed there, and up her quivering stomach.

He paused and grinned as he rested in the valley between her breasts, but then moved on until he was straddling her chest, his throbbing cock inches from her lips.

"You can't be serious?" she gasped, even as she licked her lips in anticipation. What would Craven taste like?

"It's protein," he urged, easily reading her desire in her eyes. Nola was on a sexual escapade, and she wanted more. "And don't tell me you never did this before. Your body wasn't exactly virginal when I got to it."

"Oh it's not a blow job to me," she purred. "It's more like a hobby. But I don't swallow," she added as the fire in his eyes increased several degrees.

She ran one hand teasingly over the corded muscles of his thigh and over his ass, pausing to pinch his firm flesh.

"Fair enough," he breathed, his chest rising and falling rapidly. "I have other plans for this load."

Nola grinned at her witty back and forth repartee, but soon her eyes were drawn to the hefty piece of flesh that hovered above her, his large balls rising to the base of it.

"If we are going to do this," she decided, turning serious all of a sudden, "then you are going to get off my chest and onto your back. Then you will beg me like the begging male you are."

Craven's eyebrow rose at her pronouncement. *Begging male?* He was usually the dominate in his dealings. But it would be fun to play, for a little while.

Before he could formulate a response, Nola opened her mouth and sucked his pre-cum drenched head inside.

"Damn!" he all but roared as he felt the heat of her mouth. She was on fire.

Her tongue forced him against the ridges of the roof of her mouth. He dropped his hands above her head, bending over her for support.

Then she brought her hands into play, one reaching up to cup his nuts gently but firmly, the other to grab at his ass, massaging the hard muscles there.

She tried to force him deeper, into the back of her throat, but her gagging stopped her progress.

"Easy," he murmured, trying to sooth. "Take a deep breath and try again."

He urged her onward, the silky smooth feel of her mouth driving him to new heights of eroticism. He looked down and saw her—rolling her eyes at him actually—but was caught by the sight of her stuffing herself full of him.

Nola knew what she was doing, it was just the full girth of him took her by surprise.

Ignoring his words, she eased her head back a bit then swallowed twice.

Craven blinked as he began to slide down into her throat.

Before he could blink, she has taken him all, balls-deep.

Once she had him seated comfortably, she winked at him, then began controlling her throat muscles, massaging him from within.

"*Nola*!" Craven roared, surprise evident on his face.

But Nola was not done.

Her hands began to massage his nuts, tugging gently as her hand on his ass urged him to move.

Slowly, sweat pouring from his body, and with trembling arms, Craven began to carefully move. He slid into her gripping sweetness then slid away slowly.

Nola began taking small breaths through her nose when he pulled back so that his head rested in her mouth, her tongue rapidly flicking over the sensitive crown, then opening her throat for him to plunge deeper.

Craven began to grunt as he thrust into her, and groan when he pulled back. She was beginning to play his hot buttons like she knew what she as doing.

Apparently she did know because next her hands began to caress his cheeks, running down the trench between them and gently rubbing across his rosebud.

Craven clenched first with automatic reaction, then relaxed as her fingers stimulated the nerve endings there.

He began to purr in pleasure as she began to move a bit faster.

"Damn, you are good," he sighed, then jumped as a flash of fire began to travel along his spine. "Very good.

Saying nothing, Nola added a new sensation. She began to growl deep within her throat, vibrating the whole of his cock as he was squeezed within her.

Craven's eyes popped wide open as she did this, his cock swelling even more within her.

But Nola kept a steady rhythm, easing off when she felt his balls drawing up to the base of his cock, making the feelings last longer.

Soon Craven was a shaking, soggy mass of manhood above her, tortured by a finger that teased one of his hot spots, a throat that was trying to strangle his dick, and her caressing hands that held his balls down, preventing him from exploding.

She *was* trying to make him beg!

And damn if she wasn't close.

Feeling his body began to give over to her, Nola redoubled her efforts to make Craven scream. She moved faster on his cock, her hands stroked and teased his balls, and her finger teased his opening, dropping below it to press his perineal area before dancing over his rose.

Craven felt his knees go weak and had to struggle to remain upright.

But that damn finger was pushing him over the edge.

He closed his eyes, breathing slowly, while unconsciously thrusting back against her, desperate for more stimulation.

This lasted for a good minute, though it felt like an eternity to him.

Nola's talented mouth drove him to distraction, made his hair stand on end, while her teasing was driving him to the point of no return.

Before his mind could keep up, his body took over.

Rearing up onto his knees, he opened his mouth and shouted words his brain cringed to hear.

"Please!"

Nola grunted in triumph, her eyes sparking, as she thrust her finger deep. Striking his prostate dead on.

"Nola!" he roared as she plopped him out of her mouth and her hand left off its teasing of his balls to grip and stroke his cock.

"Yes!" he hissed, eyes closed tight, lips drawn back into a grimace of pained pleasure as she stroked his prostate once more.

Nola felt his cock grow thicker, fuller than before and began to rapidly jerk him.

The head turned an angry purple, his slit dilated and she felt his inner muscles clamp around her finger.

Craven was coming and in a big way.

She felt his cock vibrate, his breath catch, then his seed, thick and white, exploded from its tip, splashing against his chest, covering her still pumping hand, as his breath sobbed in her ears.

Craven rolled backwards, his strength giving way in the face of his climax as his body spasmed and wave after wave of orgasmic release shook his body.

He felt weak, his breathing labored as a sudden peace spread along his being.

His cock sputtered one last time, then began to grow too sensitive to touch.

Nola sensed that, and left off stroking his cock to begin rubbing his thighs and stomach, gentling him until he could breath once more.

She removed her finger from his body as she leaned over him, a smile on her lips, her eyes glowing with pleasure and renewed arousal as she watched him relearn how to breathe.

When his eyes opened, she smiled at their dazed look.

Making Craven explode into orgasm was almost as good as sex with him. She felt fulfilled and arrogant, watching him come back to himself. She understood his earlier actions. Controlling his body, forcing this pleasure on him, was power-inducing. She felt like she could do anything.

When his eyes began to clear, she leaned down and took his lips in a fierce kiss, forcing her tongue between his teeth and nibbling on his full lips.

When she finally let him up for air, she again lapped at his lips, looking smug.

"Was it good for you?"

Craven groaned, then felt amazement as his face exploded in a rare blush.

Chapter Nine

Was he falling in love?

Craven lay panting on his back, his eyes slowly uncrossing to focus in on the woman who leaned above him. Nola was magnificent.

And even lying there, covered in his own cum, he was ready for more of her.

So maybe it wasn't love. It really didn't matter at this point. He just wanted more.

"Damn, I'm good," Nola, purred as she watched the heap of flesh that she had reduced the Great Master of Painful Pleasures into. It felt good, damn good.

Grunting, Craven absently ran his fingers through the mess on his chest, as if he couldn't believe that he had exploded without her inner walls pumping him, and then smiled at her.

"Human, passion is contagious. If your partner is willing and open enough, you can get them to do just about anything."

That should neatly put her in her place, he thought. After all, she did have her passionate nature awakened because of him.

"Then I must really be damn good," Nola crowed, then wrinkled her nose as she looked around the room. "But the environment needs something."

"I suppose you want roses and harps?" Craven snorted as he found the strength to rise up and tower over her. He may be messy, but he was still the boss of this operation and everybody had damn well better — what was the term — recognize it.

"No, but I am just about all fantasized out," she giggled.

"You can't be," Craven insisted as he grinned at her.

"I have little imagination," Nola returned shrugging.

"But I haven't made love to you yet."

"I don't want to make love, Craven. I want a fuck. Yes, that is my next fantasy. I want a big old nasty, sweaty fuck."

"A fuck."

"Fuck," Nola insisted. "I'll have enough of this romance crap when I go back home. Gregor is good at that sort of thing, but passion…" She shuddered. "I hope you were right earlier. Maybe I can inspire some passion in that…man."

Craven was again thrown into turmoil.

She was thinking about another man? She was still considering going back to that Gregor? After having been had by the best, by him, she wanted to go to that *Human*?

He felt so…used.

Then he felt angry.

"A fuck, huh?"

"Yup, and then I think it's time for me to get back home. They must be worried about me."

Nola paused as she looked at the man in front of her. He could make her heart weak with a word or make her senses soar with untold pleasure.

But being here with him had to be temporary. She has to remind herself of that.

If she let her feelings for this fairy, this strong sensual man, get too strong, she would never want to leave his kingdom. And then were would that leave her?

With a family that hated her guts, parents that were disappointed, and a fiancée who would be emotionally damaged almost beyond repair.

She had to distance herself.

But before she went, she would feel him deep inside of her, pulsing with life. She wanted to store up memories for the vast December her life would become after she exchanged her vows.

But the expressions that flittered across Craven's face were lost to her as she contemplated her own dismal future.

Craven had always said he wanted to experience emotions he thought were gone, but now he wondered why?

A soul-deep anger filled him, as he stared at the pretty woman who wanted to fuck him then leave.

Then a pain so deep filled his heart, he was sure that it was splintering into icy shards.

"A fuck takes planning," Craven said, his voice pleasantly neutral as he fought to keep his face void of expression. "And you need rest."

"I feel fine," Nola sighed, dragging herself out of her own dark thoughts. "But a change of environment…"

She stopped suddenly as her vision began to waver and the room began to spin like a kaleidoscope.

The dark colors of the leather room spun and swirled until her eyes and stomach rebelled and her knees grew weak.

Thought became a loud roar of air rushing by her and a pressure built up in her head.

Just before she lost control and began to scream, the room solidified, and she came back to herself with a thump.

Still a bit queasy and dizzy, Nola forced her eyes open and looked around the room she was now in, then gasped with pleasure.

It looked to be the center of a large field.

Flowers of every imaginable color and shape bloomed and fragrances zapped around her.

Buttercups and daisies, morning glories and roses, vines and stems of the most exotic orchids and blossoms surrounded her.

"Craven…"

"Rest, Nola," Craven urged, and she spun around to see him standing beside a large canopied bed.

Nola covered her mouth with both of her hands, overcome as she saw the gossamer coverings and the billowing white canopy that covered her dream bed.

Mountains of pillows covered the thick mattress while delicate butterflies were carved in and around the bedposts.

"Rest, Nola. Rest, for when I return, you will not have the energy to move for quite some time."

With that, he disappeared in a flash of bright white light and musk-scented smoke.

But Nola paid no heed to his words; she was mesmerized by the bed that lay before her and her sadness that filled her heart.

She would love Craven, she would rest in this bed, and then she would go home to the black and gray existence.

She almost felt like crying.

* * * * *

Love and Hate giggled as they watched an angry Craven storm away to his private chambers.

"Payback is a bitch," Love chortled as his brother scowled at him.

"You don't have to take that much enjoyment of it. It is unbecoming." He sniffed at his brother, but his eyes told a different story.

He did not enjoy this, not one bit.

"Craven brought it on his own self," Love insisted, grinning a grin that showed all of his razor sharp teeth—the same teeth he used to get a grip on some people's hearts, a grip that sometimes can never be torn free. "Besides, you don't want to lose our little wager, right?"

"I guess," Hate sighed, and then turned again to watch the door that Craven disappeared into. "But I say we double our bet. I am sure he is going to do it."

"Fine," Love giggled. "But be prepared to pay up when you lose."

"We are agreed?"

"Agreed."

The twin brothers turned and walked away, each anticipating the outcome of Craven's situation.

Time was running out, they both knew. But only the gods knew what Craven and Nola would do.

Chapter Ten

Craven stared at the mirror in front of him. He did not like what he saw.

His image was tarnished, weak, fading.

It was an expression of his inner torment, of the ideas and thoughts that were warring in his head.

What did he feel for Nola? He barely knew her, yet his mind was screaming to hold on to her and his body throbbing to screw her.

His silent, internal conflict was weighing heavily on his soul.

On the one hand, she had no real way of leaving. She never stipulated a time limit on her wish. So he could fuck her and leave her to the tender mercies of Oberon and Tatiana. Not to mention the several creatures who lived under the mound and would love to toy with Human flesh. That is what the old emotionless Craven would do.

But this new Craven, this Craven who felt intense desire, who felt surprised by the passion that existed within the tiny women. The Craven who rushed to protect her from Love and Hate, the one who actually took her to the Flower Bower, this Craven wanted to make tender love to her, to make her climax until she begged for mercy. This Craven wanted to learn as much as he could about her, and hold the information close to his heart.

Thus he was conflicted.

As he stared at the mirrors that lined the ceiling, floor, and walls, that conflict was reflected back at him a thousand times over.

While he waited for his sharp mind to come to some resolution, there was a loud knock at the door.

"What?" he bellowed, though his breathing remained calm.

"Craven. I desire a word with thee."

Oberon.

Great, he thought, *just what I need now.*

"What do you want, Oberon?"

"A word," the deep voice insisted.

"Then enter."

"You know that no one can face the mirrors, Craven, if they are not ready to discover what secrets they are ready to expose. I am not ready for that."

Sighing, Craven walked over to the door and exited quietly. The resolutions could be put off for a time. He would deal with Oberon and then give Nola what she wanted.

Afterwards, he would reevaluate his situation and then decide.

He exited the room, and there in the doorway, dressed in gauzy robes, was Oberon, King of the Fairy.

His long blue hair was loosely tied behind his head in a tail, and his white eyes glared in annoyance.

Oberon was at least six-feet-seven inches tall and sported the muscles that one would expect in a warrior king.

"What did you tell Tatiana?"

He raised one light blue eyebrow and waited for an explanation.

"For goodness sakes, Obie. Did you never tell her about us? I mean, you should not try and keep secrets from your mate."

Craven rolled his eyes as he stared at the magnificent warrior, the wonderful king, and a mediocre lover. That is, mediocre until he received proper training at his hands.

"My past is none of her concern, as is her relationship with you."

"But I am not screwing her now, Obie. Been there, done that, don't want a repeat."

Oberon sighed and tried to hold in a laugh as he stared at the man who, for one brief, shining moment, was his lover. Craven was aptly named.

"Our past relationship is not what I was referring too, Craven. But thanks for making her want to top your acrobatics in bed."

"Okay, so why the kingly brow and the scowl?"

Craven was already mentally distancing himself, deciding what to wear, what to dress Nola in, which room to do the deed, as it were.

"The Human."

That pulled him out of his musings.

"Nola? What about her?"

"You know that Tatiana is not fond of Humans, and this one seems to be causing quite a stir."

"Love and Hate?"

"They have some sort of bet going on about her. I hear that the cost to the loser will be harsh."

"Hate was trying to get into her literally. She was not impressed."

"The cowboy look?"

"Yup."

"Sometimes I wish we never wired the mound for satellite. Damn Western Channel."

Craven chuckled at the exasperated look on Oberon's face before he turned to look at the shorter man again.

"But that is part of the problem. She has to go, Craven. You kill her, or morph her, or wipe her mind, but she has to go."

"When I am ready."

"Craven, you have to get rid of her, or I will be forced to take action."

"Against her?"

"Against you."

"Hmm."

"I am serious, Craven, my friend." Oberon insisted as a sad look crossed his face. "I do not wish to take action against you, but the longer she stays, the more attached you will get. And I cannot allow her to stay with you here. And you will not fit in the world above. I have been there, my friend. It is no place for any decent fairy."

He clasped his friend on the shoulder and Craven winced at the feel of the power that flowed through Oberon's kingly veins.

"I will do what I must, Oberon. And I will not be rushed. I will complete this wish and then I will do what has to be done."

"Complete your task soon, Craven. The quicker you get rid of the Human, the quicker things will settle down here."

With a nod in his direction, Oberon turned and walked away, his long legs taking powerful strides that exuded power.

Sighing, Craven turned to complete his plans. He would worry about how to get Nola home later. After all, he could not just let her go, and her wish was worded for an indefinite visit. If Tatiana had a problem with that, they would cross that bridge when they got to it.

But for now, he had to go through his leather selection and get his toys ready.

It was time to fuck Nola, to give her what she wanted.

He only hoped he wouldn't lose his soul in the undertaking.

Chapter Eleven

Nola sighed as she felt warmth surround her. It felt comforting, safe, enveloping.

She snuggled in deeper, relishing the feelings that were surrounding her body, feeling cherished and loved, like never before.

"Nola,"

The soft voice calling her name was almost a nuisance as she tried to tune out everything but the warm glow that covered her from head to toe.

"*Wake up!*"

The shouted command brought her instantly awake, just in time to see the flowers, the beautiful blossoms that lulled her into a restful sleep, began to swirl and spin.

She became dizzy, disoriented as she discovered that it was not the flowers that were spinning, it was her!

She closed her eyes and groaned once but as soon as she opened her mouth to complain, the room settled and she found herself…in a dungeon.

"What…?" she muttered, confused as she took in her new surroundings.

The room was painted black—ceiling, floors, everything. In the four corners of the room, giant candelabras sat smoldering with large black candles, casting an eerie light in the darkness. On a shelf against the wall opposite her sat a strange group of implements that frightened even as they aroused.

She looked up, and before her eyes a light began to glow. It spread across the ceiling, growing in intensity, taking on a rectangular shape, until a mirror took form. She was left staring in shock, for she saw a woman covered from head to toe in leather.

She looked down, and sure enough, it was her!

Her legs were encased in what had to be custom-fitted chaps. They fit her like a second skin from ankle to hip while leaving her crotch and ass free.

Strapped across her chest was the strangest bustier she had ever seen. It lifted and held her breasts high and tight, the cups only high enough to expose her hardening nipples. The clothing exposed and offered her breasts like pastries in black leather wrapping.

Around her neck was a thick padded leather band — a collar with a metal D ring glistening in the front. She reached up and felt its confining ungiving leather, and trembled at the symbolism.

Her hands were covered too, but with leather gloves that traveled from her wrists to her biceps, leaving her fingers free.

The outfit was simple, but the feelings it evoked within her body were a lot more complicated.

She stared at the mirror and then down at her body, still not quite believing what she was seeing.

She looked powerful, strong, dominant. She was everything she ever hoped to be and was afraid of becoming.

She shivered as an untold sense of power filled her.

A wicked smile worthy of Craven himself spread across her face.

She was a leather goddess, powerful enough to take on any man. She was strength and sensuality combined in one tight package.

She was Nola. And the world had damn well better remember it!

"Beautiful,"

Nola gasped and turned at the sound of the voice.

Speak of the devil... It was Craven himself.

"All that's missing are the boots and the whip. But we will not be using that, my dear."

Nola blinked as Craven seemed to just grow into view.

And what a view!

He was also dressed in full black leather, but a harness of hard shiny leather was across his chest, pulling tight around his pecs, and emphasizing the muscular perfection while highlighting his nipple piercings.

It wrapped around his ribcage, as if testing the strength of his flesh and bringing attention to his well-developed abs.

Two leather armbands rode tight and proud on his biceps, showing the strength of the muscles while giving him a menacing appearance.

At his wrists was a pair of matched gauntlets, shiny with small silver loops that jingled as he moved closer to her.

A pair of tight black leather pants covered his legs like a second skin, showing off his corded thighs and thick calves to perfection.

On his feet here a pair of square-toed leather boots that gave him the look and the feel of a master.

"Did you borrow those from Hate?" she asked as she took him all in.

She had to resist the urge to growl *'woof'* as a slow grin spread across his face.

"Actually, he gets his fashion tips from me."

"I can believe it. But why the leather trip, Craven? This is a bit unusual."

"This is the gear that I intend to fuck you with, Nola. Per your request."

"But I never expected this."

"You get what you wish for. You wanted a fucking, a fucking you shall receive.

Before she could move, her pretty princess bed seemed to melt from underneath her, the coverings twining and lifting until she was suspended in mid air.

Almost like creeping vines, the covers wrapped around her legs, slid across her back, wrapped around her arms, until she was settled rather comfortably in a black silk swing. There was even a headrest so that her neck would not be strained.

Nola had never been in this position before. She was a bit nervous, but not frightened. Craven would never hurt her. But this leather sex, this was something that she had only contemplated in her deepest, darkest fantasies.

"I...I don't know what to do," she breathed as some of her unease began to transform into a tingling need.

"Just lay there, Nola. Lay there and enjoy my control of your body."

He started at her neck, licking and biting at the firm flesh, making her moan and toss her head back, exposing more of herself to his roving mouth,

His hands went to her exposed nipples, plucking and pulling at her sensitive flesh, making them stand out in hard peaks.

"I am going to fuck the hell out of you," he murmured into her ear before driving his tongue in, making her writhe in pleasure. She never knew how sensitive her ears were until be began to suck at her lobes.

"Craven, I..."

"Shh. Before I gag that pretty mouth of yours," he purred, pulling away from her tempting, tiny ears and driving his tongue deep within her mouth.

Their tongues dueled for supremacy, filling them with the flavor of the other, leaving them wanting more.

"You need a toy," Craven mumbled as he broke away from the kiss.

Reaching a hand out, a slender cylinder flew off the shelf and into his hand.

Smiling wickedly, he held the small silver shaft up for Nola to see.

"It's so tiny," she murmured as she wondered what he was going to do with it.

"Perfect for what I have in mind."

He twisted the base and it began a low humming. It was a vibrator.

With a wave of his hand, her bottom was lifted higher and all her secrets exposed.

"What are you going to…?"

A warning glance from him made her question fizzle.

Nodding, he reached his hand out again and a small black bottle floated within his reach.

"This will ease things a bit, while heating them up. A lot."

He stood between her spread upright legs and tilted the bottle.

The heated oil drizzled across her shaven crotch, coating her folds of flesh in the shiny substance. It slowly tricked down, past her opening to slide across her perineal area to her rosebud.

She shivered and jumped in her silken sling as heat washed across her body. Even her nipples contracted, as if there was a direct line from her crotch to them.

She closed her eyes and moaned.

"So pretty," Craven cooed. "The oil on your flesh. Did you know you are dripping wet, Nola? Even without the oil, your body shows me how much it needs this."

Stepping closer, he let his fingers follow the trail of the lubricant across her feminine lips around her opening, to that bit of skin that separated her cunt from her anus.

There he pressed lightly, hearing her moan as her nerves were stimulated, sending deeper desire flashing through her body.

He brought the buzzing, pulsing metal close to her, letting it rest for a moment against her clit before slowly circling her opening.

Nola whined, high-pitched and feminine, music to his ears as her body lunged in the direction of the dildo.

"No, no," he admonished as he ran the metal cock over the left side of her clit, the most sensitive side. "That space is reserved for me. I have another place in mind for this."

He lowered the dildo again, rolling it over her rosebud, sending fire through her spine.

Nola gasped at the sensations that buzzing thing was creating in her. No one had ever touched her so intimately, but it felt dangerous, exciting and taboo. Her blood began to rush in her veins and as she silently demanded penetration. Her body told her it would be pleasurable, and her body would never lie to her.

"Not yet," Craven teased as he applied light pressure to her, not opening her, just teasing her opening.

He bent low and took one hard nipple into his mouth.

Nola bucked up toward him, offering herself more fully as the heat of his mouth encircled the throbbing tip

Craven sucked at her deeply, rolling his tongue over the hard nubbin of flesh.

Nola's body reacted so beautifully he could not help but be affected by it.

He felt his cock harden and lengthen down his thigh within its leather confines, straining for release. Pre-cum bubbled to the tip, soaking his pants and making the head more sensitive. He was hard as nails, wet as morning dew, and ready for action. One hand slowly stroked his cock-head through the leather as he smiled. He was almost ready.

Nola bucked up against Craven's mouth, against that dildo, *anything* to make the pleasure last.

Craven brought his fingers into play, rubbing along her wet lips, teasing her clit, stroking and petting her.

He loved to watch her head whip from side to side, her eyes glazed and her luscious lips parted, gasping for breath. She was beautiful.

Shaking those thoughts out of his head, Craven decided that it was time to get back to work. Looking down at her writhing ripe body, he knew she was ready.

Stepping back, he unlaced the front ties of his pants, letting them part to expose his hardness.

"Nola, are you ready to be fucked?" he asked, his voice almost singsong.

"Craven," she whimpered as she tried to reach for him. But the silk wrapped around her wrists, preventing her from moving as it slithered along her exposed body parts, adding another layer of sensuality to the proceedings.

"I think...yes."

She nodded her head, body straining towards his like a moth to the flame.

Craven peeled his pants low enough to expose his flesh, dampened by sweat and desire.

The smell of hot leather and hotter man filled the room, making Nola inhale deeply of the arousing scent, causing her mouth to water.

Stepping up to her, Craven again ran the little vibrator over her rosebud, teasing the entrance a bit, before sinking just the head inside her ring of muscle.

Nola gasped at this penetration. Fire shot from her opening to her clit that began to demand attention of its own.

But restrained as she was, she could only whimper her approval and plead for more.

And Craven was willing to give more.

Teasingly, he slid the metal cock inside a bit, before withdrawing, widening her, stretching her for its full penetration, the oil easing his way.

Again and again he twirled the vibrator, sinking in a bit deeper each time, leaving her panting and shaking, a sexual thing wanting to be had.

"Deep breath," he whispered as he began to apply a steady pressure.

Nola first felt like she was being ripped in two. She closed her eyes and gritted her teeth. But riding along on the wings of the slight pain was an overwhelmingly intense pleasure that left her shaky and unsure of herself. She felt like she was being reborn, like there was no longer a virgin part to her body.

Trembling, she gave over to this new sensation, forcing her body to relax and accept the invader, and in doing so welcomed the fierce biting pleasure that caused her to moan and bite her lip in lust.

Dildo securely placed, Craven moved in for the kill.

Taking his cock in hand, he ran the large, plum-colored tip over her clit, adding to the wetness there with his pre-cum, circling the sensitive button until a sob escaped Nola's throat.

Slowly, he eased himself down, teasing her entrance, sliding inches in, far enough to stretch her muscles into accepting the large head, then pulling out again.

Over and over he penetrated her with just the head, making the nerves at her opening reverberate with spine-tingling need.

This want flowed through her body from where he teased, to where the vibrator sat, shaking her insides and causing her to scream in passion.

"Please, Craven!" she wailed, her hand fisting in the material, holding onto it as it centered her body, preventing it from flying to pieces. Uncaring of who may be listening, Nola threw back her head and screamed. "Now! Please Craven. Fuck me! Please!"

"What I wanted to hear," Craven growled as he reared back and slammed home, hard and deep.

"Yes!" Nola screamed, her inner muscles immediately spasming around him, milking him as white lights flashed behind her eyes and her body convulsed in climax.

Her sphincter clamped on to the buzzing toy, increasing the intensity of her explosion, making it last far longer than she thought possible. Nothing could be better that that!

And then he began to move.

Craven felt Nola obtain her release, but he wanted her to have more.

He knew that she would be sensitive after such an orgasm, but he also knew that her body was just warming up.

He slowly began to thrust, plunging deep and grinding his hips against her, rotating his hard cock in her clenching pussy.

"No," Nola whimpered as a pleasurable pain filled her. Her clit burned and her body began to overload. It was too much too soon.

But Craven continued, slowly and steadily, a grin on his face as his hair began to stick in wet tendrils to his body.

Slowly he began to pick up the pace and her resistance melted into growing desire.

She began to arch her hips up, thrusting back, forcing him in deeper.

Her denials turned to pleas for more as she closed her eyes and let these feelings swamp her.

Faster and faster Craven moved, until she matched him thrust for thrust, then he reached down and grasped the handle of the dildo.

"Craven!"

Nola screamed and jerked as Craven began to thrust the dildo counter to his movements within Nola's wet sheath.

She began to wail wordless screams of passion, begging for more as he manipulated both of her openings, dragging her to heights she had never before reached.

Nola was trapped inside a primal fury that grew stronger within her.

Unable to move to release her feelings, the tension built higher and higher, forcing her to dizzying heights of ecstasy.

Her head whipped from side to side, her throat numb from the screaming, sweat beading on her flesh, and still she wanted more!

Craven's breath rasped from his lungs as he pumped like a piston. He used his free hand to grab the sling making it swing harder, faster into him, adding to the strength of his lunges.

He was lost; all thoughts of control vanished as he closed his eyes and gave into his instincts.

He pummeled her, he slammed her, he damn near killed himself as he tried to thrust deeper into her body all the way to her soul.

But his kind of animalistic passion could not last.

Even as he opened his mouth to scream out a denial, he felt his nuts slam to the base of his cock and the first scalding shots of his life force rocket through his cock.

"No... damn... fuck, Nola!"

One lone roar of passion-pained release filled the air as Craven gritted his teeth, arched his back and let his climax fly.

Feeling him, seeing him reach this level pushed Nola over the top again.

She shrieked her pleasure as again her muscles convulsed around him, squeezing him deeply, trying to suck in his spirit, as her soul broke free of its earthly bonds and shot through the universe.

Craven lunged uncontrollably, without rhythm, as spurt after spurt of his seed exploded from his cock, his body torn between desire and pain. He relished both sensations.

Finally, his orgasm began to ease, his body unclenching from its spasm as he fell forward onto Nola, the sling stretching to accommodate them both. He pulled the dildo from her body and let it fall to the floor with a clang.

Nola panted, trying to relearn how to breathe and think as she felt his large warm weight settle on her. Instead of his weight being uncomfortable, he felt...comforting and enveloping.

Much nicer than the leather, she thought.

"Are you okay," he panted, breathing deeply between each word.

Nola moaned her consent, nodding her head, for every other part of her was numb.

"Damn, I I..." He stopped before he finished that statement.

Tiredly pulling himself up, he grinned down at the sweaty, shaking slip of a Human who had turned his world inside out.

She didn't seem to notice his slip, and that was all right with him.

Slowly he began to pull the leather from her body, sliding each piece away and exposing her tender flesh.

"Craven?"

"Shh," he admonished. "We need a washing."

He pulled the tight leather gear from both of their bodies, and with a snap of his fingers, the room began to sway.

A large scented tub rose from the ground and Craven eased the now naked Nola into his arms before lowering her into the tub.

She hissed as the hot water hit her sore flesh, but soon moaned in delight as the heat began to sink into her abused muscles, easing their strain.

But the greatest pleasure was Craven sliding in behind her, until she was cupped along his body, feeling his swelled but not hard cock rest against her ass.

"Shh, Nola," he soothed as he began to rub her arms, spreading the scented water over her. "After this bath, we rest. Then we have much to discuss."

Chapter Twelve

Nola drifted, lost in a sensual haze. Her body was limp with exhaustion, suspended in a dream-like haze.

Her mind was at total ease, awash in the lingering ecstasy that seemed to move her in a between-place where she was content to drift, languid and lost.

"Damn, you are beautiful," Craven purred, and Nola realized that she was not floating. She was being carried.

She was suspended within the cradle of Craven's arms.

And even more surprising, she felt safe.

Safe and cherished were emotions that she was not familiar with in her life. Three wee emotions that she always associated with love.

But love was a person—kind of—here in this place.

And that more than anything served to remind her that her stay here was temporary.

She had to protect herself, and allowing herself to feel—to feel anything—was out of the question,

She would not even attempt to categorize the emotions that she felt for the man that carried her so easily in his arms.

That would be dangerous, and Nola always played it safe.

There was security in safety, which was why she was getting married soon.

There was nothing safe with Craven, in loving Craven, for feeling anything for him at all.

She had to be casual. Her safety depended upon it.

"My word, Craven. What did you do to the female?"

The voice was low and royal, and that was strange enough to make her attempt to open her eyes.

But it as the man himself that impressed her.

Pale blue hair hung nearly to the floor in a long tail. His eyes appeared just as pale.

He had the carriage of a warrior, the stance of the soldier, and the presence of a king.

"Oberon," Craven sighed. "Don't you have anything better to do?"

Oberon? *Oberon.* It was the King of the Fairies himself.

"No. Pleasing my queen is the best thing I can do. So in doing my best, I must insist that you send the Human home. *Now.*"

Craven halted with his sweet bundle in his arms and felt something new.

He felt fear.

"By your silence, I am to assume that you agree."

"Well, I didn't say that."

"What do you mean?"

"Yes Craven, whatever do you mean? And the Human would appreciate it if you stopped speaking of her as if she didn't have a brain in her head."

Both men looked down at her, disbelief etched on their faces.

"Human? Do you not know who I am?"

"Can you tell me in two titles or less?" she said without thinking.

Her mind was all set to go home and away from Craven and the desires he was bringing out in her. It was too dangerous to stay here, and if she had to apply to the King himself, she would.

"And this is the creature you defy me for? Are you sure it is able to think?"

"That was sarcasm," Nola felt the need to explain.

"Well, it is at least well-endowed," Oberon allowed, his eyes stuck on her oh-so-abundant bosom.

Nola blanched, then blushed as she realized that she had gotten so used to being naked in this place, that she forgot that she was in the raw.

Her arms instantly went to cover her bosom and exposed crotch.

"Now see what you made her do?" Craven uttered, completely at a loss with his ex-companion and King. "Now I have to train her to be nude all over again."

"You are correcting me?" Oberon's eyebrow rose up as he glared at the wayward fairy. "And don't change the subject. Send the creature home now."

"Train me?" Nola's eyes widened at his words. *Train* her, as if she were a pet?

"Oh, hush," Craven snarled, earning a glare from the two other people in the hall.

"By all means," Nola growled as she struggled out of his arms. "Send me home now."

It is for the best, her mind insisted. She felt as if she had been shown the doorway to some fantastic world, some paradise, and now was being forced to leave with only a sampling of the delights it held for her.

Pain was building in her chest, but she was used to that. She had to get out of this place before her *want* of Craven turned into a *need.*

"I can't," Craven finally admitted, his face screwed up in an attitude of displeasure.

"Can't or won't?" Nola asked, her eyes narrowing as panic began to blossom in her chest.

What had she gotten herself into? She had to leave now.

"Can't," Craven growled, crossing his arms defiantly.

"Why?"

Oberon and Nola shouted the question at the same time. The looked at each other in disbelief, then turned shocked looks to Craven.

They wanted, no, *needed* answers.

"Because there was no escape clause in your wish."

"What?" Nola cried, incredulous.

"You must be joking," Oberon added. "No escape clause? What were you thinking?"

Craven slowly let his eyes roam over Nola's naked body, making her cross her arms again and shake her hair forward to cover her breasts.

Both men appraised her nakedness and exchanged similar wicked looks.

"Okay, I can see why you would be distracted," Oberon allowed. "But she cannot stay here. You have to find a way...or I will find a way for you."

That last sounded ominous to Nola's ears as she stood between the two proud men.

Oberon seemed insistent, but Craven seemed...

Nothing. His face was blank.

Then it began to dawn on her that maybe this is what Craven did to all of his women.

The crystalline feelings of joy she had developed in his arms exploded, each shard slashing her heart open.

"Is this a game to you?" Nola hissed as she stared at Craven. "Do you bring Humans here, get your jollies off, and then have the big guy get rid of the evidence when you are through?"

"Nola," Craven began tiredly.

"*No*. Is *this* what you do, Craven? How many before me have fallen for your cheap tricks and lies? How many have you seduced and then left to rot in some bog?"

"I have never..."

"I want to go home," Nola shouted. "Home, Craven. Take me home. I don't care how you do it. You did this to me. You got me here with your promises and your teases, and now you leave me to die? To die at the hands of a man that should not exist, who does not exist in my world?"

"I am not a man, Human," Oberon felt the need to point out. "I am of the earth and of magic."

"Whatever," she screamed as tears and real fear began to blossom on her face. "I don't want to die. I want to go home and marry safe plain Gregor and never have another day of excitement in my life, so long as I am alive."

Craven stared at her, conflicting emotions running through him.

He wanted so much to comfort her, to tell her that everything would be okay, and to beg her not to leave, but he couldn't. He was of dark desire and black sensuality. He could not be soft or romantic, or caring, or...falling in love.

"Answer me. Send me home." Nola screamed, tears running freely down her face.

Continued silence.

"Then damn you to hell, Craven. Damn you and what you make me feel."

Turning, she took off down the hall, straight for the first door she could find, the door to the Mirror Room. She tugged twice, hard, and then the lock gave.

Chapter Thirteen

The pounding of her heart drowned out all thought as Nola slung open the first unlocked door she came to and raced inside.

Then she froze as the room began to shimmer and spin around her.

At the center of this vortex of light was a large S-shaped mirror.

As fast as the world began to tilt, it righted itself and Nola found herself staring at images of herself.

From floor to ceiling, there were reflections of herself, and some of them were quite scary.

There she was, a lustful look in her eyes, and across the room, her image looking sad and lost. In front of her was her image, eyes at half-mast and face filled with lust. And beside that, another image of her face raised up and filled with love.

"What is this?" she asked, her eyes filling with horror as all the images, all the aspects of herself, turned to face her. And then she knew.

She was looking at, inside the core soul of herself.

Slowly, she walked to a reflection closest to her, reached out her hand and gently caressed the image.

Her mirror self was crying and she knew why.

They were tears for what could have been.

"This is all me, what's inside of me?"

All the faces nodded, and it was a bit dizzying to see…her, in all phases of emotions, nodding at once.

Nola carefully touched the mirror closest to her again. The face stared back, large brown eyes liquid with some unnamed emotion.

It was beautiful in its sadness.

"What could put such a look on my face?" she mused.

Then the large mirror in the center of the room began to spin.

Drawn almost against her will, Nola approached, each measured step filling her with dread.

Faster and faster the mirror spun, casting flashes of light against the mirrored walls.

Then just as suddenly, it stopped.

Trembling, Nola raised her eyes and saw an image of Craven, in all his naked splendor, hair being blown by some unseen wind.

"He would make me cry," she whispered as she realized that all of these emotions she was feeling were a direct result of being around Craven.

"But I need to get back home," she said, voicing her thoughts. "If I remain here, I will die. Or Craven will drive me crazy. My future is with Gregor."

The mirror pulsed, rippled, and the image of Craven returned.

"No. Craven is not my future," she insisted. "He just doesn't mean *that* much to me."

Then the picture of Craven disappeared and a picture of herself took its place.

But this picture was hideous. Her visage was twisted in a hideous mask, eyes lowered in hate and despair.

"What is this?" Nola asked, horrified as the picture of herself began to deteriorate, twisting into some creature from the pit of her worse nightmare.

Slowly she backed away, but the faces, the ugly hurtful faces, followed, their condemning eyes on her retreating figure.

Giving into her fright, she turned and tried to race from the room, forgetting that the walls were covered in mirrors.

As she did, even more horrific images of herself glared at her, condemned her.

Her breath caught in her throat and the taste of bile filled her mouth as her fear turned into horrified fascination.

Then she was racing to where she thought the door would be, pounding on it, screaming for someone to let her out.

Glancing over her shoulder, she found no pity in the many eyes that stared back at her, only condemnation.

"Please. Let me out," she wailed as she slid to the floor, a image of herself staring up at her matching the one on the mirror she pounded on desperately.

The opening of the door was a shock, but a welcome one.

She leapt to her feet and tore from the room and straight into a pair of strong, comforting arms.

"It's okay," the deep voice crooned as he rocked her.

The door was slammed shut and she was lifted into a pair of muscular arms, her face buried in long, luxuriant hair.

"Craven..." she began, then paused she caught a whiff of the man who held her.

It was not her Craven, but as she looked up through the long red hair, she knew she was in the arms of Hate.

Chapter Fourteen

"Where is Craven?" she asked, her voice still shaky, but recovering. "And what was that place?"

"Craven is with Oberon," Hate said as he swiftly carried her from the hallway and into a—gasp and swoon—regular room.

There was a bed and everything.

No moving wall hangings, no haunted bathtubs, no mirrors scaring the hell out of her. A regular room painted a plain boring white with a simple four-posted bed.

"You will be comfortable in here," Hate continued as he set her on the bed and seemed to pluck a robe out of thin air.

Handing it to her, he continued, "And the room you were in is Craven's favorite haunt, the Mirror Room."

"If he enjoys that," Nola whispered, trembling as the memory of her disintegrating face crossed her mind's eye, "then maybe he brought me here to use and get rid of."

Shaking his head at his own folly, Hate sighed and took Nola's hand, and surprisingly, she let him.

"Nola, Craven can enter that room without any fear because he knows what's in his heart. He may be an unscrupulous bastard, but he has always been honest to a fault. That room holds no horror for him because he understands himself."

"So I guess I am a liar then," Nola sniffed as she pulled on the robe, admiring the royal purple color and the silky warmth it provided.

"What did you see?" he asked softly.

"I saw me. At first it was wondrous, Hate. I saw so many aspects of my personality, things that I never knew before I met…him. Then when I said… I asked a question I wasn't ready to hear the answer to, and the room went haywire. It made me look positively evil, Hate."

"So, you were lying to yourself."

"What?" She arched her eyebrow as she stared at Hate, knowing there was some truth to his statements, but refusing to believe it.

"If your image turned ugly from simple emotions, you were lying to yourself. If you lie, you poison your inner being, and the room was showing you that poison. Well, the effects of it on your soul, at any rate."

"But… The room had to be wrong. No one can predict the future."

"True, but it can project what you feel in your heart, and what you desire most."

Nola turned her head away, shaken to the core by what Hate was telling her.

"I won't ask what your question was, Nola, but I have the idea that it has to do with Craven."

"Where is he now?" she had to ask as she turned to face him, accepting what he was telling her as truth.

She could never lie to herself for long. Craven was that important to her, and growing more important by the moment.

More important than her life? Doubtful, as she only knew him for a short time. But he was still important.

"Probably getting executed by the King and Queen for treason while he argues with them to let him change your wish."

"*What?*"

"Remember," Hate sighed as he watched panic fill her eyes. " 'Be careful what you wish for and how you wish for it.' Word your wish carefully, because you just may get *exactly* what you wish for."

Chapter Fifteen

"So what do you have to say for yourself, Craven?"

He rolled his eyes at Tatiana and turned to face Oberon.

"I can't send her home. That was not part of her wish."

"Well you have to do something, my friend," Oberon said as he seriously looked at his ex-lover and close friend. "It has been a long-standing rule that Humans are not allowed to stay. You knew this, and yet you let this woman coach you into..."

"If anything, I coached her," Craven said, still looking bored.

The inner chambers were cleared of all, save Craven and the King and Queen. It was a special privilege that Oberon granted Craven—privacy for these proceedings.

"You are not making a good case for yourself, my friend," Oberon sighed as he glanced over at his mate.

"Yes, Craven, you act as if you really care for this Human. Like someone of your nature could care for anyone other than himself."

"Now that stung," Craven growled, anger easily coming to him. "And that was uncalled for, Tatiana. Or are you still upset because we parted and I took up with that Brownie from County Cork?"

Tatiana sniffed and turned her eyes away from Craven. Okay, so maybe she was a little put out by his treatment of her, but that was besides the case. There were no humans allowed in *Tier Na NÓg*. Everyone knew that.

"This is not about me, Craven," Tatiana insisted, blushing a bit as her King raised one eyebrow at her. "This is about your human pet."

"Nola is no pet, Tatiana," Craven all but growled as he stared at his Queen. "She is intelligent, passionate, loving, and very generous."

"Yes, we heard how generous she was from the inner chambers, Craven," she drawled. "You sure can pick screamers."

Both men turned to stare at her.

"What?" Tatiana said defensively. "Everyone could here her wailing '*Oh* Craven. *Yes* Craven. *More* Craven.' It was loud."

"What my Queen means to say," Oberon interjected, "Is that the Human must go, one way or the other."

Oberon was dead serious. There was no joking or teasing involved. They were at the heart of the issue.

"If I send her home, I break my word, my given oath."

"And for that you will be punished," Oberon reminded him. "Better if I send her to the next realm."

"*No.*"

Oberon raised his eyebrow at his subject screaming at him.

Instantly aware of his faux pas, Craven took a calming breath and tried to reason with the King.

"Forgive my impudence, but I cannot see the woman punished or killed, Oberon. She has done nothing to warrant this. She just wished for passion."

"Then you will send her home."

"And then you will be punished," Tatiana stated blandly. She might be irritated with Craven, but he was still a likeable friend, an excellent sexual tutor, and…well, he was just Craven. She worried about his decision.

"I cannot let her be punished for my oversights," he stated again, flicking his hair behind his shoulders and tapping his front tooth nervously with his fingernail.

"Then you will break your word, your binding oath, and willingly accept you punishment."

Craven inhaled deeply, and closed his eyes as the words of his King penetrated his mind.

He would be an oath-breaker until he paid for his sin. Repayment could take months if not years, and he would lose something he valued, some essential part of him.

And he knew not what.

In all of his years of existence, he had only heard rumors of oath-breakers, stories that put a shiver of fear in children's hearts and kept rebellious fairies in line. Now he faced that fate, and for what?

For a Human who shouted at him and treated him worse than a servant? For a Human who only wanted him for a good fuck, who used him to get her sexual satisfaction and then would go running back above the hill to marry some demon-spawned, passionless human? For the woman who never considered his feelings in all of their dealings, as long as the orgasms kept coming?

"I accept my fate," he said calmly, his heart pounding in true fear.

It was within his nature to be honest with himself. And he did feel something for Nola. It may not be love, but it was powerful. More powerful than the lust that originally guided him and the unhappiness that made him give in to her foolish wish to be fucked. It was the thing that made his eyes water with longing and his lungs burn to breathe in her air every time he saw her.

It might not be love, not this early in the game, but it was something. Something worth fighting for.

Oberon sighed as he looked at his friend and companion, and regret filled his eyes.

"Oh, Craven."

Chapter Sixteen

"What do you mean, *executed?*"

"Well, do you expect him to do nothing while the woman he cares for is threatened?"

"Cares for me?"

"Honestly, Human," he sounded rather exasperated. "Do you think he would defy the King and Queen, threaten his brethren, and give you exactly what you asked for without making you wish for more things, entangling you deeper into a web of deceit?" He looked at her as if he thought her more intelligent than that. "*Think,* female."

"But he said he couldn't send me home," Nola argued.

"Because you didn't ask to go home when you made your wish."

"So they are going to kill him?"

"Or punish him as an oath-breaker, something that hasn't been seen since the Druids walked the land and the people were known as Picts."

"But…"

"Craven will see to it that you get home, female. And it will cost him dearly."

"Damn him to hell," Nola exploded. "Damn him and damn me for making that stupid wish."

"Wishes are not stupid," Hate insisted. "You just have to be careful…"

"What I wish for, yes I know," she finished. "But if I had just married Gregor, none of this would matter."

"And you would have been miserable."

"Well I'm fuckin' delirious with joy now," she shouted. "If I had never met him, I would never have known what I was missing. And I would be home and no one would be trying to execute the man I…"

"You what?"

"Man I was starting to love," she replied quietly.

Now that she said it, it seemed easier to accept.

"So what are you going to do?"

"I'm going to fight for him."

"Good. And when are you going to do it?"

'Right now."

She leapt to her feet, filled with new purpose.

"Which way?"

Flinging the door open, he pointed down the hall to the inner chamber. "That way."

"Great."

She stormed from the room, eyes blazing with fury.

As soon as she was out of sight, the somber serious look on Hate's face disappeared. A full-blown smirk took its place.

"Humans. They are so easy."

Chapter Seventeen

"Craven, are you ready to face Our judgment?"

Inwardly, Craven trembled in fear, but outwardly, he showed no emotion. He was the ever calm, ever cool, Craven.

"I am ready to accept my punishment."

Oberon looked at his friend, a look of sadness entering his eyes, then he began to speak.

"It is Our judgment…"

"*Wait.*"

Oberon raised one eyebrow, surprise showing plainly on his face, as Tatiana's eyes speared the interloper.

"What is this *creature* doing here?"

Her eyes assessed the Human who entered into her domain, and found her decidedly lacking.

This was the thing that Craven was going to accept punishment for?

"This *creature*," Nola snarled, "Is here defending a man who does not deserve to die. Sure he is manipulative, and thinks of his own self all the time, but he is an honest man."

"Human," Oberon sighed, trying to stop the scene before it began.

"*No.* If there is some way I can undo my wish, I will. I'm the one who jumped before thinking. I didn't read the fine print or even believe in magic. So can't we go back and change my wish? There has to be some precedent."

"Actually, there is not. But I am…"

"So you are going to slaughter the man for giving me my wish? Is that fair? I mean, I thought that was what you guys were supposed to do, you know, go around granting wishes."

Robe flapping, she turned to face Craven, almost astounded to see him dressed in a pair of leather pants and shiny leather boots.

"Nola," Craven began, but was interrupted by the Queen.

"How dare this Human try to dictate matters in our realm? You are nothing to us, mortal. You are an insect, a baby in our eyes. You mean no more to us than a grain of sand trapped beneath our boots."

"Actually," Craven interrupted. "I kind of like her. A whole lot."

"You dare," Tatiana was growing angry. This human had no place here; Craven was defying their rule. This had to stop.

"I don't want her harmed," Craven stated. "It was my fault for not giving her a way out. She should not be punished for wanting what any of us desire, to have our wishes come true."

"Can't we forget I ever made that stupid wish?" Nola wailed out loud.

"That is exactly what we are going to do."

Three voices yelled at Oberon.

"What?"

"We are going to do exactly what you desired. We are going to forget the wish ever happened."

"You are?" Nola's eyes lit up with joy.

"But not quite the way you want it to happen. You will forget about ever being here, Nola. You will forget what you learned at Craven's hands. You will forget all knowledge of our existence. It will be as if you were never here."

"But…"

Forget all that she knew about passion, what she had learned about herself? Was Craven worth the discoveries that she had made, the feelings she had felt, the new emotions and self-confidence running through her body?

Turning her eyes in his direction, she once again beheld his masculine beauty that made her want to follow him into the unknown and trust him enough to experience all that he had to offer.

"Is he worth it, Human?" Tatiana asked, curious about her reply.

"Yes."

"Good. When you leave here, you will retain no memory of your time spent here. I wish you well, Nola, and I hope you learn to remember magic. For it is all around you. It always has been and always will be. You just have to learn to recognize it."

"But what about Craven? He said that he had to be punished."

"He will. Having all memory of him stripped from your mind is punishment enough. He was beginning to love you deeply, Human. And now he will begin to lose that emotion after you leave. Also, he will have no power over you to seduce you or trick you into coming back here."

Craven sucked in a deep breath as if he had been delivered a mighty blow to the chest. He would save her life, but in the doing, he would lose his Nola. Forever.

"Oberon..."

"No, Craven. My decision is final. The moment she leaves this chamber, her memory will be no more. Learn to accept your punishment, Craven. And next time, use a bit of wisdom when granting your wishes. That is all. It is my judgment."

Oberon motioned for his mate to rise, and taking her arm, exited the chambers.

"Now what is this toy you saved for me?" he asked as they disappeared from sight. "You said you got it at an orgy. Of all places."

Chapter Eighteen

"I guess...I guess I will be leaving after all," Nola whispered as she looked at her dream man. "I am glad that you are not going to die."

Craven exploded into laughter at her words. Without the woman who granted him leave to experience such emotions, he was already dead. He was sure that no one would ever make him feel like Nola. No one.

"Nola, Nola. I haven't the words."

He took her into his arms, felt her soft body press against his, and closed his eyes, lost in regrets about what could have been and what would never be.

"Well, at least you didn't say you loved me. It's not like I would remember anyway," she smiled, trying to lift the heavy weight that settled on her heart.

"That would be lying to myself, and that is something that I will never do. But I will say that I was learning to love you, Nola. That what I felt for you I have *never* felt for another woman. And I have had so many women, Nola."

"And I am just special?" she giggled, remembering once he told her she was just like any other woman, a bit more passionate than most, but like any other woman.

"I didn't know you then, Nola. Now I find myself learning all about you, and wanting to know more. But it will not be."

"Craven..." she began, but he placed his finger against her lips, silencing her.

"Be happy, Nola. Marry...Gregor, and be happy."

Before she could say anything else, he pulled back from her and led her to the door.

Nola turned to look up at him. She had to run her fingers through his hair just one last time.

He lowered his lips slowly, and the brush of his skin against hers caused the same electric shock, making her body come alive.

And then he was gone, pulled away as if it were too much for him to take.

"Good bye, Nola," he breathed as he pushed her through the door.

Lights exploded around Nola, sucking the air from her lungs and making her head whirl.

She was falling, but she was falling up.

She opened her mouth to scream, but no sound could escape. She felt pressure building up in her body, felt it make her ears pop and her eyes feel as if they were going to shoot from their sockets.

Just when it got unbearable, she found herself looking up at the sky.

Only it was green.

"*Nola*," she heard someone scream as she realized that it wasn't the sky she was looking at. It was grass.

Groaning, she tried to get to her feet, but before she got very far, strong hands wrapped around her waist.

"Gregor?" she asked as she was pulled, too quickly, in an upright position.

The world spun on its axis.

"I was worried," he whispered as he ran his fingers over her body. "Then I saw you fall. What were you doing out here?"

"Clearing my head," she said as she began to pick the blades of grass from her clothes. "Remember when we used to play here? I was the fairy queen and you were my prince."

"And soon you will become my queen."

He smiled a self-satisfied smirk that made her want to ball up her fist and smear his nose all over his patrician face.

The thought surprised her, made her blink and reevaluate her thinking. When was she ever this violent?

"Um, yeah," she answered distractedly as she contemplated her chances of making a break for it.

I mean, my family can't stay mad at me forever, right?

But he was speaking again, giving her nerves a queer tingle that signaled her body to flee, to run away, to get to safety. His banality was going to drive her insane.

Forcing a smile that looked more like a grimace to her lips, she interrupted his monologue — of floor coverings of all things.

"That's very…interesting, Gregor. But, um, I have to go now."

She rose to her feet and took one tentative step away from him. What was she doing, marrying this guy? He would have her sitting in a corner and babbling like an idiot within a week. And the thought of him naked… *Ish.*

Still smiling, she took another step and then another. How far was it to the border anyway? Maybe if she started walking now, she could hit Dublin in about a week and make her way through England as a wandering storyteller…or something.

"Where are you going?" Gregor asked, his voice dispassionate as always. "The house is in the other direction."

Before her walk developed into a full-out run, her mother crested the hill and took charge of her.

"There you are, sweetheart. Time to get ready for the ceremony. And Gregor, you know that you are not supposed to see her before the wedding," she admonished.

Damn, Nola wailed to herself as she was led to the house for the dressing. *I almost made it. I was almost free.*

Chapter Nineteen

Craven sat on his chair at the height of the orgy and felt nothing.

Sure the bodies humping around, thrusting and gyrating were an interesting enough spectacle, but he found that his heart just wasn't interested.

"So, look at how the mighty have fallen,"

He looked up to see Hate standing there, a wicked smile on his face.

"What do you want?" Craven had no time for foolishness. He just wanted to be left alone.

"In the middle of an orgy? Yeah right. This weekly tradition of yours has gotten quite popular. Word has spread and folks as far away as America are dropping in to participate."

Craven snorted when he realized he had spoken his thoughts out loud, but turned his attention back to the shifting forms in the room.

"It has gotten quite big, hasn't it?"

"And that should make you quite proud, Craven."

Hate tossed long locks of his hair behind his shoulders, exposing his naked body in all of its glory, before turning to face the man again.

"But you are not happy."

"Is there some point to this visit, Hate?"

"Well, there is some point. I heard what happened, and let me tell you, I was pleased as punch."

"For my pain?"

"Because you were beginning to love the Human. Love bet me that you would never feel anything for someone other than yourself. I told him that you would love the Human, for she was pure of spirit. That would appeal to your jaded soul. He lost; I won. And now he owes me a few favors."

"So that was the bet." Craven could not even work up enough emotion to care that his contemporaries were betting on his life, like it was a game of bones.

"Care to make it double or nothing?"

"What are you talking about, Hate?"

Craven finally pulled his attention away from the crowd and focused in on the redhead.

"Simple, prove that Nola still has feelings for you. Prove that once your body is awakened to passion, it can never go dormant again."

"But Nola has no memory of me. How can she remember what was stripped away?"

"Oberon never said that you couldn't meet her again, just that you couldn't work your magic on her. If she was truly as passionate as everyone was led to believe — and we all heard her screams — then like will recognize like. She will be attracted to you by virtue of your, um, spirit."

"Spirit?"

"Oh, come on, Craven. You exude lust like most people wear perfume. Of course she will be able to feel it with no magic from you. You nearly choke us with your aura, and that is when you are depressed and sulking as you are now."

That earned him a glare that was returned in equal measure.

"Now, what are you going to do? You wanted the woman; you took punishment after you broke your promise to her. We all know that you sent her home. Oberon only took her memory. So what are you going to do?"

Craven sat for a moment, looked at all the sensual things that surrounded him, and still felt nothing. Only one thing could make him feel again. And that was Nola.

"I'm going to go and crash a wedding."

"Good show," Hate crowed as Craven stood and disappeared in a cloud of smoke.

"Fairies in love are almost as easy as Humans," he giggled, then went to find his brother. There were a few things he wanted done on earth, purely for entertainment.

He wanted Adrian Paul to pose nude for erotic book covers. He wanted a few annoying boy bands to hate each other enough to break up, especially the Back Ally ones and the ones that were supposed to be human temperature but left him cold. He wanted Metallica to get back together—that band rocked. He wanted a melding of heavy metal, rap, and classical to become very popular: he wanted to piss off the conservatives: and he wanted Jerry Springer to start showing the fights again. The fights were some of his best work.

Besides, after all that Love did to change things, the old boy deserved to suffer.

With a smile on his lips, he dove into the orgy headfirst and was soon sucking and fucking with the best of them.

Chapter Twenty

Nola stood before the Holy Man, eyes crossed in boredom, as he seemed to drone on and on.

What was taking so long, anyway? Just say a few words and get this disaster started, she thought as she stiffened a yawn.

She looked over at her groom and…

Could a man get more middle-of-the-road?

Even dressed in his wedding finery, he still looked about as exciting as watching grass grow. No, at least there was growth there. He looked exciting as watching paint dry.

Ooey, sticky paint. Drying in a thick coating, pushing out all of the air, suffocating in its intensity. That is, until someone splashed a little paint remover on it and made the paint disappear.

She looked over at her groom again and sighed.

Nope, he was still there.

Maybe some big monster, like the kind that liked to plague Tokyo, would come and smash the house, carrying away Gregor as he sat there calmly waiting to be eaten.

Never happen, she sighed to herself.

Maybe the earth would…

Hold the phone, who was that?

Sitting—rather, lounging—in the first row was a man like none she had ever seen before. She wondered who brought him. *And where was his leash?*

He was dressed all in black, uncompromising silk, from the Nehru collar to the cuff in his baggy pants. His hair was raven's wing black and blended with his clothes. His eyes were the strangest shade of turquoise, and were glued to her face.

He winked at her.

Wow, she thought. *This is getting interesting.*

The man moved, laid one arm across the back of the empty chair next to him, which caused his tunic to part and expose the silver of one shining nipple bar. *Woof.*

"Our vows?" a voice intruded in on her thoughts.

"Huh?" She turned dazed eyes to Gregor.

"Our vows, sweetheart. I know our marriage is making you...blah, blah, blah."

His words transformed into gibberish. She turned and watched as the strange man tossed his hair over his shoulder and smiled at her. When he noticed her attention was fully on him again, he tapped his front tooth with a long black fingernail. Eroticism was his cologne, and he wore it well.

"Nola. Nola?"

She blinked and turned to Gregor.

"What?" she asked her voice weak from longing as she turned from the man in black.

"I asked you if you would be my bride."

"Um, can I think about that for a minute?" she asked, then slapped her hands over her mouth as she realized what she said.

The whole wedding assembly gasped and murmurs began to fill the room.

"What?" The usually complacent Gregor actually managed a small flush of embarrassment.

"Um, what I meant was... Oh I don't..."

Then the man in black stood, as if ready to leave.

But before he turned to walk back down the aisle she just crossed, he looked at her, as if to say 'make a decision now'.

She looked at him, then back at Gregor.

Decision made.

Tossing back her veil, she called out, "Hey. You. Boyo." She was already leaving the platform as her words reached his ears.

"Me?" he asked quietly, a smirk attractively lifting his full lips.

"Yeah, you. You leaving?"

"Yes. I hope you have an exciting…" he looked back at Gregor. "Peaceful…um, adequate life."

"I didn't ask you all of that. But I what to know if you have a car."

"Motor bike. Why?"

"I need a lift."

He smiled again and nodded once.

"Sorry, Mum," she called out as she raced down the aisle, leaving Gregor slacked-mouthed with shock, probably the first real emotion he'd shown in years. "I'll call you when I get there."

"Nola," her mother screamed before fainting in her father's arms. Her father sighed and caught her falling body, and shook his head at his daughter, as if to say today's youth make no sense.

Turning, she grabbed the stranger's hand as she raced down the hall and out the back door.

I don't even know your name," she giggled. "But there is something about you."

"I am Craven," he laughed as he led her outside and to a huge black Harley.

"I hope so," she giggled. She fought with the heavy folds of her marriage robe as she mounted on the back of the bike.

"I am also the Master of Carnality, Lord of Painful Pleasures, Prince of…"

"I always liked royalty," she purred as he climbed on the bike and she wrapped herself around him.

"Where to?" he asked.

"Your place," she decided. "After you make my fantasies come true, I want to learn a lot more about you."

"Works for me."
And they were off.

Epilogue

Craven lay back in his bed, sighing with pleasure as a rumpled, damp, and definitely orgasmic Nola gyrated above him.

Her wedding finery was lost somewhere in a tangle of black silk, her expensive silk robes a colorful accent to the stark color.

She had shed her clothing along with her inhibitions as soon as she had walked through the door of the remote thatched-roof cabin.

He gasped, tossing his head back as she bent low, tugging his nipple bar between her teeth, and making his chest throb with a pleasurable pain.

His hands fisted in her hair, holding her closer to the sensation, silently demanding more of the same treatment.

Nola was only too happy to comply.

With him buried almost painfully deep within her, she rotated her hips and clutched handfuls of his flowing hair as she again tugged at the silver bar that pierced his nipple. Then she clamped her inner walls around his thrusting cock, making him moan in delight at her cleverness while making the sensation within her sheath multiply almost unbearably.

His hands released their hold on her head and shifted to her hips. Holding her writhing form fast, he abruptly thrust upwards, impaling her, and making her eyes roll back in her head as she felt her orgasm approach.

"Craven!" she gasped. "So good! Don't stop. Never fucking stop!"

In response, Craven tightened his hold on her and rolled them off to the side, until he was on top. He was large enough to complete this maneuver without having to pull out.

Once in position between her wide-spread thighs, he gripped her ankles and pulled them over his shoulders.

"Is...this...what...you...want?" He punctuated each word with a pounding thrust that left her gasping for breath and pleading for mercy — for him to stop, for him to do it all again.

"Ohh," she gasped from between gritted teeth as she felt her body stiffen in preparation to launch her into heights unknown.

Her neck arched, throwing her head back and her mouth opened to emit one solid shrike as her muscles began to wring the seed from his body.

"Shit!" Craven gritted out as her unexpected release triggered his own.

Uncontrollably, his body slammed into hers, his hips worked like pistons as he lost control of his larger motor skills.

Unintelligible grunts and moans escaped his lips as he thrust into her one final time, going as deep as, well, *humanly* possible as his cock erupted, sending spurt after spurt of his essence deep within her womb.

Finally with a sigh, his body relaxed against her trembling one, muscles exhausted and fatigued after this strenuous session of love play.

"This is not like me," Nola muttered as Craven rolled off to the side, pulling her to snuggle in close as his softening cock slipped from her sheath with an audible *pop*.

"Maybe I am what you always wished for," he offered as he began to lazily run his fingers through her damp hair.

She tilted her head up for a moment, and then nodded as if some question was settled in her head.

"Well besides running from weddings at the last minute, I am going to be a doctor."

"Well," he replied in the same amused vein, "I make wishes come true."

"And you live in a thatch cottage?"

"It's a night job."

"And during the day?"

"During the day, I am here to fulfill your ever desire."

He leaned down and kissed her on her cute stubborn little nose.

"Really," she snorted.

"Well, I am royalty," he responded, lifting one eyebrow.

"And you crashed my wedding too...?"

"Protect you from the evil prince. He would have stolen your soul."

"Uh huh."

She rolled her eyes at the stranger—who was not a stranger—in her bed.

"Nola, do you believe in fairy tales?"

"Like the hero rescues the maiden and happily ever after? Are you a writer?"

"No...I am a fairy."

Nola froze for a moment, looked down at his cock, still slippery from their most recent activities, and snorted in laughter.

"Could have fooled me. I mean, I am missing some of the same equipment you have."

While she was still chuckling over her own little joke, Craven snapped his fingers and the room began to spin.

"Tell me Nola," he whispered as the flower bower began to bloom around her. "What is your wildest, most wicked wish? I guarantee I can make your wishes come true."

Also by STEPHANIE BURKE:

- Dangerous Heat
- Hidden Passions Volume 1
- Hidden Passions Volume 2
- Keeper of the Flame
- Lucavarious
- Merlin's Kiss
- Seascape
- The Slayer
- Threshold anthology with Shelby Morgen

A WISH AWAY

Written by

MARLY CHANCE

Chapter One

"So, I'm basically invisible, neutered, lacking all sexual vibes. Polly, it's infuriating." Tiffany leaned back in her chair and shook her head. "I've been in the friend zone for so long that he's never gonna see me any differently."

Polly looked at her friend and nodded sympathetically. "See, that's the problem. He thinks the two of you are best buddies."

Tiffany sighed. "We *are* best buddies, dammit. I've known him for six years. You know, that's a long time to suppress lust."

Polly laughed. "Well, you weren't exactly suppressing *all* lust. You've dated. You've been through relationships with Thomas the Total Twit and Jake the Jerk. And he's had his share of blonde bimbos, too." Polly made a face and stuffed a crispytate in her mouth, chewing thoughtfully.

Tiffany grabbed another crispytate, but paused before it reached her mouth. "Yeah, but we're both single now." she said indignantly. "Do you think he just doesn't find me attractive? I mean, I'm ordinary, I know that. I'm no blonde bimbo, but I'm not a troll. I have my good points."

Polly studied her friend seriously for a moment. "Well, I find you attractive. I'd have sex with you if I was into the whole girl/girl thing." Tiffany's short dark hair and her gamin face with those sparkling blue eyes had snared men more often than the oblivious Tiffany realized. In spite of the joking tone of the conversation, Polly wondered why Tiffany never seemed to understand that her quiet loveliness had an appeal all its own to men. She winked and nodded. "Yep, I'd do you if I was a guy for sure. I think he's blind—must be all that overexposure to a single hair color. He's gone blonde blind and doesn't recognize attractiveness in brunettes, anymore. You think? We could be onto a real scientific find here."

Tiffany laughed. "Blonde blind? Well, it's a thought. Beats me just being invisible. Hell, I'm getting desperate. Maybe I should just strip. You know, leave the room when he's over for supper tonight and walk back in stark naked. He *is* male. Stark naked trumps hair color any day of the week."

Polly took a sip from her drink. "Hmmm...true. He's gorgeous. No lack of testosterone there. It might do the trick. Just jump him." She thought about it for a minute. "Yeah. You know, this plan has merit. He's bound to see you differently if you flash him."

Tiffany shook her head and tried to stop laughing. "Polly, I was joking. I can't flash him. I can't walk out naked. Rejection would be bad enough. Naked rejection would be too horrible to contemplate. I'd have to move. Preferably off-planet. And change my name. Then I'd spend years in mind-maintenance fixing my damaged psyche."

Polly laughed. "Hey, I never said it was without a certain risk factor. But I'm betting it would work. "

Tiffany sobered a little. Sipping her drink, she tried to figure it all out. It was ridiculous really. She had a good life. She did a good job as an accountant. She paid her taxes and her bills on time. She had great friends. She was happy. *But* she wanted more. She wanted passion. She wanted some excitement. She wanted...Zak.

It was impossible to pinpoint the exact moment her attraction to him had deepened. The first day she met him she'd been attracted. He was gorgeous. He was six foot three inches and had an incredible body. He had been moving into her apartment complex in the building across from hers. She had been walking through the parking lot just as he had been carrying boxes toward his place. The large transpo vehicle was parked out front and he had emerged from the back of it with his arms loaded.

She had given him one brief glance of appreciation before turning to go into her place. Then she heard a loud crash. Turning around, she saw that he had dropped the top box. She heard a muttered curse that sounded foreign. She walked over and asked, "Hi, I'm Tiffany Simmons. Can I help?"

He had put the remaining boxes down and was bent toward the smaller box on the ground. At the sound of her voice, he jerked upward in surprise and spun around as if expecting a fight. His hands had been clenched.

She remembered clearly how her heart had pounded and her mouth had gone dry. Up close, he had taken her breath away. His dark brown hair was pulled back in a stubby ponytail at his neck. He had silver gray eyes that seemed to look all the way into her soul for a minute. His broad shoulders and big chest looked mouth-watering in that dark blue shirt he had been wearing. His pants were faded and hugged the muscular contours of his body. She had been mesmerized.

He had stared at her intently for a moment, and then grinned. He said, "Thanks for the offer, Tiffany. I'm your clumsy new neighbor, Zak Lextin. I think I can manage these boxes but I would love something cold to drink. My transfer unit isn't programmed yet."

Her heart had gone into overdrive instantly. So, she brought him a cold drink and it had been the beginning of a friendship that had lasted six years. In the beginning, she *had* hoped for more. Looking back on it, she could be honest with herself and admit that particular point. But at the time, she had pretended that friendship was all she wanted.

With an inward grimace she admitted with brutal honesty that she had settled into the comfortable routine of friendship. This happened primarily because he had never given any indication that he wanted more. Her subtle attempts to catch his attention had been met with oblivious, friendly good humor. Oh, they would joke about sex with each other occasionally, but there was always an underlying understanding that it was a joke.

Over the years, they had been good friends to each other. He was a very private man, but he was decent to the core. When he spoke of his past—which was rare—he seemed almost homesick. She knew he was from one of the distant planets but could never bring herself to question him too closely about it. It seemed like such a painful topic to him and he appeared so uncomfortable whenever she headed in that direction with a conversation that she always dropped the subject. So, she had respected his boundaries and found a friend who brought laughter and a lot of joy to her life.

She sighed. Just not sex. And there was the problem. About a month ago the erotic dreams had started. Well, erotic dreams didn't quite cover it. She'd been having full-blown sexual episodes at night. She would dream vivid and realistic images of him touching her with his mouth and with his hands. They were her own little personal porn trips starring the two of them each night. The mere thought of those dreams made her feel excited and guilty.

Her mind might be saying "we're buddies and I don't need to mess that up," but her body was saying, "I'll take multiple orgasms, Ms. Thinks-Too-Much, and you can find another buddy." The conflict was making her crazy. The image from her dream last night of him filling her, sliding in and out in a slow sensual glide, flashed into her mind. She swallowed. Night after night she would wake up wet and aching, with her heart pounding and her entire body yearning for release.

It was bizarre, really. She thought she'd put him in the neat category of best buddy after six years with her libido in firm control, and now sex had to rear its ugly head. Why now? It had gotten to the point where she could barely look him in the eye. She knew he sensed something was happening with her, but she also knew he hadn't completely figured it out yet.

Even if she managed to get his attention, what then? She wasn't sure how to make the transition from friend to lover smoothly. What if they went to bed and then broke up later? She couldn't stand the thought of losing him. However, she didn't think these feelings were going to disappear either. If anything, they were growing stronger.

He seemed oblivious to her as a woman, but she certainly wasn't doing a good job of hiding her growing feelings. Things were going to change—she knew it in her bones. The big question was if they were going to change for the better. She winced. Somehow it wasn't looking good for the home team.

"Earth to Tiffany. *Hello.* Remember me?" Polly's voice penetrated Tiffany's thoughts and she gave a guilty start.

Polly gave her another sympathetic look when she saw Tiffany was paying attention again. "All kidding aside, you're going to have to figure something out, Tiff. It's making you miserable. Zak may be blind when it comes to your attraction, but he's not blind when it comes to your well-being. He'll notice you're unhappy and he'll demand to know why. Zak's very protective of you. Geez, remember how he got when Jake let you down? I thought he was going to put Jake in a med-unit for sure. You were the only one who could calm him. "

Tiffany smiled, although it was a little wan. "Yeah, he was ready to hunt him down and beat him senseless. I started crying and Zak just stood there looking at the door and then looking at me." She brightened a little. "And then he just yanked me right into his arms."

Polly grinned. "You should have seen his face, Tiff. The man looked three kinds of miserable. He was patting your back and glancing toward the door and then sighing. It's actually funny now that you're not a sobbing wreck."

"Gee thanks. Not exactly my finest moment." Tiffany made a face and was glad she could laugh about it now. "Hey, I have a lousy record with birthdays, but that one was the worst. I was expecting a surprise party and was worried that arriving home early would mess up the surprise. Instead, I walk in on Jake and Danita doing the wild thing. I was surprised all right. Way surprised." She grinned. "Of course, they looked outright astonished."

Polly smiled and shook her head. "You're well rid of that jerk. He didn't deserve you. And this birthday bad luck is pure nonsense." She checked her arm-pc and then widened her eyes dramatically. Her voice was gently mocking. "Why, Tiffany, I do believe you've made it halfway through your birthday this year with no great disasters. Another twelve hours or so and you should be in the clear."

Tiffany grimaced. "Oh, I *really* wish you hadn't said that."

Polly interjected, "A wish! Wait, we forgot to have you make a wish."

Tiffany leaned forward. "Polly, I love ya, but you're killing me here. Let's not do the wish thing. It's tempting fate. I swear I really do have weird birthday karma or something. Making a wish would boomerang on me for sure."

Polly merely chided, "Nonsense. You have to make a birthday wish. I have forgone the traditional cake. I have given in to your request for no party and have instead paid for an ordinary lunch at our regular place on our regular lunch hour. *And* I had to argue with you to let me do the paying. The least you can do is make a wish."

Tiffany smiled ruefully. "One wish?"

Polly nodded, looking somewhat put out. "One tiny wish. It should at least seem a *little* like your birthday."

Reluctantly, Tiffany gave in. "Alright one little wish. Let's see…I wish…"

She heard her arm-pc alarm going off and realized it was time to head back to work. She looked at the diners all around her in the restaurant. Everyone was eating, paying no attention to the two of them. It was a perfectly ordinary, uneventful day.

It was ridiculous to be so superstitious. Besides, birthdays *ought* to be celebrated just a little. She had let several years' worth of coincidental bad birthdays throw her off. It was a new year. She was thirty-three. To hell with superstition and bad birthday karma. She closed her eyes and wished silently with all her might, "*I wish Zak would notice me, really notice me and I wish I had a little more excitement in my life. Wait. Is that two wishes?*"

As the last beep of her alarm died away she glanced toward the door. She felt her heart leap into her throat as Zak burst into the doorway of the diner, looking grim. His eyes searched the occupants of the diner with one decisive sweep and then landed on her. She was shocked. What was he doing here at this time of day? And why did he look so deadly serious?

He strode toward the table quickly and then stopped to look down at her. His tone was as grim as his expression and he sounded impatient. "Tiffany, I'll explain later, but we need to leave right now. My *real* name is Zak Ren'Marna and I'm from Kerla in the Zertica Galaxy. There's a killer after you. It's my fault and I'm sorry. I'll protect you. Come with me."

Polly choked on her drink, but Tiffany just asked, "What?"

Zak leaned down until he was inches from her face. He said simply, "Leave with me now. Trust me. I'm your promised and you're in danger. I'll explain later. Right now, we need to go."

He placed a brief, hard kiss on her mouth, leaving Tiffany stunned. "Zak, are you okay? I don't understand. You're not making any sense." She stood up from her chair and felt his forehead. "Are you feverish? You don't feel feverish."

Zak jerked at her touch and then grabbed her hand. He began tugging her toward the door. Tiffany was moving reluctantly. She turned back toward Polly and said, "Polly, I'll call you. I don't know what's wrong with him, but..."

Polly wondered what had gotten into Zak. She nodded at Tiffany and sent Zak a puzzled look, wondering if he was actually playing a practical joke or setting up a birthday surprise.. No matter how crazy Zak sounded at the moment, he would never hurt Tiffany or let anyone hurt her. Regardless, she'd get to the bottom of this mystery soon enough. She waved to them and called out, "Don't forget the flash plan. And have some fun, for goodness sake. Happy birthday!"

As Tiffany disappeared through the door, Polly muttered, "Zertica Galaxy. A killer. And Zak's her promised? That must have been one *hell* of a wish."

She touched a series of buttons on her arm-pc and then grimaced as her subordinate's voice spoke unintelligibly in her ear. She sighed and waited until the noise stopped. Then she spoke patiently, "Jack, you need to turn the volume down before I go deaf."

Jack's voice was lower now and he sounded sheepish. "Sorry, sir. Again."

She smiled. "No prob. Now listen up…please get me all the information you can about a Zak Ren'Marna from Kerla in the Zertica Galaxy. And Jack…better make it fast…"

Chapter Two

Tiffany stopped in her tracks outside the diner as she spotted an airtranspo parked right out front. Zak was pulling her toward it with determined strides, but she planted her feet. "Zak, that's not your vehicle."

Zak pulled a little harder. "It is now. Get in and strap tightly. I don't want to kill you in an air crash before the killer does."

Tiffany frowned. "Very funny. Zak, I *hate* airtranspo. I like walking. Walking is better. Can't we just walk to where we need to go? Hey, I'll even run. Running could be good...or underground transpo..."

Zak shook his head impatiently and half shoved her toward the side door he had opened. "Tiffany, get in or I swear I'll put you in myself. I'm not playing here. This is dangerous."

Tiffany stepped into the airtranspo reluctantly and watched as he slammed the door behind her. She sighed. Maybe he wouldn't have the ignition card to start this thing. Maybe it was some kind of weird practical joke or birthday surprise.

He ran to the other side and quickly popped the driver's door. Climbing through, he muttered, "Strap in." He yanked his straps down from the overhead and gave her a hard look as he waited for her to do the same.

Rolling her eyes, Tiffany pulled the protective shield and straps from the ceiling compartment downward. She jerked the shield into place across her chest and then tightened the crisscrossing straps until they were snug. With another glare in Zak's direction, she snapped the locking device into place on each side of her.

She saw Zak remove the ignition card from his pocket and was shocked. He was serious. He really was going to start this thing. She *hated* air travel. Zak had better have a damn good explanation for inflicting airtranspo on her. It would serve him right if she hurled her lunch all over him during this little trip.

Zak started the onboard computer by inserting the ignition card and looked at the map that had popped up on the monitor. He quickly programmed a series of co-ordinates. Tiffany watched him grimly. Finally, she said, "For the record, I am finding this experience less than amusing, Zak. Please tell me you didn't really steal this thing."

Zak looked over at her as he started the ignition sequence. His face registered his amusement for a moment. "I stole it. And I plan to steal another in a day or two. We'll steal as many as it takes. In the meantime, just think of it as *desperate borrowing* if it makes you feel any better."

Tiffany said sarcastically, "Gee, won't the judicial system be impressed with that reasoning. 'Your Honor, we weren't really stealing, we were…eeeehhh…'" her voice ended in a shriek as the vehicle took off. The force knocked her backward in her seat.

For the next few minutes she didn't talk as she focused on staying conscious and breathing deeply. Zak had them traveling at a speed that made conversation impossible. She gave him an evil glare as he watched the monitor in front of him. She switched her gaze to the screen and saw the red dot representing their vehicle moving through air space at an alarming speed, zigging around other dots/vehicles. In desperation, she closed her eyes.

There were no windows for a reason, she reminded herself. All airtranspos had highly advanced onboard navigation and tracking systems — with avoidance and alert mechanisms. There was no need to worry that they would hit anything. She knew it intellectually but somehow it never made her *feel* any better. She liked seeing where she was going. She liked being able to avoid obstacles in her path. Depending on a computer to do it for her just went against her inner sense of control. She avoided airtranspo like the plague because of it.

She spent the next half hour silently fuming and planning all of the things she was going to say to him when they landed wherever the hell they were supposed to land. When the vehicle finally stopped, she opened her eyes. The monitor flashed a picture of the outside of a rather notorious, seedy motel on the outer edges of the city. They had traveled in what had to be circles for thirty minutes only to end up *here*?

Tiffany gave him a look that should have scorched him in his seat. "Well, Zak, you certainly know how to show a girl a good time on her birthday. You shouldn't have. And it's such a *nice* motel, too — with a reputation for sneaky sexcapades with hourly companions. Our own little torrid love nest. If you think you're getting laid in this rathole after this fiasco, you can think again."

She raised an eyebrow at the speed with which Zak unstrapped and then turned to her. She watched him in furious silence as he moved until he was leaning over her. His face was inches from hers. She tensed.

He said huskily, "Oh, I'm getting laid alright. Rathole or not. You've had this fuck coming for six years, darling. There's not a chance in hell that I'm giving up now."

Tiffany knew her mouth had dropped open when he gently brought his hand up and closed it for her. He placed a quick kiss on her mouth and then she vaguely heard the click of her straps being unlocked. He leaned backward and began to climb out of the vehicle. Tiffany sputtered, "I cannot believe you just said that..."

Zak leaned down until she could see him in the frame of the doorway. He grinned. "Tiff, there are lots of things you're going to find hard to believe, but that's only the beginning. If you want to find out more, you're going to wait right here while I get a room. I'll be watching you from the office, so don't even think about making a break for it."

Tiffany thought about it...for a minute. Her remark about getting laid had been a typical joke, although there was real annoyance behind it. She'd never expected him to say what he had. What was going on with Zak? She wanted an explanation. Besides, in spite of the shock she was feeling from his attitude, she was feeling an undeniable sense of excitement, too. Apparently, Zak had noticed her in a major way. She wanted to hear his explanation for this whole bizarre episode. She gave a brisk nod. "Fine. Hurry back. But this better be good."

She saw with a sense of renewed shock the way his eyes drifted over her body with blatant appreciation. He winked and said, "Oh, it will. I'm counting on it."

Then with another cocky smile, he slammed the door. She sucked in a deep breath and tried to calm her rioting pulse. That man was going to give her a heart attack. What had happened to her oblivious buddy? He had never looked at her with such obvious…lust…in all the years that she had known him. It shocked and excited her more than she would have thought possible.

In spite of her aggravation with him, she smiled a little. It looked like her life was becoming more exciting by the moment. Her smile turned into a frown. What if Zak was right? What if someone really *was* trying to kill her? That would be bad. She looked at the monitor again and grimaced. Dying would be bad, but dying at the Little Layaway Motel would be too tacky for words.

Chapter Three

Zak opened her door a few minutes later and Tiffany looked up at him in surprise. His expression was serious once again. He was scanning the surrounding parking lot and then turned to give her an impatient look. She climbed out of the airtranspo and muttered, "Gee, that was fast!"

Zak nodded. "Yeah. Let's get into the hotel even faster and then we'll talk."

"Good. You'll talk and I'll listen. Then *you'll* get to listen. I have quite a bit to say at this point." She kept pace with his long strides as he walked to a room three doors down from the office. The doors to the motel were painted in different colors. The door they stopped in front of was painted black with a large red #3 on it. She wondered briefly what they would find behind door number three. She'd never been to the motel before but it had such a notorious reputation that even *she'd* heard the rumors. As Zak punched in his code, the door swung open and she stepped back in shock at the dark and forbidding interior. She said, "Um...you know, Zak, this might not be the best room for this conversation."

Zak flashed her another impatient look and said through clenched teeth, "Tiff, get in there. *Now.*"

Tiffany gave an indignant sniff and moved through the door. She said over her shoulder, "Look, if I *really* have a killer on my trail like some bad book plot, then I'll be much more cooperative. But keep in mind, you've been dragging me around and blabbing about people trying to kill me — and you *know* how stupid that idea sounds. I'm an accountant, Zak. I'm ordinary. I'm not the type who has to run from killers. I've never even gotten a judicial violation notice. I'm the eternal boring nice girl. You sound completely nuts."

She heard the soft click of the locking door behind her as her eyes began to adjust to the gloom of the room. The walls were black and there was a very large bed to the left against the wall with a satin bedspread of deep red. She heard Zak say softly, "Lights, optimum."

The lights came on and the room was fully revealed. Tiffany felt her heart jump as she took in her surroundings in more detail. There was a holographic statue in one corner of the room. It was a miniature nude couple in a rather interesting embrace. The woman was handcuffed to a wall and the man was on his knees, his mouth moving between her thighs. Her head was thrown back and she appeared to be moaning in helpless ecstasy as she writhed and pulled on the chains. Tiffany swallowed past her dry throat and quickly averted her gaze. She looked to the right and saw the lifesize and very real set of cuffs hanging from the wall. She took a step back and nearly bumped into Zak.

Zak chuckled and said, "Relax, Tiff. You're safe for the moment. I'd love to do what you're obviously thinking, but explanations first. I need you to take what's happening seriously."

Tiff took a hasty step toward the chair on the left side of the bed, moving around Zak's big body carefully. She was feeling off-balance and nervous. Deciding the sturdy red chair was safer than that wickedly carnal bed, she walked over to it. She sat down and placed her arms on the armrests realizing immediately that it wasn't safer at all. She saw Zak's sudden grin just as the chair attacked.

It shifted underneath her and large straps sprang from the sides. Tiffany exclaimed, "What the hell?!" as two straps emerged from the sides of the chair and locked her arms in place against the armrests with an audible click. She pulled her arm upwards, but the straps were snug. She pulled harder, but the straps did not give. The material was soft, but very strong. She was stuck.

Zak laughed. "You should see the expression on your face! Tiff, that was classic! Well, you're not going anywhere for the moment and it seems I now have your undivided attention."

Tiffany snarled, "Yeah, well get me out of these things."

Zak smiled. "I think you're fine for the moment."

Great. She was now strapped to a chair until Mr.-I've-Lost-My-Mind decided otherwise. She'd landed in some kind of bizarre birthday farce where even furniture could not be trusted and Zak decided *now* was the time to be cute. Men. Tiffany gave him a look that promised retribution and said flatly, "Start talking or start planning on how to get away from me when you're done here. One of those things may save your life."

Zak's face grew serious. "I'm not sure where to begin."

Tiffany gave him a scathing look. "Gee, the beginning would probably be appropriate. I already know the ending."

Zak settled his body on the edge of the bed across from her. As he leaned forward, Tiffany was extremely aware of his body on that bed and his proximity. She felt heat rising inside her and reminded herself that however delicious he looked, he was in major trouble at the moment.

Zak said earnestly, "I'm from Kerla in the Zertica Galaxy. I know I never talk about my past, but it's because I've been in hiding. "

Tiffany interrupted, "Zertica is so far way, Zak. I don't know anything about it except for textbook stuff. And you're a systems technogeek. Why would you need to hide so far from your home planet?"

Zak winced. "The preferred term is compbiotech specialist, Tiff, as you well know. It wasn't my profession that led to the trouble. I was in the wrong place at the wrong time. A simple case of…"

Tiffany nodded and muttered, "Weird karma. I know how that goes, believe me."

Zak's mouth curved but then he grew serious again. "Believe it or not, I witnessed a murder. Actually, I was a witness along with another guy who happened to be at the same corner late that night. It was one of those weird times when no one should have been out. The weather was bad. I had worked very late and was in a hurry to get home. It's usually deserted at that time of night. But not that night. That night there were four of us on that road."

His eyes were staring through her as if he could see it even now. Tiffany felt as if she'd been punched. Zak was serious. He had really seen someone killed.

Zak hesitated and then said, "When I rounded the corner, I saw a guy who looked a little drunk, as if he'd come from a party. He was stumbling around. There was a man at the door of one of the *suernes*—houses—I mean. He had his palm on the print-lock to open it. The drunk stumbled toward him, mumbling. The guy at the door half-turned, saw the drunk, and then the door began to open. He turned and took a step forward toward the door. Then the drunk pulled out a lasgun and fired it right into the back of the other guy's head."

He said carefully, "Suddenly, another man rounded the corner. He stopped as he spotted the lasgun and the dead guy. There was this weird moment when I knew the killer was probably deciding which of us to shoot first. I actually ran toward him and the other guy did, too. He spun and shot at me first because I was closest I guess. I dodged and then I heard this sound."

He looked at her wryly, as if he had a hard time believing it had really happened. "He'd hit a pipe filled with *Perinon*. It's used in the heating process on my planet. There are pipelines connected outside most buildings. There was this hissing sound and then an explosion. That's the last thing I remember. It knocked me out. When I woke up, there were people and enforcers everywhere."

He shook his head and said with chilling calmness, "I was told later that the assassin that night was Jero Merlez. He's a professional killer. The Kerlan government has been trying for years to catch him, Tiff. He's considered one of the best contract killers on the market. They occasionally get the proof they need to mind-wipe him but then in the rare case when there's a witness, the witness mysteriously dies before Merlez can be located and brought before a council. The other witness from that night was killed while under government protection. Merlez *never* leaves any live witnesses—he's very good at his job."

Tiffany felt her spirits sink at his words. Zak was completely serious. He was staring at her earnestly. His expression was grave and he looked tired and bleak. She asked with dawning sympathy, "You had to come all the way here to be safe?"

Zak shifted restlessly on the bed. "If it had been just me, I would have tried to find him before he found me, but I have a younger brother and sister... Merlez might have hurt them to get to me. The government made the arrangements. I was supposedly killed in an accident. No one but my brother and the government knew otherwise. They gave me a new identity. My identity and location are known to only two people. One is my Kerlan contact and the other was my human contact here."

Tiffany said, "Now that's one hell of a witness protection program you guys have."

Zak smiled, although it looked strained. "Generally, it's highly effective. I was given the language and culture implant chip to allow me to successfully blend in here on Earth. Earth is so much larger than our planet, but similar in some ways. The government made arrangements for my journey and gave me a new identity. I was allowed to keep only my first name. They arranged my new job—even my housing. Everything was very well planned. They were supposed to catch Merlez quickly and then I would be free to return to my normal life."

Zak looked down at the floor a moment and then raised his eyes to her face. "That was six years ago. *Six years.*"

Tiffany looked into the sad face of the man in front of her and felt the ache all the way to her soul. What must it have been like for Zak? He had been jerked out of his life and sent to some distant planet with no friends and no family. He couldn't tell a soul so much as his real name. He had done nothing wrong and yet he had suffered for years. It must have been so difficult. She murmured, "Zak, I'm so sorry. That must have been so hard for you. And so lonely."

Zak's face tightened briefly. He said grimly, "That's the problem, Tiff. It was lonely. Except for you. It all comes back to you. I've put you in danger and it's all my fault. My own damn selfishness. I'm so sorry."

Tiff started to move forward to hug him. He looked so sad and regretful. When the straps held her in place, she said instead, "Zak, you've never been selfish. You have a lot of faults, but that's not one of them."

Zak shook his head. "Tiff, you've been the one real bright spot in this mess. You made my life so much better in so many ways. I tried to keep my distance, but it was hopeless. You're not the kind of person anyone keeps a distance from. You're so warm and so giving."

His face was a picture of self-blame. "I didn't want to put you in danger, but as the years went on and we grew closer, I convinced myself that Merlez might never be caught. I was existing in limbo and I really thought that it might last forever. I needed you, Tiff, like my next breath."

Tiffany sighed. The time for plain speaking was here. "Zak, I need you, too. You're my best friend in the world. In any world, actually."

Zak winced. "Well, some friend I've been. I've repaid your friendship by putting you in danger."

Tiffany asked, "But why? What's changed? Why the sudden freaking out and hauling me away with dire threats of a killer?"

Zak folded his hands in front of him. He cleared his throat and looked extremely uncomfortable. "Hmmm...well, that's a little hard to explain. How honest do you want me to be?"

Tiffany felt a jolt of excitement at the sudden intensity in his expression. He was looking at her in a way that made her shift a little uncomfortably, too. "Totally honest."

Zak nodded. "You and I have been careful to keep within certain boundaries in our friendship. The attraction between us is very strong. It has been from the beginning. Initially, I tried to keep my distance as I said. Then, I tried to focus on others who were interested in only short term…er…relationships to fulfill certain…mutual needs."

He said with obvious frustration, "It was both helpful and infuriating when you became involved with others, too. I tried to keep my feelings hidden or make them go away. But it's been so long, Tiff, and I want you so much."

Tiff heard his words with a sense of total shock. He had wanted her for *six years*? He had been hiding his feelings for *six freaking years*? She gave him a look of total exasperation. "You're an idiot, you know that?"

He grimaced. "Thanks for the understanding. I was trying to keep from hurting you, Tiffany, when I left to go back to Kerla. I was also making sure that if Merlez did find me that you wouldn't get hurt. I've been careful to keep most of our interaction at your apartment or mine. Haven't you ever noticed and wondered?"

Tiffany laughed. "I thought you were the hermit type, Zak. The original Mr.-Let's-Eat-At-Home-I-Hate-Crowds. Besides, we've been out with my friends sometimes."

Zak smiled. "True — as a group."

Tiffany shook her head. "But Zak…"

Zak interrupted, "I can't stop wanting you. I've tried. And I'm Kerlan, Tiff."

Okay, so he was Kerlan. She searched her memory but couldn't come up with any specific information about Kerlans. Uh oh. Were Kerlans even biologically compatible with humans? She ran her eyes over Zak's body in sudden panic. She'd never seen him unclothed. "Are Kerlans...um...that is...Zak...are you...can you...can we..."

She felt her face flushing scarlet and closed her eyes. Great. Could she screw this whole thing up any worse? Her best friend starts explaining that a killer is after them and she's asking questions about whether the two of them can get it on? Tiffany to libido – back the hell off and give brain the helm for a minute. She opened her eyes to see him regarding her with a hungry look.

"Oh yes we can. Kerlans are very similar biologically to humans. That's one of the reasons Earth was picked as my destination. But, Tiff, Kerlan males are different in some ways."

Tiffany moistened her lips and watched as he tracked her movements with his eyes. It was getting hot. Very hot. Very fast. She was suddenly extremely aware of her body. Her nipples felt sensitive. Zak's eyes, usually silver-gray, were nearly black. He was aroused. So was she. She shifted and was nervously conscious of the wet heat between her thighs. She needed to focus here. "What kind of differences?"

Zak's voice was husky. "We get aggressive. We have strong sexual appetites. The biggest difference, though, is when we find our promised."

Tiffany could feel her heart pounding. Aggressive? Strong sexual appetites? Oh. My. God. "You called me that before. Your promised."

Zak's face gentled. "When a Kerlan male forms a bond with a special female, she is called his promised. It is similar to the bond between spouses here on Earth. However, once a Kerlan male bonds, he begins to..." He hesitated.

Tiff burst out, "Good grief! Begins to what? You're killing me here!"

Zak was obviously choosing his words carefully. "You know how humans and animals give off scent? It's a method of attracting the opposite sex. Well, Kerlan men begin to do the same thing once their emotions are fully engaged and they are life bonded, only it goes one step further. We begin to project images..."

Tiffany had a sudden thought. She kept her face neutral, but it wasn't easy. The dreams. The incredibly vivid erotic dreams she had been having night after night. "Zak, can human females pick up these images?"

Zak watched her face carefully. "I asked my Earth contact that same question, among several others. There have been some human and Kerlan promise pairs, but I have never met any. There were things I needed to know. He contacted his Kerlan counterpart. The answer is yes."

Zak had been...She kept her voice steady and tried to stay calm in spite of the graphic sexual pictures that were running in a loop in her memory. "You needed to know?"

Zak nodded. "You're my promised, Tiffany. I was beginning to lose control and I knew it. Until I was able to claim you sexually, the images weren't going to stop. I could control them while I was conscious. But at night, when I was sleeping...I'd lose control and project...I knew it was happening from the intensity of the dreams...It's been torture trying to keep control every waking moment."

His eyes darkened further and his voice was husky. "I needed to know if you would receive my thoughts. I was told you would probably experience them as very erotic dreams."

Tiffany swallowed. Oh yeah. You could say that. "What else did your contact tell you? On second thought, Zak, I'd really like to get up from this chair now. I need to think and I don't want to be strapped down to do it." She silently cursed. Even she could hear the nervousness in her voice.

Zak stared at her for one long moment. He stood up and knelt by her chair. She held her breath. He reached out and she froze, but he just pressed a button on the side of the chair. The straps retracted and Tiffany hurried to get up. She nearly stumbled because she was moving so fast.

She was several steps away from him when she heard his voice behind her. It was half-promise, half-threat. "I'll have you strapped down again, Tiff. Never doubt it. And next time you won't be *thinking* either."

Tiffany spun around in surprise. He stood beside the chair and faced her. She gave a nervous little gulp and tried to think. Things were all upside down. Her whole reality had changed. Zak wasn't acting like Zak. The old Zak was sexy, but comfortable and easy. This new Zak was much more intense.

She shifted restlessly under his gaze and tried to bring her breathing under control. She was acting much too nervous. His words were exciting her. Arousal was not helping her to think. "Zak, we need to slow down. Fine, you started asking questions because the two of us were feeling…because we were getting more involved…"

She winced. No way was she bringing up love. If he loved her, he was going to say it first. This promise business was confusing. It sounded like he loved her, but she needed to hear him say it. And she was too off-balance and unsure with this sudden change in him to assess her own feelings clearly. And no way was she discussing those dreams.

Zak looked amused at her words. "More *involved*? Yes, we were getting more involved – from your face, I'd say night after night we were probably *involved*. How long have you been receiving my images, Tiff?"

Tiffany decided to avoid that line of questioning for the moment. Even an idiot could see where that conversational path would end. She needed more answers. "Answer me, Zak. Why the sudden danger?"

Zak's entire face changed in an instant. His tone was full of regret. "Gorden was killed. My contact here on Earth. He was murdered this morning. All I can figure is somehow the increased interaction with his Kerlan contact must have tipped Merlez off in some way. I don't know. All I know is Merlez contacted me with Gorden's arm-pc. He told me that my old and *dearly departed* friend had proven most helpful and that he was coming for me, Tiff."

Fear swept Tiffany and she shuddered. "Zak, you have to get away from here right now. Far away where you can't be tracked."

Zak nodded grimly. "Yes, that was my first reaction, too. I thought about taking the first transport, *any* transport, out. Then, I thought about why he'd used the arm-pc."

Tiffany exclaimed, "To track your location! He didn't know where you were! He must have been hoping to keep you on long enough to trace your coordinates."

Zak said, "He was nearly successful, too. When I realized he had locked onto my location, I ran like hell. He probably showed up within minutes. I got all the way to the transport when I had a sudden thought. You. I couldn't leave you."

He raked a hand through his hair. "But I couldn't put you in danger. I realized Merlez would no doubt be expecting me to try to get offplanet in a hurry. Then I thought about my conversations with Gorden. Tiffany, Gorden was a careful man, but he would save data much too often for my comfort. I argued with him about it more than once, but he claimed that it was safe."

Zak blew out a breath and his face grew grimmer. "Merlez has Gorden's arm-pc implant. It'll run at least twenty-four hours on backup power outside of Gorden's body. Merlez could access information until then — once he breaks the code."

Zak paced back and forth now. "He would have found you. I told Gorden your name, where you lived, where you worked, everything, when I was talking with him. Gorden was my friend and I was worried about what was happening with us, Tiff. I don't know how much Gorden stored, but there's a good chance Merlez will find out. I couldn't take the chance that he might hurt you. I was frantic to find you. Then, I remembered your birthday lunch with Polly."

Tiffany remembered his grim face as he walked through the diner door. No wonder. She felt another shaft of fear and tried to keep her voice steady. "So now there's a good chance this maniac is after both of us."

Zak stopped and said simply, "There has always been a plan in place in case of exposure. I placed a call from public access at the transport to my Kerlan contact, Rojda. I didn't actually speak to him because he wasn't available. I followed the plan and left a code word. We'll meet him in forty-eight hours at the prearranged place. It'll take him that long to get here. In the meantime, all we have to do is stay alive. Kerlan authorities will be all over the place trying to catch Merlez at that point. We'll figure out what comes next after that."

Tiffany nodded slowly and said, "Okay, we stay alive. Good plan. I'm for it."

Zak smiled. "Yes, I'm for it, too."

Tiffany said, "We could go to law enforcement here. Explain and ask for protection."

Zak shook his head. "No. I don't trust anyone but you. Merlez killed the other witness from that night, Tiff. He was under protection by law enforcement. It's suspected that Merlez bribed one of the enforcers guarding him. I'm not placing our lives in a stranger's hands. I'm paranoid, but I'm alive because of it. I'm not stopping now."

"Are we safe for the moment?" Tiffany worked to keep calm.

Zak took a step toward her. His tone was reassuring. "We're safe. He has no way of finding us right now. His haste this morning was a miscalculation. It's not like him. A lot of this doesn't make sense to me. How did he find out I was alive? How'd he find Gorden? If he had simply broken Gorden's access code and studied the arm-pc data, he could have surprised me. Something is pushing him, but I don't know what. He killed Gorden and contacted me rather than choosing stealth. It's not making sense."

Zach rubbed a hand over his face in a familiar gesture of weariness. "I placed an anonymous call to Earth authorities via public access telling them that Gorden was dead and who was responsible. Now Merlez's options are more limited. It will be hard to look for us while Earth authorities look for him. We need only stay here for two days and be careful."

Zak looked her in the eyes. "I promise you, I wouldn't say it if I didn't believe it, Tiff. The real danger comes when we leave this place. Merlez will be hunting us and he's very good. He may eventually find the emergency plan in Gorden's arm-pc. If so, he'll know where we're meeting Rojda and when. We'll be taking a huge chance to go to that meeting, but it's the only way to get to Rojda and find out what's happening. Until then, we stay here."

Tiffany's thoughts were racing in circles. What was going to happen to them? Even if they weren't found, what happened next? Would Merlez be at the meeting? Was it better to go into hiding? Her mind was in total turmoil. Her emotions were all over the place.

Zak probably loved her. It looked like he had *noticed* her for six damn years. A crazy alien hitman was trying to kill both of them. She might have to run away with Zak to some distant planet for the two of them to be safe. And wouldn't *that* be the mother of all airtranspo rides? Excitement was entering her life on a bitch and a half scale. Freaking birthday wishes.

Tiffany looked around the motel room and it suddenly seemed like a very small place. "What the hell are we going to do for the next forty-eight hours?"

Zak's face changed and then he slowly smiled. In six years he had perfected the art of imitating her and he had her down pat. He drawled, "Well, gee, Tiff, we're in the Little Layaway Motel in the Cuffs-Enough Room with possibly less than 48 hours to live. We're promised. We've wanted each other for six years. What do you think?" His voice deepened. "Somehow I don't plan on playing cards. I think a very...unique...and...private...birthday celebration is in order."

He walked toward her and asked in a low, husky voice, "Have I mentioned how good you looked in those straps, baby?"

Chapter Four

Oh boy. Tiffany watched as Zak walked toward her. She felt the heat rising inside her with every step. She squeaked, "Zak, uhhh, I'm...you're...I never said I wanted you. You only said you wanted me. Let's just slow down a minute here and think..."

Zak smiled that sexy smile and continued to move forward. He had the look of a predator stalking wary prey. It was only then that Tiffany realized she was walking backward. She backed into the wall and knew instantly that it was a mistake.

Zak stepped forward quickly and placed a hand on each side of her head, caging her. She felt her heart racing and wondered how someone so familiar and so trusted could make her feel so panicked and so thrilled. She knew Zak would never hurt her. She trusted him completely.

And yet, this was new territory for them. Zak had never looked at her the way he was looking at her now. He looked sexy and dangerous. She swallowed. There was no doubt that he was exciting her. He hadn't even touched her and she was already wet. She watched as he leaned forward until his face was close to hers.

"Tiff, you're acting so nervous. Now why is that?" He sounded even more aroused. He brought a hand down and she felt the warmth of it caress her face. She tried to think, but it was getting harder to do while he was actually touching her. She had wanted to feel his hands on her this way for so long.

Zak asked huskily, "Could it be because you're remembering those dreams?" His hand drifted from her cheek to her neck. "Are you remembering all of the things I want to do to you?"

Tiffany swallowed. He was seducing her with that husky voice and the tender touch of his hand. She struggled to slow her breathing but her breaths were coming more rapidly. She knew her nipples were pressing against the cloth of her unidress. He was staring into her eyes, watching her face intently. She felt mesmerized, caught in the spell of his words and touch. His hand drifted to her breast and he began kneading it gently. She swallowed a moan and murmured, "Ohhh…"

Zack leaned forward and she felt the light touch of his mouth on hers. His lips were warm and moved with easy skill. Tiffany began to move her mouth in response. The kiss was non-threatening at first, almost friendly. Then she felt the first brush of his tongue along the seam of her mouth. The feel of his hand on her breast excited her unbearably. He was rubbing her nipple with his palm and using a little more pressure. It felt so good.

She parted her lips and Zak immediately took advantage. His tongue entered her mouth and began teasing hers. She was shaking with excitement. She could feel the wet velvet of his tongue against her own and responded tentatively. She felt more than heard his moan of approval. She responded more aggressively and the kiss caught fire.

For several moments, the world narrowed down to just the two of them and the feel of him exploring her mouth. Tiffany was shocked when he pulled back abruptly. Zak was breathing heavily and his face was hard.

He asked roughly, "Tiff, do you trust me?"

Tiffany looked into the familiar face of the man who was her best male friend in the world. He might look like a stranger at the moment and she had never seen that look on his face, but she knew Zak. "Yes."

His face gentled. "Good." He reached down and took one of her hands in his own. He brought it to his mouth and kissed it. She felt her heart turn over. With his other hand, he captured her free hand and brought that one to his mouth as well.

His face changed and he said in a firm voice, "Then trust me now." She felt him bring her arms over her head. He let go of her wrists and said, "Leave them there."

Tiffany knew her surprise was showing. Leave them? As her sluggish brain began to kick back in gear she saw him reaching above her head. It was only as she felt the first soft click that she realized he was cuffing her. She burst out, "Zak, about that whole aggressive thing...hmmm...well...when you say *aggressive,* you don't mean frothing-at-the-mouth feral, right?" Her voice was a little too high.

Zach paused and placed a gentle hand under her chin. "Tiffany, I would never hurt you or abuse you in any way. You know that, don't you?"

Tiffany looked into his face and couldn't help smiling at the concern she saw there. She was acting like an idiot. This was *Zak.* She said, "Of course I know it. Brief moment of panic. That's all."

He continued to stare into her eyes sincerely. "If you don't like what's happening then you say the word stop. That's it. I'll stop, Tiffany. On my life, I swear to you I'll stop no matter what. But you say anything else and I'll keep going anyway. Understand?"

Tiffany felt more than reassurance at his words. She felt the warmth and comfort of six years of solid friendship and caring. He wasn't going to stop unless she used that word. The arousal that had gone through her at that notion was shockingly strong. She nodded. "Okay."

The second cuff locked into place. The cuffs were very soft around her wrists, but very strong--the same material that had been used as straps for the chair. She flexed her arms and could move them, but not much. She was well and truly caught. She swallowed hard. She'd never been tied up or cuffed. She'd certainly fantasized about it more than once, but this was reality.

When he leaned back and smiled, she relaxed a little. It was scary in a way, but exciting, too. Her heart was hammering in her chest and she wondered what he planned to do with her now. Without thinking about it, her eyes sought the holostatue in the corner. The woman in the statue writhed and squirmed. She jerked her eyes away from it guiltily and looked up at Zak.

His smiled widened into a grin. "Tiff, that was quite a hint."

Tiffany burst out, "No really. I wasn't hinting. I…"

Zak chuckled and leaned forward until his mouth was next to her ear. He said softly, "I'm going to taste you like that. And I'm going to have you squirming like that, too. Will you scream for me when you come, Tiff? I want to hear you scream while my mouth is between your lovely thighs. "

Tiffany swallowed and felt the rush of excitement all the way to her toes. Just the thought of him doing it was unbearably arousing. She remembered a particularly vivid dream from a few nights ago when he had driven her wild with his mouth.

Suddenly, a soft computer voice could be heard from her arm-pc. "Arousal level requires system check. Please wait. Running diagnostic. No disease present. Contraceptive functioning at maximum level. Remember to reset manually as auto-diagnostic is now shut down. Proceed if desired."

Zak smiled. "I love that kind of efficiency. So tell me again, Tiffany, about how you may not want me."

Tiffany closed her eyes as embarrassment creeped in. Granted, it was highly effective and everyone had one, but it never failed to mortify her when her computer announced her syscheck. Oh what the hell. It was pretty damn obvious anyway that she was excited and aroused.

The best defense against embarrassment was to turn the tables. She opened her eyes and was moved by the tenderness she saw on his face. Why was she acting so reluctant? She must have lost her mind sometime earlier today amidst the weirdness. Screw impending danger and mad killers. Her wish, her most important wish in the universe, was coming true at this very moment. She'd wanted Zak for so long. She said, "I do want you, Zak. I want to feel you touching me. I want to feel your mouth on me. I want to feel you inside me."

Zak looked surprised and then his expression changed to pure hunger. He leaned down and kissed her roughly, obviously inflamed by her words. Tiffany felt the hard pressure of his mouth against hers and the aggressive thrust of his tongue inside her mouth. She moaned and tried to bring her body into contact with his, but the cuffs held her in place.

Zak broke the kiss and then his mouth traveled down to her neck. He kissed along the sensitive line of her throat. When he reached the curve of her neck and shoulder, he sucked gently. Tiffany leaned her head to the side and gave another moan. She had never realized that spot was so sensitive. She moaned again and distantly registered his arm-pc performing his syscheck.

Zak reached the edge of her dress just as the computer voice announced, "Proceed if desired…"

Zak muttered, "If desired…yeah…right…"

He licked along the neckline of the dress and Tiffany shivered at the sensation. She wanted his mouth on her breast. Her nipples were aching. She needed more. She muttered, "Zak, please…"

Zak's head came up and he looked at her. He said huskily, "Oh, I like the sound of that word. I will please you, Tiff. What is it you want right now….hmmm?"

He brought one hand up and slowly pushed the material of her dress down just a little. The upper curves of her breasts were exposed, but that was all. The hard outline of her nipples was clearly visible beneath the fabric. "You know what I like about this strapless unidress, Tiff? I can peel you out of it a bit at a time."

He leaned down and placed kisses along the slopes of her breast, saying in between kisses, "It's like…mmm…unwrapping… a present…very slowly… I can…savor you. "

He pulled the dress a little further down and Tiffany's breath caught. The material was as far as it could go without her nipples being exposed. His mouth moved over the skin newly available. Her breath was coming in pants now and her heart was hammering so loud she wondered if he could hear it. She'd never been so turned on in her life. His tongue swept under the fabric a bit and narrowly missed her nipple. She whimpered.

He muttered, "That's it, Tiff. I want to hear you. Don't hold back."

Tiffany realized something in that moment. There was no chance of holding back. This man was exciting her physically and emotionally at a level that she'd never experienced and she was shaking with it. She arched forward almost without thought, silently asking for what she wanted. Zak pulled the material down and she felt the moist heat of his tongue as he licked around her nipple. She muttered, "Oh that's good…Oh…"

Zak made a little hum of approval and continued to tease her nipple, licking it in slow circles. Finally, he pulled the length of it into his mouth and sucked. Tiffany felt her knees go weak and leaned back against the wall for support. He followed her with his mouth, never pausing. He continued sucking, occasionally pulling back to lick and then drawing her nipple back into his mouth again. It felt unbelievably good.

Then Zak moved to her other breast, giving it the same treatment. He brought his hand up and she felt the gentle tug as he toyed with the nipple he'd just left. She was already exquisitely sensitive from his mouth and she shivered and moaned as he rolled it gently with his fingers. Finally, Zak pulled back completely and used both hands to continue the sensual torment.

He watched silently and then lifted his eyes to her face. "You are so beautiful. I've imagined you like this but the reality is so much better. You're so sensitive to my touch. I can hear your heart beating, Tiffany. Kerlan senses are more acute than that of humans. I can smell your scent when you get aroused. I can feel the heat of your body as that arousal gets stronger. Can you imagine what you've been doing to me for the last six years? Can you imagine how hard it's been to hold back when I knew you wanted this as much as I did?"

Tiffany shook her head, feeling drugged. She was too far gone to make any coherent reply. She could understand what he was saying, though, and it just made her ache more. He sounded on the edge of control, like a man pushed to the brink.

Zak stopped suddenly and said, "Tiff, look at me. Really look at me."

Tiffany focused and stared at him. His face was drawn tight. He looked like he was in pain. He pulled the dress further down until it was below her breasts completely. He said, "I need to feel you give yourself to me. I've dreamed of it night after night. That look on your face when you come apart for me."

Zak planted a tender kiss on her mouth. Then, he knelt on the floor. He said in a strained voice, "You're my promised. Once I claim you, there's no going back. You understand? I'll never let you go."

Tiffany smiled, despite the fever in her blood and the excitement still pounding through her. "Yes."

Zak leaned forward and placed his mouth against her stomach. Tiffany felt her muscles tighten there and shivered. He was looking up at her with dark eyes as his mouth continued downward. She felt the tug of the material as he pulled it over her hips and she saw him pull back a little as the material was pulled down to her thighs. He looked from her eyes down to the nest of dark curls between her legs and she heard his breath catch. He ordered, "Step out of the dress."

Tiffany moved clumsily, feeling as if her legs were weak and not working. He was shaking her up with the intensity of his words and the excitement of his touch. She stepped out of the dress. He reached out and helped her to remove her shoes. She was left standing nude, while he was on his knees in front of her still fully clothed. She jerked when he leaned forward suddenly and put his mouth on her sex. He pulled back a little and placed a gentle kiss into her curls. He murmured huskily, "Relax…"

Tiffany felt him cup her hips with his hands and then felt his lips pressing kisses over her. She was shaking hard. When she felt the moist heat of his tongue lick into her sex for the first time, she moaned loudly. Her knees went weak again. She clenched her hands into fists and leaned against the wall for support. Zak delicately licked and sucked until Tiffany could no longer hold back her moans. He was driving her out of her mind. She murmured, "Please Zak…"

Zak circled her clit with his tongue and then pulled back enough to ask, "Please what?"

Tiffany said, "I need…" she couldn't even think of the words. She needed relief. She needed to climax. She was moving her hips against his mouth now, but he was controlling her movements with his hands on her hips. She pulled against the cuffs, aching to touch him. She wanted to feel his hard length driving deeply inside of her.

Zak muttered, "Not yet…look at the holostatue, Tiffany…"

Tiffany looked at it dazedly and then her concentration sharpened as something registered. The couple in the holostatue had changed. The woman now had short dark hair. She was staring at something to one side of the room. She was naked and her breasts were full. Her nipples were hard and her skin was flushed. She looked a little wild and intensely aroused. The man was on his knees staring up at the woman. His hair was pulled back in a stubby ponytail *and* he was fully dressed. The shock of recognition filled her. She said, "It's the two of us!"

Zak said softly, "Watch yourself, Tiff. Watch me send you over the edge with my mouth on you."

Tiffany shook her head, but felt a jolt of excitement at the forbidden idea. In spite of guilty thoughts, she couldn't tear her eyes away.

Zak murmured, "That's right." He leaned forward again and strained a little harder, pushing her closer to the edge with great skill. Tiffany pulled against the cuffs and said, "Let me loose…"

Zak said roughly, "No," and continued to lick.

Tiffany felt her knees go completely and realized he was holding her up with his hands on her hips. She arched against his mouth and pulled on the cuffs helplessly. "Uncuff me. Now."

Zak merely continued pushing her. She felt the tension gathering in her body and she bit her lip. The image of herself being pleasured by Zak depicted by the holostatue was just one more level of excitement that was driving her like a fury.

Zak ordered roughly, "Scream."

Tiffany whimpered and pulled harder on the cuffs. She wanted more of his mouth and yet the torment was making her crazy. She tried to pull back from him, but he held her tighter. She moaned loudly and the entire world narrowed to the place between her legs. Her sex clenched and her vision blurred. She let go completely. Incredible pleasure began to pulse through her and she screamed and screamed until the last wave died away and there was only the sound of her harsh breathing in the silence of the room. She looked down as Zak lifted his mouth from her curls.

He gave her a look of dark hunger as he said, "Beautiful."

He stood up slowly and she saw the large bulge of his hard cock against the front of his pants. A thrill shot through her in spite of her euphoria. He let go of her hips and she realized she could stand again on her own, barely. He reached up and unlocked first one cuff and then the second. Tiffany let her arms fall to her sides. Without any warning Zak reached down and scooped her into his arms. Tiffany wrapped her arms around his neck and said softly, "That was unbelievable, Zak."

He smiled down at her but the smile looked strained. "That was the beginning, Tiff, and yes, it was unbelievable." He strode over to the bed and put her down on top of it. Tiffany scooted back on the bed and pulled the covers back. She started to pull them back over her when she heard him say, "No. Leave them off."

She looked up at him in surprise. His tone was tight and he looked barely in control. She froze. He reached down and jerked the covers all the way off the bed. Moving back, he yanked his shirt over his head. Tiffany's breath caught. He had broad shoulders that led down to a well-defined and muscular chest. She watched those muscles ripple and felt her stomach tighten. He looked so sexy with his shirt off and just those pants still on. She watched as he toed off one shoe and then the other quickly. He removed his socks with quiet efficiency. When his hands went to his pants, he paused.

Tiffany could feel her excitement rising with every movement. When he paused, she looked up at his face. He was staring down at her and said, "I'd keep going slowly, but I can't. It's been too long. I need to claim you, now."

Tiffany swallowed. The hard bulge of his cock stood out against his pants. He looked very large suddenly. She nodded and watched silently as he unbuttoned his pants. She kept looking from his hands to his face. He was watching her, his eyes fastened on her with absolute possession.

She felt a thrill go through her at that look. Screw political correctness and careful equality. There were times when just being taken was an incredible turn on. This was one of them. She had never felt so powerfully a woman. Zak was struggling, trying to stay in control. She was turning him inside out and a part of her thrilled to the notion. She watched as he pushed the pants downward and stepped out of them. When he straightened, she felt her mouth go dry.

His cock was hard and the length of it jutted out from his body aggressively. He looked huge. He strode toward her and she jerked her gaze back up to his face. She saw his amused smile as he said, "Tiff, you look scared. You've seen one of these before, right?"

Tiffany smiled, realizing she was being silly. Of course she'd seen one before. Just not one quite so impressive and not one attached to Zak. She said sincerely, "Of course. Just...Zak...you look...beautiful to me." She immediately winced, feeling somewhat stupid. What a weird thing to say to a *guy*.

Zak faltered, and she saw a flush rise along his cheekbones. He closed his eyes. When he opened them, she saw a look of tenderness so profound that it made her chest feel tight.

He cleared his throat and said, "Thank you, Tiff."

Tiffany watched as he climbed onto the bed beside her. He turned until he was on his side facing her. She stayed turned toward him as she reached out and touched the muscles of his chest. As they jumped under her fingers, she realized how much her touch was exciting him. He watched her with dark eyes.

She moved her hand to the flat circle of one nipple and traced it slowly. She could hear Zak's breathing becoming harsher. With an inward smile, she continued with her exploration of his chest. His skin was warm and smooth under her fingertips. She let her hand drift downward onto his stomach and felt his breathing stop. She found the hard length of his cock and touched it gently. He was extremely hard, but his skin felt like velvet under her fingers. She heard him moan. She wrapped her hand around it and moved up and down slowly, simulating an act they both craved.

Suddenly, Zak muttered, "That's it. No more playing."

He grabbed her hand and removed it from his cock. He pushed her with one hand until she was on her back. Shifting until his body was over hers, he moved one knee against her legs. He said, "Spread your legs, Tiff. I want in."

Tiffany felt the thrill of his words all the way to her toes. He nudged at her legs and she opened them. Moving them until they were spread, she caught her breath as he brought his cock into contact with her sex. Most of his weight was on his hands on each side of her head. She could feel the tension in his body as clearly as she felt it in her own. He looked down at her as his cock brushed against her curls and she saw him close his eyes again for a moment.

When he opened them, he said huskily, "I can't control it. You'll get images for a moment. It's only this one time. It's the claiming. Stay with me, okay? Do you accept me freely, body to body, mind to mind, soul to soul?"

The Claiming? Tiffany felt a moment of confusion and then remembered. The dreams. She would get some images. She could handle it. She nodded. "Yes. It's okay, Zak. Let go. Just let go."

Zak nudged her opening with his cock. She felt the pressure as he entered her carefully. She swallowed hard. He was filling her slowly, pulling back a little and then pushing forward again as if making room. She bit her lip and tried to relax. He was big, but tensing up wouldn't help. He pushed further until he was nearly completely inside her. Her breath caught as she teetered on the edge between pleasure and pain. He paused as if waiting for her to adjust and then surged forward again. She raised her hips a little and felt him slide all the way to the hilt. She was still staring into his eyes, lost in him completely.

He pulled back faster and thrust forward harder. When he surged into her this time, she couldn't hold back a moan. The sound seemed to trigger something in him. The hard length of his cock rasped her inner walls as it left her and then slammed back into her. She whimpered at the wonderful sensation. She brought her hands up and gripped the muscles of his butt. They flexed beneath her hands as he moved in and out of her. She knew her nails were biting into him, but the small pain merely seemed to spur him on.

He gave a low throaty moan as if in response and thrust harder. Tiffany kept her eyes locked on his and thought, "*This is Zak…my best friend… He's inside me and I can't believe how good he feels…how right.*" Tiffany raised her hips and met his thrusts.

Suddenly mental images began to flood her mind. She was on her knees on the floor, his hard cock in her mouth. She was in the bathroom under the shower and he had her arms pinned to the wall as he thrust into her from behind. She was on top of him, her wet sex gripping his cock tightly as she moved up and down its hard length. She was strapped to the chair and he was between her legs, licking her sex. The images continued relentlessly, each more graphic and intense than the last. She felt the hard pressure of his cock filling her sex and the overwhelming feel of him filling her mind. It was too much, she gave a moan and felt her vision start to gray.

Zak said, "*No!* Stay with me."

He arched his spine and thrust harder and faster. Tiffany felt the last of the images fade away and whimpered at the loss. The excitement was unbearable. She could feel her lower body tighten and her sex gripped his cock savagely. Suddenly, the pressure inside her released and she felt the first pulses as her climax hit her. She screamed.

As her body swam with pleasure, she heard his long low moan and felt him shake. The wet warmth of his seed flooded her sex. He continued to pump into her until her screams died away. Then he collapsed on top of her. Some subconscious part of her noted that he kept most of his weight off of her, but he was still heavy. She decided that if her brain ever worked again, she'd ask him to move. Maybe.

Tiffany stared blindly at the black ceiling overhead until she could breathe and think again. She felt incredible. What had happened here was not sex. She didn't know what it was exactly, but it wasn't just sex. It was too intense. Too personal and intimate and special.

Zak finally pulled out of her and then rolled to his side. He maneuvered until he had an arm under her neck and then carefully pulled her to him. She rested her head against his chest, feeling his heart beat beneath her ear. What was going to happen now? How weird or awkward was this going to get? She had made love with Zak. Or had sex with Zak. Or whatever. She sighed.

Zak hand played with her hair gently and she heard the dark rumble of his voice as he asked, "What are you thinking, Tiffany?"

Tiffany tensed. Feeling strange, she said, "That's my line, isn't it?"

He continued the soothing motions of his fingers in her hair. "We don't have any lines here. It's you and me."

Tiffany sighed again. "I feel weird, Zak. I've wanted you for so long, but this changes things."

Zak chuckled. "Yeah. It definitely changes things."

Tiffany lifted her head and looked at him. He was gazing at her sleepily. She shook her head. "You know what I mean. Friends don't sleep together, Zak."

Zak raised an eyebrow. "Husbands and wives generally do."

Husbands and wives? Tiffany cleared her throat. This was tricky. What did he mean by that remark? The only way to know was to ask. "Er…was that some kind of lame indirect marriage proposal?"

Zak looked shocked. "*No.*"

Tiffany was shocked herself at the depth of her disappointment at that one word. With a sinking heart, she realized she could no longer pretend that she and Zak were just buddies. But the truth was, she was in love with him. She'd probably been in love with him for quite some time. She felt embarrassed and awkward at his obvious shock at the notion of marriage between the two of them.

Okay, she was rushing things. He cared about her. It would be enough for the moment. There was that whole promise pair deal, too. What the hell was a promise pair anyway? She tried to brazen it out. "Well, okay then. Right. I didn't mean that you should ask me to marry you. I meant…" She searched frantically for something to cover the awkwardness. "What did you mean by that remark exactly?"

Zak was still looking stunned. He opened his mouth and then closed it. Finally, he said, "Tiff, that wasn't a marriage proposal."

Tiffany felt indignant. No need to rub it in. She'd gotten the point. "I know. You said it wasn't. Fine." She sat up completely and scooted back from him a little on the bed. She picked up the pillow and held it in front of her chest like a shield. "I get the point."

Zak sat up slowly. Speaking very carefully, he said, "It wasn't a marriage proposal because we're already married, Tiff." He reached out and removed the pillow from her hands.

Tiffany let him, barely aware of the pillow any more. She blinked. "Married? Did you just say we were *married?*"

Zak reached out and brushed the hair back from her cheek tenderly. "I asked if you would accept me body to body, mind to mind, soul to soul. Then I claimed you as mine. What did you think I meant?"

Tiffany stared at him. "I just thought it was romantic talk. Heat of the moment stuff. Really sweet. I thought you were warning me about the images, too."

He smiled. "I was warning you about the images, but I asked for your promise. I made you mine when I declared myself in front of a witness."

Tiffany could barely comprehend this new turn. "What witness?"

Zak frowned. "Polly. At the diner. I declared I was your promised. Don't you remember? That was the first half of our claiming."

"You mean you *half married* me in a *diner* on my *lunch hour?*" Tiffany couldn't get over it. "Just like *that*?! Just 'I'm your promised' and that was *it*? Kerlan marriage ceremonies suck."

Zak frowned. His voice was defensive. "I was in a hurry. I was claiming you and trying to get you to leave with me, Tiff. Give me a break. Usually it's done at a ceremony with family and friends present, but there was no time. I don't know. I wasn't thinking really. I was just so glad to find you. I had been worried that Merlez would find you first."

Tiffany tried to sort through her feelings but couldn't seem to grasp how her life had changed so radically in a matter of hours. "But, we're not married. Not on Earth anyway. I mean, not according to Earth laws we're not."

Zak's face darkened. "We're bound together according to the laws of my people. I declared myself to you. I asked you to accept me and when you did, I claimed you."

Tiffany blew out a breath. "Unbelievable. You know, talking about it first might have been good. Explaining would have been really good. This is crazy. I can't believe I got married Kerlan style and didn't know it. That's bizarre."

Zak said coolly, "Bizarre or not, it's done."

Tiffany looked at his face and realized she had hurt him. Zak only used that tone when he was covering up hurt. She placed a hand over his on the bed. "Zak, I'm not sorry exactly. Please understand. This is something of a shock."

Zak's features softened and he nodded. "I should have explained. I was…it's been hard. This day has been so…terrible and wonderful. Gorden's death…Merlez…then finally being honest with you. Tiffany, I realized when I was at the transport that I couldn't leave you. No matter what. You're a part of me. At that point, claiming you was inevitable. Since Merlez was probably after you, there was no reason to hold back any longer. I wanted to claim you for so long that I didn't even think of waiting."

Tiffany felt hope and wonder bloom. "You love me?"

Zak looked at her in disbelief. He rolled his eyes and then smiled. "Of course. Haven't I mentioned it?"

Tiffany smiled back with dawning understanding. "No, you idiot. But you really do. Enough to freak out and half marry me in a diner even."

Zak laughed. Shaking his head, he tossed the pillow aside and then pushed her flat onto the bed. She gave a muffled shriek and laughed as she landed on her back. He came down over her until his face was inches from hers. He grinned and she felt her heart leap a little at the light in his eyes. He looked so happy.

He said, "Tiffany, I love you. Now I believe you have something to say to me."

Tiffany grinned. "Yes, I do. Zak…" She let the pause stretch out.

He looked impatient. She waited another beat and then said teasingly, "Thanks for the birthday celebration."

He gave a warning look, but there was a note of insecurity in his voice. "And…"

Tiffany's heart melted. "Aww…Zak…Of course I love you. I only wish you knew how much."

As soon as the words left her mouth, she regretted them. Oh, she didn't regret the love part, but she really regretted the wish part. Suddenly, there was a loud pounding on the motel room door. She and Zak both froze. She muttered, "Oh hell. I did it again."

Chapter Five

The pounding against the door was even louder. Polly's voice could be heard over the noise, "Zak, Tiff, let me in!"

Tiffany scrambled one way and Zak went the other. Tiffany made a grab for the sheet on the floor and wrapped it around herself, watching as Zak yanked his pants on. She called out, "Just a minute, Polly!" Tiffany walked to the door and opened it.

Polly stood there looking like she'd seen a ghost. She walked in quickly and said, "Tiffany, get out of here, okay? Right now."

Tiffany closed the door behind Polly, confused at her words. She walked to the other side of the room toward Zak. He was looking at Polly in confusion, too. Before she could reach Zak, Polly put a hand on her arm and stopped her. Tiffany looked at her in surprise.

Polly said grimly, "I'm serious, Tiff. You need to leave. I need to talk to Zak."

Tiffany asked in surprise, "How'd you find us?"

Polly shook her head. "The stolen airtranspo." She turned to Zak. "That was a mistake, Zak, and you can't afford mistakes."

Zak muttered an oath. "I planned to dump it later."

Polly said sarcastically, "Well, later is too late. I asked questions and found you'd left the diner by airtranspo. I've been watching for reports of stolen transpos and traced you here. I have a few more resources at my disposal than law enforcement, but they won't be far behind. You need to leave and Tiffany needs to come with me."

Tiffany shook her head. "I'm not going anywhere without Zak. Polly, what the hell is going on? What are you talking about?"

Polly sighed. "Tiff, I work for Covert Coalition. It's not something I advertise. I know you assumed I was a photographer and I am. But, it's a nice cover for my real work."

Tiffany was shocked. Had the whole world gone nuts? First Zak, and now Polly. Was *anyone* who they said they were? It was crazy. She said, "I don't believe it."

Polly smiled, although it lacked amusement. "Believe it. The main problem at the moment is that Zak is wanted by law enforcement for questioning in the death of Gorden Lorting." She flashed an assessing look at Zak.

Zak's face hardened. "And how do you know that?"

Polly eased her arm from her side, showing her weapon. "Well, Zak, there's a bulletin out. I should have checked you out more thoroughly six years ago. I don't like making mistakes."

Tiffany felt like she'd been punched. She looked from Polly's accusing face to Zak's hard eyes. This was a mess. A total mess. She took a step away from Polly. "You have it backwards, Polly. Zak didn't kill Gorden and he's not a killer. He's running *from* a contract killer."

Polly raised an eyebrow. "Do I have it wrong, Zak?"

Zak's face was stony, although his eyes looked coldly calculating. Tiffany felt chilled by the look in his eyes. He shrugged. "Does it matter? You wouldn't be here alone if you were sure. You suspect there's more to it or you'd have come with half a dozen armed companions."

Polly's smile was cold. "I certainly would. And I may have those companions right outside this room. There's no way for you to know, is there? So, that leaves us in a bit of a predicament at the moment. I think Tiffany should leave and let us sort this out."

Tiffany shook her head. "Polly, I don't care what you've been told. Zak's not the killer."

Tiffany felt Zak's hands come up onto her shoulders. He placed a kiss into her hair and said quietly, "Tiff, get dressed. Then we'll talk to Polly. It's okay."

Polly nodded grimly. "Go ahead. Zak, you keep your hands where I can see them. I don't believe you'll hurt Tiffany but that's about the only thing I know right now."

Tiffany grabbed her unidress from the floor and put it back on quickly, making a grimace of distaste. This whole day was one hell of a mess. Polly was with the Covert Coalition? The secret agency was known for fighting terrorism, spying on other planets, and working to keep the peace through intelligence gathering. The operatives for the CC were expertly trained and deadly. Some might sit behind a desk and some might be out undercover, but they were all put through the same training.

She was amazed to think that her goofy friend Polly, the carefree photographer who bounced from one freelance job to another was actually a spy. What next? Could this day get any stranger? Her hairdresser would probably confess to being Elvis next at this rate. As she pulled the dress into place and jerked her shoes on, anger began to replace confusion.

Tiffany looked from Zak who was now pulling his shirt over his head and standing fully dressed to one side of the room to Polly who was still holding her weapon on him. She said sharply, "For the record, I'm pissed at both of you. I mean it."

Both Polly and Zak looked at her in surprise. Tiffany sent them each a lethal look. "There are three people in this room. One of those people has been honest. Two of those people have been lying to the honest one. Guess which ones you are?"

She saw the flash of guilt on their faces but it didn't sway her. "I've been so caught up in all of this that I haven't had a chance to think it through. You've both been lying to me for years. I don't care if you had good reasons. Okay, I understand the reasons but I don't like it. I feel like an idiot. What else have you kept from me? What other secrets are lurking out there just waiting for discovery, huh?"

There was knocking at the door and everyone looked at in surprise. A low masculine voice drawled, "Zak, it's Dran. Let me in."

Tiffany arched an eyebrow at Zak. "You know, Zak. This whole plan of hiding where no one can find us was *really* impressive. What did you do, take out an ad?"

Zak said defensively, "It's my brother. He always knew I was in hiding. I placed the call from the transport to meet me here. He's early. I didn't think he'd get here until tomorrow."

Polly said sharply, "Tiff, don't open that door. Give me a minute." She walked until she was behind Zak with her weapon trained directly to the back of his head.

Tiffany rolled her eyes. "If you blow his head off, Polly, I'm going to be upset. Take it easy, will you? And Zak, who else did you call while at the transport? My mother? Your third grade teacher?"

She walked to the door and opened it. A large man, maybe six-two with dark brown hair and light blue eyes stood in the doorway. He gazed at her in confusion. He was gorgeous, but then he was Zak's brother so that wasn't a huge surprise. Tiffany said calmly, "Hello, Dran. Your idiot brother is inside here at our highly secret location. Come on in and join the party."

He slowly smiled. "You must be the Tiffany I am to protect. Hello, promise sister."

Tiffany couldn't help smiling in spite of her irritation when faced with his charm and friendliness. "Hi. Look, things are a little freaky at the moment. Try to stay calm when you see your brother, okay? My friend Polly is worried he's dangerous."

Dran gave her a confused look and then stepped into the room. Tiffany shut the door and saw him stop in surprise when he spotted Polly and Zak. His hand went to his side and Polly said sharply, "Try it and he's dead."

Dran eased his arm back out from his side. Without warning, he grabbed Tiffany and placed his hands around her neck. She squirmed but he murmured quietly for her ears only, "Trust in Zak if you do not trust me."

Tiffany stood quietly. The room was deadly silent. Dran said in a hard voice, "Drop the weapon or I break her neck."

Polly's smile was all teeth. "I don't think so. You're here to protect her. I heard you say it."

Dran drawled. "Ah, but you can't be sure what lengths I'll go to protect my brother, can you?"

Zak said, "This is ridiculous. Dran, let Tiff go and Polly will lower the lasgun."

Polly and Dran remained silent and unmoving. The tension was unbearable.

Finally, Tiffany said, "You know you guys are *totally* ruining my birthday. First Zak lies to me for six years and is running from a killer, then Polly turns out to be CC. I found out I got married on my lunch hour at a damn McDiner. Now Dran the brother- in-law from hell shows up and threatens to break my neck. For the record, this is going down as the worst birthday party in history. Merlez won't have to kill any of us. We'll do him a favor and kill each other."

There was a moment of stunned silence in the tension of the room. Finally, Polly laughed. She said, "Tiffany, I swear you have a way of cutting through to the core of things." She stared at her friend. "Tiff, are you sure Zak's the man you think he is?"

Tiffany rolled her eyes. "He's the man I love, Polly. He's no killer. Good grief, you know him, too. Think about it."

Polly sighed. "Well, hell. Okay. This whole situation seems off to me. I don't care what the bulletins are saying. I'll risk it." She lowered her weapon.

Zak turned around and stared down at her a second. Polly gave him a sheepish look. "I'm sorry, Zak. I'm the careful type."

Zak smiled. He leaned down and placed a kiss on her cheek. When he pulled back he said, "You were being careful because you're her friend. I understand. Polly, did you think I wouldn't notice the safety was on the whole time?"

Polly winced. "Hey, I didn't really want to blow your head off. I just wanted to be sure my gut instincts were right."

Dran released Tiffany's neck. Tiffany shot him a look of irritation. She said, "You know, for future reference, on Earth we don't generally threaten to break someone's neck at first meeting. It's rude."

Dran laughed. He swept her into a friendly hug, catching her by surprise. When she pulled back, he said teasingly, "But it's such a lovely neck. I was protecting my brother. I would never harm you. And yes, I have the language culture chip. I knew I was being rude. Forgive me?"

Oh this one could charm the pants off of any female within twenty feet. Tiffany smiled. "Oh, okay."

She watched as Dran's face changed. He looked at his brother fully for the first time. Both brothers stared at each other for a long, intense moment. Finally, Dran cleared his throat. He asked huskily, "You are well, Zak?"

Tiffany rolled her eyes. "Men! Zak, hug your brother for heaven's sake."

Zak flashed her a grin and then stepped forward. The two men hugged each other hard. They spoke haltingly in their language and then began to talk so fast that they were talking over each other. Tiffany smiled, feeling touched. Their joy was obvious. They were talking animatedly, grinning and gesturing. She looked at Polly. Polly was regarding the two of them with a bemused expression as if to say, "Who will ever understand men?"

Tiffany finally said, "Dran, let me introduce you to Polly. Don't forget her hug." She watched with an inward smile of amusement as both Polly and Dran flashed her duel looks of disbelief. Tiffany kept her face quite innocent. "What? We're all friends now. No hug?"

Polly snorted. "Tiff, don't push your luck."

Dran drawled, "Why not?"

He gathered Polly into his arms with lightning fast precision. Polly froze, caught completely off-guard. She felt Dran's mouth come down on hers with stunned shock. It was the kiss of a conqueror. She kept her lips firmly together and tried to remember her training. She'd wait for her moment of opportunity and then he'd pay. When she felt his hand massage her ass, she fought the rising heat. Okay, so he was a great kisser. And his hands were skillful. And she was aroused. Still, if she just kept her head, she'd be fine. He broke the kiss and gazed down at her with hard dark eyes. He said loudly, "Hello, Polly." Leaning down until he was close, he murmured for her ears only, "In the words of your culture – fair warning. Next time we kiss, I'll fuck you senseless."

Polly used every ounce of her training to appear completely unaffected. She murmured back in a low voice, "Fine. Fair warning. Only you'll be the one fucked senseless." She flashed him her best shark-like smile. "I'm particular, I'll have you know. In the meantime, back off before I decide to kill you instead." Raising her voice so the others could hear, she widened her smile until it looked overly innocent and said, "Nice to meet you, *Drain*."

Dran flashed her a look promising retribution. She merely kept her smile in place and walked carefully over to where Tiffany and Zak were staring at the two of them in amazement. Tiffany arched an eyebrow at her, but Polly shrugged and said calmly, "Now that we've all decided to be friends, let's talk about this mess."

Chapter Six

It took a while but explanations were finally finished and everyone was left staring grimly at each other. Zak and Dran were both pacing the room restlessly, while Polly was sitting on the edge of the red chair. Tiffany had been surprised when Polly offered the chair to Dran, wondering if Polly knew what the chair would do. When the chair had trapped Dran, much to his chagrin, Polly had looked directly at Tiffany and winked. Tiffany was left fighting back a smile as Zak helped his brother. Zak shook his head at Polly with obvious amusement as he freed Dran. He had then pushed the button disarming the chair permanently until it was reset.

Polly perched in it now, although she looked like she was frustrated and ready to start pacing, too. They were fighting over a good plan to stay alive at the meeting *and* even how to get rid of the airtranspo.

Tiffany was sitting on the bed, feeling tired and not very optimistic at the moment. She had listened to the others arguing until she felt her head would explode. It was time to cut through all this alpha crap and do something. She said quietly, "That's it."

Zak and Dran continued speaking and pacing, arguing, as Polly interjected with pithy disagreements from the sideline. Polly jumped up from the chair and faced the two men. The three voices were rising in volume and frustration.

Tiffany stood up and put her fingers to her mouth. She let out a short, loud whistle. Everyone froze in surprise and looked at her. She rolled her eyes. She might be known for her somewhat absurd sense of humor and easygoing personality, but she was an accountant for goodness sake. Practical and methodical should have been stamped on her forehead at birth. They were getting nowhere. It was time to change things. She said calmly, "Now that I have your attention, you will listen as I make an important observation crucial to our survival. The problem with you alpha types is that each one of you thinks you know best and that you're the only one who can save the day."

She gave each of them a glare in turn. "The only way to get through this is teamwork. I don't care about heroes or being brave, I care about staying alive. Zak you want to get rid of the airtranspo before law enforcement finds it, but you're worried about leaving me here, so you want the others to stay. Here's what is going to happen. Polly you don't trust Dran or Zak to get rid of the transpo properly, so you do it. Dran, you don't trust Polly, so you're going with her to make sure she does it right. Then, Polly, you'll work on getting the Gorden mess straightened out with law enforcement for Zak without revealing exactly where we are to anyone. Dran, afterward, you get a room and get some sleep. Interplanetary jetlag has got to be a bitch."

She looked at Zak and frowned. "Zak and I are going to eat and then we're going to bed. Big day tomorrow with the whole meet-with-Rojda-possibly-get-killed plan. So, we need to rest and relax and not kill each other prior to the meeting. If this is my last night on Earth, I'm spending it doing something other than listening to you three argue. We'll iron out the rest of the details in the morning over breakfast when all of us are thinking more clearly."

The three of them started to object and Tiffany said loudly, "End…of…discussion. This is unproductive and annoying. I'm done. The birthday girl has spoken. Don't make me wish for quiet. What I'm saying makes sense and you know it."

They regarded her with a mix of frustration and amusement. Finally, Polly said, "Fine, Drain, let's go. Try to keep up."

Dran shot a look at Polly that would have another woman quaking in her shoes. He nodded in agreement and said, "Let's go."

The two of them left, shutting the door quietly. Tiffany turned to see Zak staring at her thoughtfully with his eyebrow raised.

She asked sharply, "What?"

He smiled and said, "Tiff, I'm wondering how the military missed you. You may be fluffy and fun, but under that exterior beats the heart of a general."

Tiffany laughed. She couldn't help it. "I only resort to a group coup when my sense of efficiency is invoked. I'm an accountant."

Zak grinned. "Oh, no, you can't fool me. That was alpha. I saw it. Of course, only you would invoke weird birthday wish karma as a threat." He shook his head and laughed. His shoulders shook and his eyes were warm. "I love you, Tiffany. I really do."

Tiffany grinned. "Well, in that case...I love you, too."

Zak took a step forward and said, "So, how hungry are you?" His eyes swept her body.

Tiffany looked at the man in front of her. His hair was still in its ponytail, although strands had escaped and he looked a little wild. His eyes were hungry and dark as they stared into hers. His big body was within a few steps of touching her. Her pulse rate climbed and she said huskily, "I'm starved. Screw dinner."

Zak's eyebrows shot up and she watched as he struggled to keep from smiling. She felt a sense of confusion until she realized what she had said. She laughed. "I mean, forget dinner."

Zak's face changed and he took two more steps toward her. He asked huskily, "How about a shower?"

Tiffany had an image from one of her dreams of Zak stroking into her from behind, his body wrapped around hers in the shower. She closed her eyes at the memory and then opened them. She smiled and flirted playfully, "Well, if you insist...but Zak, won't a shower get me all wet?"

He smiled the smile of a predator and closed the distance between them. He scooped her into his arms and strode to the bathroom. Pausing in the doorway, he looked down at her and said, "Baby, count on it."

Chapter Seven

Polly wiped the last of the prints, shut the door of the airtranspo quietly, and slipped into the shadows. It was at a public mall and should be discovered soon as the mall closed down for the night. She had contacted her assistant and given him the details to get Zak out from legal trouble fairly quickly. As she walked toward the closest underground transport station, she thought about Zak's brother Dran.

He was gorgeous. There was no doubt of that fact. He was also arrogant, overconfident, and annoying. If only he weren't so sexy, she could dismiss him without a qualm. But it had been a long time since her last sexual encounter with a live human being. Hell, her batteries were low on her vibrator anyway.

One-night stands weren't typically her style, but if he would be gone to some distant planet soon, he might be worth an exception. It was just sex and sex was a healthy need. She walked a little faster.

Okay, let's face it. She was hot for the guy and he was available. Wasn't everyone allowed one night of insanity? Who would know or care? She wasn't committed to anyone. Her lifestyle and personality didn't exactly generate a lot of long term relationships. What was the harm in taking a night of pleasure just this once? He would be out of her life in days and everything would be back to normal with no one the wiser.

She saw the shape of a well-built man leaning in the shadows of the entrance to the underground transport. As he stepped into the light, she felt her system jolt. She said coolly, "I thought I lost you about two blocks from the motel."

He nodded and said equally coolly, "Yes, I know."

She took a step closer. "Why are you waiting for me? Don't you need to get a room?"

He smiled an infuriatingly confident smile that had her heart racing. She took another step closer and stopped. "What?"

He took her arm and began to walk. "If you don't want me to take you here, you need to show me how to get to your place."

She rolled her eyes, but walked beside him. "That confidence is annoying. If I weren't feeling horny and in the mood tonight, I'd tell you to go to hell."

They reached the payment machine and she slapped her palm against it a little forcefully. The machine's mechanical voice said smoothly, "Hello, Ms. Hill. How many traveling?"

Polly answered, "Two."

Zak reached out and placed his palm across the machine. The machine spoke, "Thank you. Destination?"

She said, "Grove Street Station."

The machine buzzed and then a door opened in the wall in front of them. The machine said, "Your account has been adjusted. Vehicle 28 in Section 3 is departing within 5 minutes. Thank you for traveling Subveh Systems. Please remember to lock securely after strapping in and be considerate of other passengers by turning off all audible devices. Enjoy your trip."

Polly and Dran stepped through the door and walked toward their section, dodging other passengers streaming out from an arriving vehicle. Dran's hold on her arm never slipped and he moved beside her with easy grace. When they were strapped into their seats, Polly turned her head to look at him. The vehicle would be leaving any minute. She said, "I can't believe I'm going to do this. I'm having a moment of pure insanity. You have an arm-pc implant with syscheck, right? Sheesh, I'm nuts. I'm not sure I even like you."

Dran's eyes grew heavy lidded as he stared at her silently for a moment. As the vehicle began to move, he said, "I have the implant and syscheck because I knew Zak was here and wanted to be ready if he needed me. I don't leave things to chance. And liking me or not liking me doesn't matter tonight...because you're going to love what I do to you."

The vehicle picked up speed with a jerk. Polly wasn't sure if it was the lousy public transportation or Dran's words but she felt as if her heart was in her throat and her stomach had been left a mile back. When he smiled at her slowly and her nipples hardened in a rush, she sighed. It was Dran. Dammit. And he was right. Either way, her body was already sure it liked him plenty. She checked her straps again to make sure they were secure and give herself a distraction. She muttered, "I've made the leap from horny to crazy. I knew it. It was only a matter of time."

He answered softly, "Polly?"

She raised her eyebrow. "Yes?"

He stared at her mouth for a long moment as the lights dimmed and then came back on. The vehicle was moving at top speed. "The name you'll be screaming tonight is Dran, not Drain. After tonight, you'll never forget it."

She swallowed. "Big talk."

He nodded. "Yes, but I don't lie."

Polly gave him a sad look for a moment thinking of all of the times she had been lied to and all the lies she had told in her career. In spite of the heat coursing through her body, she gave a soul-weary, skeptical sigh. "Right. Let's start off with some degree of honesty at least. We want each other and we're strangers. It's for one night. You'll be leaving soon and we'll never see each other again. No need for evasion or dishonesty. That's actually the beauty of it. Purely pleasure, no obligation. No responsibility. We're having sex, plain and simple. To put it bluntly, a fuck's a fuck. Beyond that...well, sorry, but trust me, *everybody* lies."

He said firmly, "I'm not everybody."

As the vehicle pulled into the station announcing the first stop, she felt the ground shift beneath her feet. Telling herself inwardly that it was only the slowing of the vehicle, she turned without saying another word and faced straight ahead.

Chapter Eight

Tiffany felt the warm spray of the water as it washed over her body and let out a sigh of pleasure. She could hear Zak moving around in the bathroom, but he had given her a moment of privacy by putting her down inside the doorway. As she listened to his movements, she felt her excitement build. He was about to join her. She raised a soapy hand and began to rub along her arm, imagining what would happen when he stepped inside the small stall with her. She paused as she heard a muttered curse and then nothing.

Then, the door of the shower opened and Zak appeared in the doorway. She turned and smiled at him, feeling a little awkward. They had made love but that had been a heat of the moment thing. This was, well, this was different. She was naked and he was…She caught her breath. He was naked and already erect. The muscles in his body moved as he stepped forward and put his arms around her. She felt the hard length of his cock pressing against her stomach. She lifted her head and leaned into him, grateful for the embrace. She smiled and said, "Well, hello. Nice to have you join me."

He smiled down at her tenderly, although he gave her a playful nudge against her stomach and said, "Well, I'm happy to join you, too."

He pushed her a small ways away and gave her a mock frown. "I believe you missed a spot."

Tiffany grinned. "Oh yeah? Which spot?"

Zak hit the button on the wall and soap sprayed into his hand. He rubbed his hands together slowly, working up a lather. He said huskily, "Let me show you."

Tiffany watched his hands and nearly groaned at how sensuous they looked. He was killing her. She was getting turned on by a guy's hands for goodness sake. But, then again, this was not just any guy's hands. This was Zak. And he was about to rub her body the way he was rubbing his hands together—with those same slow strokes. She swallowed.

Zak said huskily, "Turn around and face the wall."

Tiffany turned around and heard him chuckle. She felt confused for a moment and then remembered the dream. Oh yeah. She realized that he meant the wall next to them and felt foolish. She stepped and turned until she was sideways, with water streaming over her but not as strongly now.

Zak stepped behind her and said huskily, "Put your hands on the wall, sweetheart."

Her heart started racing and she licked her lips. Placing her hands on the wall in front of her, she felt the coolness of the tile. The next thing she felt was the heat of Zak's body as he stepped closer. He touched her back and she arched a little, grateful to feel his hands on her at last. As she felt him stroking slowly over her back, it was all she could do to hold back a moan. It felt wonderful. He was exerting just enough pressure to relax her and yet turn her on. He kept up the gentle rhythm, making her sigh.

Tiffany was silent as Zak worked his hands down to her waist and then to her butt. As he massaged her, the slick slide of his soapy hands made Tiffany bite her lip. She said softly, "That feels so good. Don't stop."

She felt the teasing glide of one long finger between her cheeks and stilled. Zak said smoothly, "You feel incredible under my hands, Tiff. All of you."

His hands moved to her thighs and she could feel him bending down behind her. She started to turn, but his voice stopped her.

He said firmly, "Stay where you are."

She cleared her throat and murmured, "Okay."

He continued his massage down her legs. Tiffany felt like squirming. She'd never felt so relaxed and so excited at the same time. Her heart was hammering in her chest. She felt hot and she knew she was dripping wet in a way that had absolutely nothing to do with the shower. As she felt him stand up behind her and place his hands on her shoulders, she moaned.

He said softly, "I love to hear that sound. I love to feel you shiver under my hands."

Tiffany felt his hands slide down her back and then around to her breasts. She held her breath as she waited for him to touch her aching nipples. As she felt him cup her breasts in his palms and rub, she moaned louder.

He responded by thumbing her nipples and bringing his lower body into contact with her. She felt the hard length of his cock pressing along her lower back and butt and shivered hard. Her knees were beginning to feel shaky. She leaned backward into him a bit, but arched forward at the same time into his hands.

He murmured, "That's right. Step back and spread your legs for me, Tiffany. Arch your back, baby."

Tiffany could barely understand him. She was focused on the feel of his hands toying with her nipples. She stepped back and spread her legs until her stance was wider. She felt him move one hand to her lower back and complied by arching forward even more under that gentle pressure. When his hand moved from her back around to her aching sex, she sucked in a breath and waited impatiently.

He stroked between her legs slowly, his fingers gently circling her opening and then slid upward to circle her clit. She gasped and moaned louder. She said, "More. Give me more."

He gave what sounded suspiciously like a moan, too and complied. He teased and tormented her clit until Tiffany could barely catch her breath. She whimpered. Suddenly, she felt him move his hand and she was caught by surprise as water poured over her. He was using his hand to direct the spray.

He took his hand from her breast and said roughly, "Step under the water for a minute."

She complied eagerly, anxious to have him inside her. Once she had stepped under the water and rinsed completely, she turned to him anxiously. She reached up and kissed him hard, catching his mouth with hers and thrusting her tongue inside eagerly. He met her with his tongue and they fought for control of the kiss. Tiffany felt him pushing her backward until the cool tile was pressing into her back. She shivered at the sensation.

Zak broke the kiss finally and placed both hands on her shoulders. Tiffany felt the gentle strength in his hands as he turned her firmly around. His arms slid down her arms until he reached her wrists. Wrapping his hands around both wrists, he brought them up and over her head. She felt him slide his hands until they were over hers, and place her palms flat against the tile.

He said harshly, "Step back and take me."

She stepped backward, spreading her legs and arching her back, anxious to feel his cock slide into her waiting heat. As she felt that first probing touch, she moaned loudly and pressed backward as far as her body and her hands on the tile would allow.

Zak's cock probed her wetness, sliding inward slowly as if he was trying to be gentle. As she felt the length of him fill her deeply, she moved forward a little and then pushed back. She heard Zak suck in a breath and moan softly. He pulled out of her and then pressed inward again with more speed. As she felt him slide along the sensitive walls of her sex, she arched to meet him. The water from the shower streamed over them gently and Tiffany felt the heat rising. He was thrusting into her harder and harder, going deeper inside her. Her mind stopped thinking and she was just focused on the sensation, the feel of him behind her. His hands were pressing hers against the tile, making movement impossible. It was wild and almost primal as he thrust within her depths over and over. She moaned louder.

Zak suddenly removed his hands from over hers and swept them along her back. Tiffany shuddered but left both palms where they were. One hand crept forward and he began to tease her clit mercilessly. He kept up the relentless rhythm of his strokes as she fought to keep her legs from giving way. Then, his other hand traced her spine downward, making her muffle another moan. He shoved into her hard and then pulled back. His hand swept along the cheeks of her ass and his thumb traced the crease. He circled her rear bud slowly and Tiffany stiffened with a combination of fear and shock and excitement. He thrust into her harder, stroking her clit.

His finger played along the crease of her ass, and she went over the edge with a sudden surge of wild pleasure. Her climax hit her with the force of a violent storm, the waves of pleasure crashing through her without mercy. She screamed helplessly, focused only on the clenching of her body and the pleasure filling her.

She heard him moan loudly, but continue stroking. Suddenly, he slammed into her hard and paused. His entire body shook and he groaned. She felt his cock pulsing inside her sex as his hot seed flooded her.

It was a long moment before Tiffany could breathe well enough to speak. Finally, she said, "When I can walk again, I want to strap you in that chair. And I want to be the one on top of you."

He was resting against her back and pulled upward a little, although he was still inside her. He chuckled and said, "Wellll…it is still your birthday. I don't want to ruin your birthday party."

Tiffany turned around slowly and then beamed at him. She said, "Yes, well…"

Birthday party. Wishes. She had a sudden thought. She really shouldn't do it. It was too risky. Then again, if things turned out well in the long run like they had with Zak…She remembered that hot kiss Dran and Polly had exchanged. With an inward smile, she silently made another wish. What the hell.

Zak studied her expression curiously. "What was that look all about?"

Tiffany grinned. "Oh, just wondering how Polly and Dran are doing."

Zak's voice reflected his sudden amusement. "You made a wish involving the two of them. Didn't you?"

The problem with falling in love with your best friend is that he knows you all too well. Tiffany gave him her most innocent look. "Now would I do something like that?" As she heard Zak burst into laughter, Tiffany grinned. You bet.

Chapter Nine

Polly took a deep calming breath as her door came in view. She started to press her hand on the id-lock, when Dran spoke behind her.

He said firmly, "No. One moment."

Polly turned to look at him in surprise. The hallway was deserted and quiet. The two of them were alone. It was safe. There was no threat that she could discern. With some degree of bafflement, she asked, "Why?"

Dran pushed up his sleeve and hit a combination of buttons on his arm-pc. In the silence of the hallway the low mechanical voice of the computer said, "Instituting syscheck…"

Polly felt the heat flood her checks. Of course. She should have thought to get this out of the way right up front. It was the practical thing to do. No need for embarrassment or feeling foolish. As she listened to the computer continued running the diagnostic and announce that it was okay to proceed, she pushed up her own sleeve and punched in the activation code. The voice of her computer performing the syscheck and declaring her okay sounded loud to her own ears. The silence continued as she stared at him, her heart pounding.

Finally, his mouth curved in a smile. He said gently, "Polly, open the door."

Polly nodded jerkily and turned around, feeling clumsy. Right. The door. She pressed her palm to the id-lock and heard the slide as her door opened. She swallowed and walked boldly into the apartment, hearing his footsteps behind her. The door closed with a barely audible click.

She turned and met his eyes squarely. Determined to cover her sudden awkwardness, she asked, "Would you like a drink?"

He shook his head and said, "No." His hands went to his shirt and he drew it over his head with casual normality.

Polly saw the width of his shoulders in the dim light of the room. She had left lights at sixty percent. His skin was smooth and dark. His muscular chest was clearly defined and seemed to gleam in the soft light. His nipples were flat round disks surrounded by a light covering of dark curly hair.

Polly sucked in a breath and tried to still her pounding heart. He looked like gorgeous, mouth-watering, sexual temptation incarnate.

She cleared her throat, trying to think of something, anything to say. Her voice emerged husky and low. "Would you like something to eat?" She watched as his eyes darkened.

He said slowly and distinctly, "Polly take off your clothes if you don't want them ripped." He bent down and removed his shoes and socks. His hands moved to his pants and he lifted an eyebrow at her. "*Now.*"

Polly felt a dark thrill at his words. He sounded predatory and aggressively male. In spite of the danger of the situation, she felt strongly that he wouldn't hurt her. He might fuck her brains out, but he wasn't going to hurt her. She reached down with shaky hands and hurriedly took off her clothes. She felt clumsy and awkward in her haste, but she couldn't help it. She wanted him so much, far more than she had anticipated. When she was completely nude, she took one step forward and stopped to face him.

He was completely nude as well. Her eyes dropped to the large hard cock thrusting forward from his body and she felt an undeniable sense of need so sharp it stole her breath away. She let her eyes wander from his lean hips to that hard cock past the masculine thighs and legs to his feet and back up again. Her eyes finally landed on his face and she knew in an instant that tonight was going to be out of control. He was staring at her as if he planned to eat her alive and had every right to do so.

He said huskily, "You're beautiful. And for tonight, you're mine. There are no rules, just pleasure. As much pleasure as you can take. And then, I'm going to push you harder and you're going to take more. Come here."

Polly took a step forward and then stopped. His words rang in her ears like a battle cry. She shook her head. "No. You come to me. And we'll see who pushes harder."

Dran smiled slowly at her words. He walked forward until he placed his hands on her shoulders. When she jerked a little under his touch, he smiled wider. "This time will be fast and hard. There's a long night ahead of us and plenty of time for you to push all that you want. You're welcome to try." He reached out abruptly and palmed her sex. Stroking her gently, he teased, "I guess I'll show you how to come, too."

Polly was shocked at the sensation of his hand boldly moving between her legs. She was already wet, and his fingers slid slickly along her flesh. As he teasingly probed and circled, she lost her breath on a moan.

Dran leaned down and took one nipple hungrily into his mouth. Polly bit her lip at the sudden wet heat pulling at her breast, causing her to feel pleasure too sharp for words. She felt him circle her hard nipple with his tongue and boldly push one long finger inside her sex. She was so slick and ready for him that he slid inward easily.

Within seconds, she felt a second finger join the first. Her legs began shake and she felt the heat rising inside her with a ferocity that was unbelievable. She brought her hands up to his head and tangled them in his dark hair, pulling him closer to her. Finally whimpering, she muttered, "More, dammit. *More.*"

Dran stood and picked her up into his arms. Polly gave a muffled exclamation of surprise at the suddenness of the move and then grabbed for his shoulders desperately as he strode toward her kitchen. She had a bar separating the living room and kitchen. She felt a wild surge of hunger as she felt him place her gently on the counter facing him. He spread her knees and stepped between them in one smooth motion.

Polly said, "This is…"

It was all she had time to get out before he placed both hands on her hips and pulled her toward him. As she felt her sex come into contact with the hard thrust of his cock for the first time, she said, "*Wow.*"

He was poised at the entrance to her sex. Polly held her breath as she waited for that first intimate plunge. Instead, she felt him move one hand up until it was under her chin, forcing her to look him in the eye.

He asked roughly, "What's my name?"

His name? Polly fought through the haze of desire to recall why that information was important at the moment. She remembered his earlier statement and said huskily, "Dran."

He brought his hand between them, guiding his cock until the head was just inside the tight entrance of her sex. Feeling the blunt tip of him sliding into her, she fought to relax and enjoy the sensation. He was huge, but she was going to take him. She was going to take him and enjoy him and utterly savor this night of madness.

She whimpered as he pulled back just a bit. She said, "Give it to me now." She arched forward, trying to force him deeper inside. She didn't want slow and considerate. She wanted hot and hard and fast and mindless. As he slid further inside her, she wrapped her legs around his waist and muttered, "I want it all. *Now.*"

Her words seemed to set off something inside him. He cursed and thrust forward hard, filling her roughly with one long powerful stroke. He arched his spine and pushed until the tip of his cock could go no further. Then he paused and gasped, "Did I hurt you?"

Polly shook her head. His cock stretched her inner walls tightly. She was filled, teetering on the fine edge between just enough and too much. She moaned and murmured, "It's good. So good."

He muttered, "Yes. It will be better." He withdrew and thrust forward again with more force. He moaned and his hands tightened on her hips, threatening to bruise. He began to stroke her with the rapid, violent strokes of a man pushed past the limit of civility. He claimed her savagely and ruthlessly, an animal claiming his mate.

Polly met his thrusts, tightening her legs and then arching upward to take more of him. She threw her head back and moaned loudly, drunk on the feel of him inside her and the intensity of the passion between them. She no longer felt like herself. She had lapsed into some primitive being, greedy and desperate only for more pleasure, more feeling.

He snarled, "Say my name."

She whimpered, "Dran." As he rewarded her with another forceful stroke, she heard the slap of their bodies. His hands on her hips pressed a little harder, just short of pain and she smelled the tangy scent of arousal, sweat, and sex. She drew in a harsh breath and said in a voice that didn't even sound like her, "*Dran!.*"

He stroked in and out fiercely, not letting her catch her breath, keeping her pinned to the edge of release. She moaned and fought the impulse to scream.

He said roughly, "Again."

She felt the rasp of his cock as he withdrew and then plunged deep within the slick clenching walls of her sex. She was hot, aroused beyond caring. Nothing mattered but this feeling. Nothing. She screamed, "Dran!" and tightened her sex around him. With the force of a punch, she was hurtled over the edge of the cliff into oblivion. As pleasure pulsed through her, she dimly heard his low throaty moan as he joined her in release and barely realized that the scream echoing in her ears was her own voice.

Dran collapsed against her, his head buried in her shoulder, breathing raggedly. Polly struggled to breathe. She felt boneless, as if she were floating. When he lifted his head, she eyed him lazily, too content at the moment to move.

She saw the sleepy male satisfaction on his face and nearly smiled, charmed against her will. When he leaned forward and placed a gentle kiss on her lips with surprising tenderness, she felt the first stirrings of unease.

He leaned away, staring into her eyes for a long moment, and then said with peculiar solemnity, "Hello."

Polly stared into his face and wondered why that one word sounded so much like a promise and a threat.

Chapter Ten

The next day the four of them met at the motel. It was a somewhat grim day filled with planning, arguing, and trying to figure out how to survive while catching a killer. The only moment of levity came when Polly spoke for the first time in a strangely hoarse voice. Tiffany raised an eyebrow and asked, "Polly, your voice sounds strained. Are you okay?"

Polly flushed, looking away from Dran and said, "I'm fine. A twenty-four hour thing. I'm sure it's only temporary."

Dran's voice rang with challenge as he said, "Best take care. Temporary can become permanent."

Polly flashed him a look. "Not in this case."

Dran watched her with hooded eyes and merely shrugged. He turned to Zak and began to question him about the meeting.

Tiffany eyed Polly skeptically and asked, "You going to tell me what that was all about?"

Polly said firmly, "Not a chance."

Tiffany grinned. "That's what I thought. Oh well. I guess I'll let you keep your night of wild sex with Dran a secret for now."

Polly's expression was pure exasperation. Her face flushed even more. "Can we stay on topic here or do you want an orgasm count?"

Tiffany laughed and placed her hand over Polly's. "Okay, I'll stop teasing you. I'm just...glad for you, Polly. You look...happy."

Polly smiled a little. "Well, thanks."

Then the four of them returned to the grim task at hand. They went over the options carefully, trying to plan every scenario. What if Merlez was waiting in ambush? What was the best way to draw him out later if he didn't show up? When Zak mentioned the location of the meeting, Tiffany rolled her eyes, too appalled to speak.

Zak looked at her in question. "What?"

Tiffany said sarcastically. "I just can't believe it. A warehouse? At night? You've read the books and seen the movies, right? This is such a bad idea. It's a cliché, I'm telling you. Merlez will be in there waiting to blow your head off. Or else he'll catch me outside. My life had turned into a series of bad plots. I'm so *not* liking this whole idea."

Zak smiled. "Clichés are clichés, Tiff, because there's usually some truth to them. The warehouse was chosen as the meeting location long ago because it's remote. Meeting at a public place endangers other innocent people. It's completely logical."

Tiffany nodded her head. "Right. Okay, fine. But when Merlez jumps out from behind a box, I'm going to be very ticked off. I mean, extremely aggravated."

Zak laughed. "Yeah. I know."

Tiffany frowned, "And the girl usually gets shot trying to save the hero. Or else the hero gets shot and nearly dies tragically in her arms while declaring his love. Nope, I'm not liking this idea at all."

Zak grinned. "I've already declared my love." His expression sobered abruptly. "All kidding aside, Tiff, you're not going to get shot. I wish you would stay here at the motel. I really think it's safer than at the meeting. If only I could be sure..." He was frowning, lines of worry creasing his forehead.

Tiffany saw the concern on his face and felt her heart melt a little. "Zak, I'm joking but I'm serious, too. I'm worried about you, too. We'll face this thing together. We'll be fine."

Zak nodded his head, although his eyes still looked grim. "Yes, we will. And when it's over, there are some things we need to discuss."

Tiffany smiled. "Like where we're going to live?"

Zak's face softened and the look of tenderness he sent her melted her further. He said, "Yes, and how soon I can convince you to marry me."

Tiffany felt her heart jolt in her chest. "I thought we were already married?"

He placed his hand over hers and said, "We are married according to my world, but I want a commitment from you in the eyes of your world, too. I know I didn't really give you much choice about it before." He flashed her a look of love, with just a touch of uncertainty. "Will you marry me?"

Tiffany took a deep breath, filled with such joy that she wondered if her body could contain it. She looked at the man she loved so much and said simply, "Yes."

He kissed her softly, his mouth moving against hers tenderly. When they drew apart, Tiffany sighed. She murmured with absolute determination, "I won't lose you."

Zak brought her hand to his mouth and kissed it gently. He looked into her face and said solemnly, "No, you won't."

Tiffany felt a chill as she thought of the upcoming meeting. She hoped they were right.

Chapter Eleven

Zak, Tiffany, Polly, and Dran paused outside the warehouse speaking in low voices, wearing identical grim expressions. The building looked deserted and eerie in the moonlight. Dran had rented a vehicle and they had parked some distance away so that they could approach the building quietly. Zak hadn't lied when he called the location remote. The rundown building was situated beside the river in farming territory. There were no other buildings even close. It had been out of use for years, although Tiffany wondered if the government had used it in the past for covert meetings. Staring at the warehouse, she put her hand on Zak's arm and said, "I don't like this. I have a bad feeling. I think Merlez is in there waiting. And where the hell is Rojda and the rescue crew? This doesn't look right."

Zak's voice was reassuring. "Rojda and his men are probably inside. Tiff, everything's going to be fine."

Suddenly the distinctive sounds of lasguns being used came from the warehouse. They could see blazes of light through the windows and hear voices screaming. The four of them ran forward, ducked down, and crouched behind a large bush. Tiffany could hear noises like things were falling within the warehouse. There was the sound of footsteps echoing in the night. And then silence. Total silence.

Tiffany looked at the others. Polly, Zak, and Dran had their lasguns out and ready. She had refused to take one, saying she'd probably shoot herself by accident. She hated guns. There was no point in carrying one if she didn't know how to use it. Besides, she wasn't completely helpless.

A masculine voice called out from the warehouse. "Zak, are you out there?"

Zak muttered, "It's Rojda." He called back, "Yes!"

Rojda yelled, "Stay where you are until we make sure we have him. We've got a man down but he was hit in the face. I need to make sure it's him. There was also more than one person who came in. Give us time."

Tiffany felt the hard cold press of metal against her skull. She swallowed. She said quietly, "Zak…"

Zak, Polly, and Dran were peering around the bush at the warehouse, lasguns gleaming in the moonlight. Tiffany said loudly, "Merlez has a lasgun against my head."

The three of them spun around and she saw the look of disgust and anger cross their faces. They had been so preoccupied with the action in front of them that they had not expected an approach from behind. It was a stupid mistake.

Merlez said calmly, "Very good, my dear. Everyone stay calm. Drop your weapons."

Tiffany saw the hesitation. She swallowed and said, "Drop them, guys. He's a killer, remember? And it's gonna be hard to miss when he has the lasgun to the back of my head."

The three of them dropped their guns. As each one hit the ground with a soft thud, Tiffany tried to focus and keep calm. This was it.

Merlez's voice continued coldly from behind her. "At last. Zak, before I kill your whore, I wish I could make you pay for the last six years."

Zak eyed Merlez grimly and asked, "What do you mean?"

Merlez said bitterly, almost conversationally, "It was my last hit. I was retiring. Instead, I've spent six years hiding, moving from planet to planet. They have pursued me relentlessly. I am not pleased. It's a shame I can't torture you before killing you. It would give me a great deal of satisfaction. Normally, I don't waste my time, but for you, I would make an exception."

Tiffany felt a chill all the way to her soul. There were times in life when evil crossed your path. There was no question, no other word for it, there was only the deep internal knowledge that you were in the presence of something dark and evil. This was one of those times. She knew intuitively that Merlez was more monster than man.

Tiffany braced herself and bluffed for time, "Thank goodness some clichés really are true. Merlez, we have you surrounded. You shoot me and you'll be dead, too."

She heard the quiet chuckle from behind her. "Oh, really? I don't believe you, my dear. I think Rojda and his men are quite busy with my hired help in the warehouse."

Then there was the sound of Merlez sucking in his breath and the distinctive hum of a lasgun on ready. Tiffany remained absolutely still. There was silence for a moment and then another masculine voice said, "I think she's telling the truth. Drop the lasgun, Merlez. My name is Rojda Perilnere and you are hereby declared a ward of justice."

Merlez cursed. "I'll kill her. At least I'll have the satisfaction of hurting him."

Rojda's voice was cold and calm. "If you do, I'll kill you. Not exactly a good deal for you, is it? Drop the weapon now."

The tension was unbearable. Tiffany looked at Zak in the moonlight. His eyes were glittering at her and his hands were clinched in fists. She could see that he was ready to spring at any moment. If she waited, he'd play the hero. She knew it. She said, "Zak, I love you."

Zak surmised her intention just a second too late. For Tiffany time seemed to slow and yet crash in on her at lightning speed. Her heart was hammering and her vision seemed to have narrowed. She knew she'd never get a better chance with Merlez distracted by Rojda.

Tiffany screamed her head off, startling Merlez. At the same time, she fell into a crouch, bringing her arm up and wind-milling it outward, sweeping the lasgun from Merlez's hand with a clean, practiced motion. Then, with all her might, she used her other fist to drive upward between his legs. She heard his agonized wail, just as Rojda's lasgun went off, missing

Merlez and almost hitting Zak. Merlez went to his knees and Tiffany brought her elbow upward, smashing it into his jaw. He fell to the ground, out cold.

There was a moment of confusion and yelling and hands pulling at her. Tiffany was swept into Zak's arms. She could feel his heart racing beneath her ear and his shaking body. He was holding her too hard and saying, "I can't believe you did that. I can't believe you did that." He pushed her away from him and shook her. He yelled at her, *"Don't you ever do that again!"*

Tiffany felt her own body shake now as what had happened began to penetrate. She nodded jerkily. "Okay. Zak, it's okay."

Eventually, things settled down and were sorted out. According to Rojda, Gorden had betrayed Zak. They were still investigating, but Kerlan and Earth authorities had verified that much information while investigating Gorden's death. Rojda made arrangements with Zak to testify before the council in a few weeks, but said he would notifiy Zak of the exact details later.

When everyone had calmed down and Merlez was on his way to Kerla with Rojda, Tiffany found Dran, Polly, and Zak staring at her. Assuming they were still upset over Gorden's betrayal of Zak, she said grimly, "I know, I can't believe Gorden was corrupt either. Zak, I'm sorry your friend betrayed you."

Zak shook his head at her. He said flatly, "He paid for it."

She nodded sadly. The three of them continued to stare at her. Finally, she demanded, "What?!"

Zak said, "Tiffany, where the hell did you learn to do what you did to Merlez?"

Tiffany said, "Well, I took that defense class a year ago. Don't you remember?"

Zak closed his eyes. When he opened them, he said, "I thought it was some kind of self-protection class. I had no idea they would teach you *that* kind of thing."

Tiffany grinned. "Well, they did and they didn't. Did I ever mention I was the junior kickboxing champion of my college class?"

The three of them eyed her in surprise. She laughed. "Hey, you three think you're the only ones who can have secrets?" She beamed at them proudly. "And I'd like to point out for the record that the ditzy brunette beta accountant without the weapon saved the day. How's that for surprises?"

The three of them began to laugh. Tiffany grinned. Zak was right. Sometimes life was a cliché and clichés were often based on truth. But, in her experience, just when you thought you had it all figured out, life threw you something unexpected. Like a wish. Or a secret agent friend. Or a brother-in-law. Or a contract killer. Or love. You just had to go with it and hope for a happy ending. And be prepared to defend yourself against the bad stuff.

Zak shook his head at her and said, "Remind me never to get you mad at me. And don't ever do that again or I'll..."

Tiffany raised an eyebrow. "Yes?"

He wrapped her in a hug. "I'll never let you out of my sight."

Tiffany laughed. "Some incentive to stay out of danger. Oh well, don't worry. My birthday is over. The bad guy is caught. Everything should be back to normal soon. My brief career as a damsel in distress is officially over."

Zak hugged her hard. He murmured, "I love you, Tiff. Let's go live happily ever after now. What do you say?"

Tiffany relaxed into his embrace. "I say yes."

Chapter Twelve

Tiffany looked at the image of herself in the mirror with amazement. She looked almost...beautiful. Her skin was glowing against the stark white of her wedding gown. Her face was lightly flushed and her eyes glittered with excitement. She looked exactly the way a bride should look—radiant, expectant, in love. She saw Polly step up behind her in the mirror and smiled.

Polly sighed. "Tiffany, you look so beautiful. Absolutely perfect. Zak's going to be struck mute when he sees you."

Tiffany smiled inwardly at the thought. Oh she hoped so. She said aloud, "Thanks. I feel so happy today. I can't believe how right this feels. I can't believe how perfect this *moment* feels."

Polly smiled, although a shadow crossed her face. "You deserve to be happy, Tiff. Zak and you love each other and you'll be happy together."

Ralph, her hairdresser, chimed in, "And girl, your hair is perfect, too."

Tiffany turned and surveyed him, unable to stop the grin from tugging at her mouth. "Yes, my hair does look perfect. Ralph, as usual, your artistry knows no equal. You are the king of hair."

He beamed at her and drawled, "Thank you, *thankyouverramuch.*"

Tiffany was shocked as a sudden thought occurred to her. No way. She'd known the slightly overweight and balding man in front her with the dark hair and incredible blue eyes for years. Elvis was dead. Everyone knew Elvis was dead. Why, for her hairdresser to be Elvis he'd have to be at least...she mentally calculated...well, much, much too old to be alive. She frowned and flashed him a narrow look. Unless Elvis had actually been Preintellian. They could live for thousands of years. Nawwww. She shook the thought off with a grin and caught Polly staring into space, again. That had been happening a lot lately.

Tiffany stood up and walked over to her friend. Polly blinked and looked at her in question. Tiffany said, "Polly, everyone deserves to be loved. You never know what or when life will throw love in your direction."

Polly said, "Thanks, Tiff, but my life is exactly the way I want it. I know where I'm headed. I know the score."

Tiffany smiled broadly. "Yeah. But no matter how orderly and predictable your life seems, things can change in an instant. You never know what might happen. You may wake up some morning and find order turned to chaos. Polly, trust me, love may be only a wish away."

Polly went pale. She narrowed her eyes. "Tiffany, on your birthday, you didn't make a wish involving me, did you?"

Tiffany tried to hold her innocent expression. "Would I do *that*?" She hugged Polly and Ralph quickly and then said hurriedly, "Better run, happy ever after is waiting!"

As she stepped through the door, she heard the distinctive sound of Polly saying vehemently in a tone of panicked denial, "*Nooooo! Tiffany!*"

Tiffany smiled to herself as she heard her name called in a wail. Yep, sometimes, your friends knew you only too well.

Also by MARLY CHANCE:

- Oath of Seduction: Seducing Sharon
- Oath of Challenge: Conquering Kate

SERENDIPITY

Written by

JOANNA WYLDE

Prologue

Able and Mali crouched in the pantry, watching the kitchen through a crack in the slightly opened door. Mom was out there. She was talking to Jax, the man who had checked into their hostel yesterday. Something about him made Able nervous, although Mali liked him a lot.

Of course, what could you expect from a little sister? Mali wasn't old enough to understand that Jax was dangerous, maybe as dangerous as their father had been. But what could you expect from a three-year-old...at seven, he knew better.

"What are they talking about?" Mali whispered, biting her thumbnail nervously. Able sighed in disgust. Mali never seemed to understand *anything*. It was almost scary how much she didn't know about the world. If he wasn't around to take care of her...

But he would always take care of her, he reminded himself. He was the man of their family now. Mali and mom needed his protection, something he'd better not forget.

"You have to be quiet and listen," he whispered back. "I'll explain everything later, but I want to hear what they're saying. If you keep talking we'll miss everything."

Mom was speaking now. She was upset; he could hear it in her voice.

"You know, I'm sick and tired of men who think they need to take care of women," she said harshly. "I had a husband who *took care* of me regularly, and I wouldn't wish marriage on any woman. It's a trap, and Calla's falling into it. It's a trap," she repeated.

Mom was right, Able thought. They had all been trapped with dad. He hurt them. Of course, Able was able to take dad's licks, but it had been too much for Mali. He looked down at his sister protectively; remembering what her little face had looked like, all bruised. He was glad dad was dead. He wished Aunt Calla wasn't leaving. Mom was right. Marriage was a trap, and Aunt Calla was falling into it. Just thinking about it made the lump in his stomach swell and burn.

Jax was talking now. The sound of his voice made Able's stomach feel worse, but he forced himself to listen.

"That's not true," Jax said. "For a Saurellian—"

"Don't give me your crap," Mom replied. Her voice was strong, and Able was proud of her for standing up to him. She stood and paced across the floor, arms folded in front of her. "Get out of my kitchen, get out of my hostel. You brought him here; you're responsible for this. Go back to Saurellia, because I don't ever want to see you again."

Able's expression turned grim and his head started to throb. Not only was Jax a threat to their mother, it was his fault Aunt Calla was leaving to get married. This was too much...somebody had to do something to stop him. The sound of his voice caught Able's attention again.

"I'll give you some space, Sarai," Jax said. "But I'm not ready to leave Hector Prime just yet. I'll see you again."

"Don't threaten me," Mom replied, her voice sounding tight and harsh.

"I would never threaten you," Jax said. "And I'll never lie, either. I'm not your ex-husband, Sarai. I'm a good man, and I won't hurt you."

He left the room, leaving mom alone. Able sat back on his heels trying to think. Mali watched him carefully, her small face twisted in concern.

"What's wrong, Able?" she asked in her soft, little girl's voice. She plucked at his shirt, looking for reassurance.

"Well, I think he likes mom, and wants her to go with him like Aunt Calla's going with Seth," Able whispered back. Mali's face crumpled, tears welling up in her eyes.

"You mean mommy might leave us?" she whispered despairingly, her small face pinched in pain. "What will we do without mommy?"

"Oh no," Able said, pulling her small body on to his lap. He held her close, rubbing her hair with one hand. It was so hard sometimes, trying to explain things to her. "Mom would never leave us, Mali. You don't have to worry about that. But Jax might want to stay, and that's not good."

"You mean stay and be with mommy?" Mali asked. "Like a daddy?"

"Yes, although we don't need him," Able said fiercely. "You remember what dad was like. He was horrible. We don't want another one of those, do we?"

"I suppose not," Mali whispered back. Daddy had been mean. He used to hurt her, and hurt mommy. But still...

Jax didn't seem like daddy. He seemed different. Nicer. She had even seen him in the garden earlier that morning, and he'd waved at her. She'd been too afraid to go near him, but she remembered how nice he looked. And he'd been tall enough to get her flying disk out of the tree in the garden. It had been stuck up there for two days. Not even mommy had been tall enough to do that.

"You know," she whispered. "Kally likes her daddy. He plays with her all the time. Kally's mommy seems to really like him, too. Maybe not all daddies are like ours was."

"We don't need a father," Able replied fiercely. "You and mom have me. I'll take care of you."

"I know you will," Mali replied softly. "You've always taken care of me, Able. But sometimes I wish I had a daddy, like Kally."

Able sat up, spilling her on to the floor.

"That's a stupid wish, Mali," he said. "We have to get rid of him. It's just you, mom, and me. That's all we need."

"I don't think it's a stupid wish," Mali said, grabbing the shelf to steady herself. She stood up and looked down on her brother, small fists on her hips. "And besides, I can wish for anything I want, and I want a daddy. There's nothing you can do to stop me."

Able just stared at her in disgust. Sometimes there just wasn't any point trying to reason with a little sister. They just didn't understand.

Chapter One

He was out there. Watching her.

He'd been watching her for days. Seven days, to be exact.

That's how long it had been since Calla left with her new man, Seth. Unfortunately, Seth had forgotten to take his big, stupid friend Jax with him.

Sarai rolled over in her bed, punching the pillow to soften it up. Her room was too hot. She knew how much more cool and comfortable the air would be if she could open the sliding door to the garden, but if she did he might take it as an invitation.

He'd been trouble from the minute he'd set foot in their small hostel. Usually they catered to students. After all, Hector Prime was one of the best places in the quadrant to study biology. From desert to jungle, the planet-wide nature preserve had something to offer everyone. But the only thing Jax wanted was right in her bedroom.

Sarai rolled again, settling on her back. What was it about him? She hadn't been able to sleep that first night, so she'd gone out into the garden, her private refuge. He had been waiting for her then, too. A twist of desire coiled through her at the memory. He'd touched her in the darkness, and she had lost control.

His hands, tugging at her gown, had been rough and calloused. She could still feel the way they caught against the smooth skin of her belly, before dropping lower…

Unconsciously, Sarai raised one hand to her breast and fingered her hardening nipple. He had touched her there, too. She remembered the scrape of his finger, back and forth against her taut flesh. Mirroring his actions with her own fingers, she twisted in her bed as an ache spread through her body.

He had been so hard.

She dropped her hand lower, searching for the space between her legs that would give her relief. She hated how much she needed to touch herself, but she knew from experience that once the ache started, it had to be appeased. Otherwise she would toss and turn for the rest of the night.

She found the small nub, then started slowly rubbing it, back and forth. Slow and steady. What was he doing there in the darkness? Did he ache, too? Was he touching himself like she was? She could just about picture him.

He would be leaning back against the bench, legs splayed out before him. One hand would drop slowly to the bulge in his crotch, testing it. It would grow, lengthen under his hand. Would he grip it? Would he work it up and down between his fingers, or simply finger the head softly?

Her own fingers were moving faster now, and she gave a little whimper at the thought of the smooth, hard length waiting for her in the darkness.

All she had to do was open the sliding door and she could have him. He would be on her in a heartbeat, pressing her back against the soft bed. Being kissed by him was an experience in and of itself. His tongue, thrusting inside her, taking what he wanted. He had no mercy when he kissed. It was a brand, a mark of ownership. Her lips burned with the memory.

She thrust the image from her mind, forcing herself to focus on her own movements. Thinking of him wouldn't help. It would just make things worse. She needed to focus on the pleasure she could give herself. She had been massaging her nipple as she rubbed her clit, but the feelings were becoming more intense now. She couldn't do both things, she couldn't concentrate. Back and forth, harder and harder. She could feel the pressure building, but she wanted more.

She wanted him.

His cock was like a pillar of granite. So hard, so deep. He'd plunged into her like he had something to prove. When he'd come to her that night, it felt like the first time she'd ever been with a man. He'd stretched her open; she'd been splayed beneath his strength. Completely helpless, she had no choice but to give into the ecstasy his touch could bring.

Heat rose in her. Her fingers were moving so quickly now that it took all her strength not to arch up beneath her hand. Was he watching her? She'd pulled the drapes, but they were all too sheer. Did he know what she was doing?

What would his tongue feel like on her? She could imagine it, slippery and hot, darting back and forth against her aching center. Would he tease her, bringing her close to the edge before falling back? Or would he keep moving, bringing her to orgasm time after time? She'd never felt a man's tongue there, but she'd heard it was a wonderful thing. If only she could feel something like that...

The pressure was intense now. It pushed against her, and she felt like she was climbing to the top of a cliff. She could see the end, she was so close to it, but she couldn't quite make it over. Her fingers flew faster and faster, seeking desperately to provide her with some relief. She had to get some relief, or she would die. Either that, or she would call out to him to come to her.

No.

She wouldn't do that.

She pressed harder, her body shaking from the strain of remaining perfectly still. The sensations built up in her, heart pounding. Her breath was coming in ragged breaths, but she held her position. A swooshing sound, the sound of her own heartbeat, filled her head.

Just a little more.

Around and around. *Don't think about him, his hard cock stuffing you so full that you feel like you might choke,* her traitorous mind whispered. *Him pounding against you, your whole body shaking from the force of his thrusts.*

Her treacherous body wasn't listening, though. There was an empty hole where his cock should be. Her entire body was ready to explode, but there was no one for her to explode against. Her fingers flew, her mouth opening in a silent gasp of aching need. Against her will, her head arched back against the pillow as the orgasm hit her. She shuddered under the onslaught of sensation, biting the back of her hand to keep from crying out. What would he see if he were watching her now? What would he think?

That night in the garden she'd seen the look on his face as she came, every muscle in her body clenching his tightly. His face had been filled with a pleasure so intense it was painful to watch. But she wanted to watch it again.

Slowly, her breathing returned to normal. She allowed her hand to drop to the mattress. The sound of her heart faded, and she let her hands fall to her sides. After a few minutes her breath was slow and steady again. The ache was better, although she could still feel a trace of tension.

She rolled onto her stomach, punching the pillow to soften it up. Then she lay her head down and forced her mind to calm. Would the night never end?

Finally, after another hour, she finally relaxed enough to fall asleep. Morning would be there all too soon.

* * * * *

Jax sat in the dark garden, watching Sarai's room. It would be so easy to go in through the door, to push her back on the bed and kiss her until she gave in to him. And she would give in, he already knew that. Her response to him from the first time he'd touched her had been incredible.

A physical response wouldn't be enough, though. Not to convince her she needed him in her life.

What was she doing in there, he wondered? Was she sleeping, thinking of him? Did she have any idea how much he wanted to be with her?

She was his life mate—he was certain of it. He had spent the first thirty years of his life believing he'd be alone forever. After all, he'd had no life mate among his own people, the Saurellians. Until a few weeks ago he'd never heard of a Saurellian finding a lifemate anywhere but Saurellia.

But now there was new hope. His friend, Seth, had found Calla. And Sarai had been with Calla.

What was life like before Sarai? It had only been a week, yet in those few short days his entire life had changed. He was frustrated, of course. He had made love to her in the garden that first night, but she hadn't let him touch her since. But even though the frustration was maddening, the sheer joy of her presence filled him.

He felt alive, complete.

The sound of her voice curled through him every time she spoke, touching corners of his soul he'd thought were long dead. And her children, they were beautiful. Little Able, a child who thought like an adult. He would be a challenge, Jax realized. He felt threatened by the thought of his mother having a new man in her life. Their father, Calvin, had been a horrible man. He'd hurt the entire family deeply—Jax's only regret was that Calvin was already dead. He would have liked to kill the man himself.

And Mali.

She was a little angel, a smaller version of her mother; only this version accepted him with open arms. She had been shy at first, but now she ran up to him every time she saw him, demanding hugs.

But no matter how much her daughter loved him, Sarai would hardly speak to him. He wanted to sweep her into his arms, to take her with him to his homeworld and make her his. And by Saurellian law he was entitled to do that; she was his lifemate, after all, a bond created by the Goddess herself.

Simply taking her wasn't a real option, though. He'd realized almost immediately that if he ever wanted to win Sarai over, he'd have to woo her. She'd already been forced into marriage with one man. He had to prove he was different than Calvin, no matter what else happened.

He couldn't prove himself to her unless she gave him a chance, though. He needed to show her that he wanted more than her body, that he didn't need to control her. He wanted a partner, not a servant.

Unfortunately, she didn't seem to want him at all.

He would have to change her mind.

Chapter Two

Sarai was stirring a pot of porridge over the stove when Jax came into the kitchen. She could sense his presence immediately, of course, but she didn't acknowledge him. There was no way she'd let him know just how aware she was of his every move.

She lifted the porridge and turned to pour it into the bowls she'd set out.

"Mali, Able, do you want sweetener in your cereal?" she asked brightly. Then she turned and allowed herself to see him lounging against the doorway, arms folded in front of his chest.

"Yes," Mali piped up, looking excited. Able grunted, glaring at Jax. At least one of her children hadn't gone over to the enemy, Sarai thought dryly.

"Do you have enough for me to have a bowl?" Jax asked softly. The question seemed innocent enough, but his voice was dark and silky. It caressed her ears, reminding her of how he had sounded as he came into her that night.

"No," she said tightly, walking over to the table and setting down the bowls in front of the children. "Food isn't part of the arrangement here. I've told you that before. There are any number of places in town where you can find breakfast."

Jax simply smiled at her, and then sauntered across the kitchen to the table. She glared at him forbiddingly, but he ignored her. Coming up beside Mali, he swung one leg over the bench and straddled it next to the small girl.

"Good morning, Jax," Mali said brightly, carefully balancing her spoonful of cereal and blowing on it. "Would you like some of my breakfast? Mommy always gives me too much."

"No thank you, sweetheart," Jax said, catching Sarai's eye. "I'll get something later. You'll need all your food so you have energy to play today, and do your studies."

Mali nodded, stuffing the spoon in her mouth. Sarai pursed her lips. She'd already asked him several times not to come into the kitchen, but she didn't want to make a scene in front of the children. They'd been through enough without having to watch that. Instead, she filled her own bowl and turned to the table. Jax watched her as Mali chattered on about her plans for the day. Able glared.

"Are you done with your food?" she asked finally, and the two small blond heads nodded in unison. "Put your bowls in the sink, and go on outside."

Mali hopped up and carried her bowl to the sink. Able followed more slowly, watching them carefully.

"It's all right, son," Sarai said, giving him as open a smile as she could manage. "You go on and play with your sister. It'll be time for your lessons before long."

"All right," he muttered, and stomped out the back door behind Mali. Silence fell over the kitchen.

"Mali tells me you had to carry pails of water for the vegetables yesterday afternoon," Jax said in a smooth, drawling voice. "She told me the water wasn't working right. Do you know what's wrong with it?"

"No," Sarai said tightly.

"Have you called anyone to fix it yet?" Jax asked, watching her face carefully.

"No," she replied, refusing to meet his gaze. "I don't want to spend the money right now."

"I can take a look at it if you like," Jax said lightly.

"And what would a soldier know about irrigation?" Sarai said sharply.

"Well, I wasn't born a soldier," Jax replied calmly. "I was born on a farm, and I used to work on the irrigation equipment with my father. They have farms in Saurellia, you know. Even soldiers have to eat."

Sarai was startled. She'd never thought of Saurellians as farmers. They were soldiers, conquerors. They came and took things; they fought the Empire. They didn't fix broken pipes.

"Well, I can't stop you," she said, standing abruptly. She scooped up her plate and turned away from him. "But I don't want you bothering me here. You need to leave."

"Sarai," Jax said quietly. "You can't just brush me off forever. I'm not going away. Why won't you at least give me a chance?"

"I don't want you in my life," she said tightly. "I don't want any man in my life."

Jax came up behind her. She couldn't hear him move, but she could sense his presence with every fiber of her being. She tried to look relaxed, but she felt like screaming. She was trapped, she couldn't move.

"I'm already here," he replied, all but whispering in her ear. "I'm not leaving. We can't just leave this thing between us unfinished."

She whirled to face him, startled by how close he was. His chest was just inches from her face. His shirt was open just a bit at the neck, and a few dark hairs from his chest caught her attention. They were coarse and curly. She already knew what they felt like. They had been wiry against her hands that night.

She could smell him, too. He smelled a little like the soap she kept in each of the hostel's rooms, and a little like himself. *Jax.* She took a deep breath, hoping to calm herself. Instead she inhaled more of his scent. A thrill at his presence ran through her body. She could feel herself starting to tremble. Steeling herself, she took a deep breath and stared straight into his eyes.

"You have no idea what I've been through in my life," she said. "I'm free now, and so are my children. We've lived under a man's control before. I won't go back to that. Ever."

Jax reached one hand up, lightly brushing her cheek with the backs of his fingers.

"I don't want to control you," he whispered. He leaned over and brushed a kiss against her ear. "I want to make love to you, and be with you. Nothing more than that."

She held herself still, longing to lean into him.

"Give me a chance," Jax continued. "And I'll prove it to you. I don't expect you to accept anything on faith."

Sarai closed her eyes tightly. He was too intense, too much. She wanted to touch him, feel the smooth silk of his skin under her fingertips, the wiry hair of his chest. What had he said? Give him a chance? She had to get rid of him somehow. Maybe she could use his own words against him, she thought desperately.

"You want a chance?" she said, opening her eyes. His face was only inches from hers, his gaze focused on her mouth. He licked his lips, and something inside her clenched. If she leaned forward even the slightest bit, they would be touching. "If I give you a chance, will you go away?"

A stillness came over Jax.

"Yes," he said slowly.

"I'll give you a week," Sarai said nervously. She could feel tension radiating from him. He was like wild predator, one who wanted to devour her.

"A week isn't enough," Jax replied softly. "I want a month. And during that month you have to let me touch you."

"No," she said quickly. She already knew how dangerous his touch could be.

"Yes," he replied firmly. "You want me to promise to leave you? Well, I'll leave if after a month you still want me to. But you have to let me touch you whenever I want. And I want to sleep in your room."

"I won't have sex with you," she said in panic. "I won't ever have sex with another man unless it's *my* choice. I won't give you that kind of power over me."

"I didn't say you had to have sex with me," he replied smoothly. His eyes were intense, compelling. His fingers brushed her cheek again; it was impossible to think. How did he do it? How did he make her melt like this?

"If you don't want to make the deal, I can't force you," he continued. "But it's the only way you're going to get rid of me. What do you say?"

"Two weeks," she said desperately. "A month is too long."

"Three weeks," he whispered. His lips brushed against hers, his body pressed her back against the counter. She could feel the entire length of him. His frame was hard with muscles, and against her belly an unmistakable bulge jutted.

Against her will, her hands rose to grip his waist. She wanted him to pull her against him, to lift her up onto the counter and thrust into her. She took a deep breath.

"Three weeks," she whispered. Could she last that long? She would have to. She had seen his determination; this might be her best chance to get rid of him.

He groaned as she agreed, his mouth taking hers in a kiss unlike any she'd ever experienced. His lips were rough, commanding her to open to the onslaught of his tongue. His arms came around her like bands of iron, molding her to him even as one leg thrust between hers.

He thrust into her mouth like a marauder, a warrior, and she let her head fall back under his strength. He plumbed her depths, thrusting again and again even as his lower body ground slowly against her pelvis. She could feel her nipples tightening, and moist heat built between her legs. How was she going to survive three weeks with this man? She couldn't even survive three minutes!

"What are you doing to my mother?" Able's voice cut through the kitchen, filled with disapproval and dislike. Jax stilled instantly, and Sarai all but whimpered as he pulled his lips from hers. He stood back from her, and turned to face the boy.

Sarai's son was standing there, both hands on his hips and his face twisted with dislike. She groaned inwardly, disgusted by her own behavior. She had allowed this man to maul her in front of her child, a child who had seen first-hand the horrors his father had committed.

"I was kissing her," Jax said lightly. "Does that bother you?"

"Yes," Able said, his face grim. Sarai rubbed a hand against her forehead. How was she going to explain this to Able?

"I don't plan to hurt her, and I won't do anything she hasn't agreed to let me do," Jax said, keeping his tone friendly. "But I wasn't making her do anything she didn't want me to do."

"Is that right, Mom?" Able asked, turning his accusing gaze to her. She sighed, knowing he would be upset if she said yes. For a moment she considered saying no, covering up her part in the kiss. But she had never lied to her children before, and now wasn't the time to start.

"Yes," she said. "I agreed to let him kiss me."

"Oh," Able said, at a loss for words. He looked confused, and suddenly very young. "Why did you do that?"

Sarai gave a choked laugh, wondering what to tell him. *Because I can't control myself? Because I made a deal to get rid of him? Because your father only hurt me, but when this man touches me I feel like I'll break into a thousand pieces, and it feels good?* None of them were answers she could give her son.

"Because sometimes men and women like to kiss," she said finally. Able's face grew dark again.

"That's a stupid reason," he said after a brief pause. Then he whirled and ran out of the room.

Sarai slumped back against the counter.

"I'm a terrible mother," she whispered, looking up at him with haunted eyes. "How could I let you do that where my children might see? This deal we've made, none of it can happen around them. They are my life, they are far more important than you. Can you understand that?"

Jax nodded, his gaze inscrutable.

"As long as you understand that at night you're mine, I'll make sure I don't touch you in front of the children."

"Thank you," she replied. "I can't have them getting hurt over this. They've already been hurt enough."

Jax reached one finger to her chin, and lifted her face so he could look at her directly.

"I understand," he whispered, dropping a quick, light kiss on her mouth. He straightened, then spoke again in a louder voice. "I'll go take care of that pipe now. Let me know if you need anything, all right?"

He turned and strode out of the room.

* * * * *

He could win her over, he knew it.

Sarai was inside getting the children ready for bed. He sat outside her bedroom in the garden, waiting for her. It had been dark for hours; she'd kept the children up well past their bedtime. She was avoiding him, using them as a shield. But eventually she would run out of excuses.

He saw the light come on in her room, and the outline of her body against the drapes. If she had any idea how sheer they were she would faint, he thought with amusement. Every night she gave him a show, as she got ready for bed.

She untied her apron and started removing her clothes quickly and efficiently. Turning as she pulled off her dress, she was briefly silhouetted. Long, slender legs, shapely breasts that were still fairly firm, even after two children. Her blonde hair hung down her back like a curtain. *What would it look like over her naked body?* he wondered. That one night they'd had together had been all too brief. He'd never gotten the chance to see her as he'd fantasized so many times. He wanted her astride him, her head thrown back in pleasure and her breasts bouncing. Her hair would be wild and free, offering him glimpses of her body even as she rode him through the night.

He hardened at the thought, blood rushing to his groin. A familiar ache spread through him, making him groan.

Her room went dark. It was time to make his move.

He rose and walked silently over to the sliding door that separated them. He tested the latch, noting with amusement that she'd kept it locked. As if a lock would be able to keep him out.

He knocked softly, but she didn't respond. Probably hoping he'd go away. She would have no such luck tonight. By promising not to touch her in front of the children he had given up valuable time with her during the day. He wouldn't allow her to waste any of their nights together. He pulled a small laser pick out of his pocket and had the door open within seconds. In addition to being raised on a farm, he'd spent some time in juvenile detention for petty theft during his unruly youth, something he hadn't felt like mentioning to her earlier.

The skills he learned there came in handy at times.

He slid the door open and stepped quietly into the room. She was lying on the bed, pretending to be asleep, but she knew he was there. He could tell by the catch in her breathing that she was as aware of him as he was of her.

"Sarai, you promised," he whispered, trying to keep the desperate need he felt out of his voice. Her presence called to him, it took every bit of strength he had not to press her back against the bed and thrust his cock into her until she screamed. She was so hot, so tight. He bit back a groan at the thought. "You didn't think I'd forget, did you?"

"I had hoped," she whispered. She sat up in bed, clutching the covers in front of her.

"I don't think so," he replied, gliding across the floor to her bed. "I've been dreaming about this moment all day. I can't wait to touch you."

"No sex," she said tersely. "You promised no sex."

"I don't need to come inside you to enjoy being with you," he said quietly. He pulled his shirt over his head impatiently, then kicked off his shoes and pants. She shrank back as he pulled the covers back and slid into bed.

"What are you going to do?" she asked nervously.

"Just hold you," he said, reaching out and pulling her into his arms. She turned away from him, so he gently nestled her back against his chest. Her tight little ass nestled against his hard length and his breathing grew ragged. The only thing separating him from her hot opening was the thin cloth of her shift, worn from many washings.

She was tense, and as his hips pressed against hers involuntarily, she stiffened further. He sighed, and forced his body to remain still. She wasn't going to make things easy.

Her hair smelled clean and fresh, like the flowers she grew in the garden. He dropped his nose to it, inhaling deeply. Her head was resting on one of his arms, the other arm holding her loosely against him. He gave her several minutes to get used to his presence, then slid his open palm along her stomach.

She stiffened again, but this time he ignored her, allowing his hand to slide slowly up her body until he was cupping one of those beautiful breasts he'd seen outlined through the window. The fabric of her shift was so thin it was useless in providing her any protection from his touch. He grunted triumphantly as the nipple hardened against his fingers. He played his fingers back and forth, and her breath caught.

"You like that, don't you?" he whispered against her ear. It was a smooth shell beneath his lips, and he dropped little kisses on it and the back of her neck. She squirmed, murmuring something.

"No," she said, but her nipples betrayed her. Her breasts swelled under his fingers, silently begging him for more.

He let his hand drop, smoothing the fabric of her shift along her stomach. Her stomach muscles twitched as his finger trailed lower, and she shifted her legs restlessly, pressing them together. The motion forced him to stop for a moment, breathing deeply and trying to maintain control. Her ass was wiggling against him so much, he felt like a rocket about to go off. It would be so easy to slide his leg between hers, to hold her open for his thrust.

But he couldn't do that, not until she asked for it, he reminded himself. He had made a promise; he couldn't afford to blow this. Not if he wanted to keep her in his life.

He allowed his fingers to drift lower, until he could feel the thatch of her hair under the fabric. He pushed one finger experimentally toward the opening there, and moisture started soaking the fabric. She was definitely enjoying this, even though she seemed to be doing everything in her power not to show it.

He let the finger trail up, smoothing its way across the tiny nubbin of her clit. She twitched, and his hips thrust against her spasmodically. She pressed back into him, trying to escape his finger. Instead, she pushed against his cock so hard he thought he might explode. He wiggled his finger, and was answered by a wiggling of her little butt. He sighed in pleasure, then started moving his fingers in earnest.

He pressed down against her clit, rubbing it back and forth even as he applied the pressure. The fabric was becoming soaked with her juices, and her breath was coming fast. So was his, and against his will he started rubbing his cock against her ass. It jutted up against her, sliding back and forth in her crack, cradling his erection.

His fingers moved more quickly, and he tried pushing into her a bit with them. The fabric wouldn't let him, though. He briefly considered trying to work the fabric up, but he was afraid to stop moving for even a second. He didn't want to give her a chance to change her mind; something he knew would happen if he gave her any time to think. Instead he slid one finger on each side of her clit, tugging and pulling it back and forth, increasing the tempo of his movements as her breathing caught and become ragged.

He could feel the blood in his body pooling in his groin, and he started thrusting against her body, rubbing his engorged flesh between them. He realized that by pushing harder against her clit with his hand, he could not only bring her more pleasure, but she would jerk her hips back into him. Each jerk pushed his cock deeper between her ass cheeks. His breath started growing ragged.

She was grinding against his hand now, making ragged, whimpering noises and muttering something under her breath. He pulled her even more tightly against him, his hips writhing slowly against her from one side while his hand worked her harder and harder from the other side. She jerked against him spasmodically, grunting and moaning. He knew she was close. He straightened his index and middle fingers, pulled the fabric taut as he thrust them into the mouth of her cunt. He rubbed back and forth roughly, dragging the fabric roughly across her swollen flesh. She stiffened, spasmed against him and a keening noise came out of her mouth.

Unable to control himself, he thrust against her back violently. In that instant she came, squealing, her ass cheeks tightening around his bulging cock. The squeeze was so strong it was almost painful. He thrust once more, then his own orgasm hit him. He gasped; clutching her pelvis to him so hard there would be bruises in the morning, and spraying his seed into the fabric of her shift. Again and again he jerked against her in ecstasy, grunting harshly into the mass of her hair.

Gradually the sensations faded, and he loosened his grip on her body. Neither of them spoke in the darkness. He had lost control; he'd had no intention of coming himself. His entire goal had been to give her pleasure, not to explode all over her like an untried youth. He would make it up to her.

Gently moving away from her, he pulled her damp shift over her head and threw it on the floor. Then he rolled her onto her back and leaned over her, propping himself up on one arm. She stared up at him with a dazed expression. A wave of smug pleasure washed through him. She'd been as affected by his touch as he'd been by hers, regardless of his lack of control. She opened her mouth and took in a breath, preparing to speak.

Before she could say anything, he covered her mouth with his. His tongue swept in, exploring her depths. His fingers found her clit again, still dripping and hot from her orgasm. She reacted to his touch instantly, her hips rising under his touch and her arms reaching up to clench his shoulders.

He thrust his fingers into her hot opening roughly, this time without the fabric to separate them. She was slippery and wet, pulling him to her. He lifted his mouth from hers, and she stared up at him, eyes pleading for another release.

"Please," she whispered. "I need—"

He cut her off with another long, slow kiss, all the while working her clit and exploring her cunt. She squirmed against him, moaning into his mouth. Then he sat up abruptly and stepped off the bed. Wrapping one hand around each of her ankles, he pulled her body toward the edge, kneeling between her spread legs. Draping one leg over each of his shoulders, he leaned forward and touched his tongue to her clit.

Delicately, he parted the folds of her flesh, swirling his tongue around the sensitive nub. He opened his mouth wider and sucked gently. She squirmed and bucked against him, her entire body shivering.

"That feels so good," she gasped. He paused, looking up to find her leaning back on her arms and watching him. The sight of her, flushed with passion, her lips bruised by his kiss, was incredibly erotic, but it wasn't enough. He wanted her screaming, losing control and begging him to fuck her.

His head dipped again, his lips and tongue tugging harder on her flesh. Again and again he thrust his tongue into her willing flesh, until she dropped back against the bed and started bucking against him. He wrapped his arms up and around her legs, holding her steady and renewed his attack.

She was twisting and moaning so much that he could tell she was getting close to her completion. He stabbed into her with a series of tongue thrusts, then started wiggling his tongue back and forth against her stiffened clit. She shrieked, her entire body tensing, and came with a heave of her hips against his mouth.

He pulled her down into his arms, cradling her body against his and kissing her forehead and face. She was drenched in sweat and breathing heavily. With shock, Jax realized she was crying. He pressed her head to his chest as a series of sobs shook her body. What the hell was going on? He'd been trying to please her, not make her cry.

Carefully lifting her limp body, he laid her in the bed and crawled in next to her, pulling her against him. She cried in silence for a while, then snuffled noisily, turning her head away from him.

"Let's go to sleep," she said finally, to his surprise. Didn't she want to talk? Women always wanted to talk, especially when they'd been crying. He was out of his depth.

"Sarai, I think —" he started to say, but she cut him off.

"No, I just want to go to sleep," she said. "I said you could touch me. Talking wasn't part of the deal, so shut up."

She was right. Talking hadn't been part of the deal.

Eventually her breathing evened out and he could tell she really was asleep. His own rest was harder to find, his thoughts racing as the hours passed. If he couldn't win her over with sex and she wouldn't even talk to him, what chance did he have of convincing her to stay with him?

Three weeks, he reminded himself. Three weeks, and then he was bound to leave. There had to be a way to convince her she needed him as much as he needed her. He just had to find it.

Chapter Three

Sarai slid slowly and quietly out of Jax's embrace. He was sleeping deeply, his sooty black eyelashes resting against his cheeks. She'd awakened to find him holding her close, his body wrapped around hers protectively. It felt good to be held, something she hardly dared admit to herself. She felt safe in his arms.

It was a feeling she couldn't let herself get used to.

His touch last night had shattered her control, forcing her to face up to the reality that she wasn't complete and independent in herself. It made her feel weak, useless. Maybe she really was the kind of woman who needed a man to survive...No. She was more than that, and she couldn't let herself forget it.

She padded over to the chest of drawers where she kept her clothes and pulled out a fresh dress. Many of the women on Hector Prime wore jumpsuits or pants, just like the men, but her own upbringing had been more conservative. Despite the fact that she had left the Pilgrim way of life behind for good, she still wasn't quite able to bring herself to wear what she thought of as men's clothing.

That didn't stop her from dressing Mali in the same coveralls that all the other little girls wore, though. For the thousandth time, Sarai looked in the mirror and swore to herself that her daughter would have a better life than she had had. She glanced at the bed as she pulled on her clothing. Falling into the sack with any handsome man who crossed her path wouldn't make it any easier to give her daughter the kind of life she deserved, she told herself sternly. No matter how good Jax made her feel, she had to remember what was really important—her family, and her independence. There was nothing more important than that, nothing.

She quietly opened the door and made her way down the hall. It was still early; hopefully the children wouldn't be up quite yet. They'd had a late night. Time to start breakfast and pretend nothing had happened. Able was already worried about Jax, and Mali was halfway in love with the man. It would be best if they had as little to do with him as possible.

* * * * *

Able crouched in the bushes, watching Jax throw the flying disk to Mali. She was giggling hysterically, thrilled at the attention the man was giving her. Each time Jax threw the disk, he was careful to keep it slow and steady, so she actually had a chance of catching it. Able curled his lip in disgust. Mali was too stupid to see what Jax was doing—he would use them to get to mom if they let him.

The leaves beside him rustled, and he turned to see one of the furry little mammals that lived in the garden watching him. It held a large nut in its paws. Boy and animal held each other's gaze for several minutes, then Mali shrieked in the background. The animal leapt away in fright, leaving the nut behind.

Able reached out and picked it up thoughtfully, turning to eye Jax and his sister. It felt good in his hand, with a nice heft. Able clenched his fingers around it. Mali had dropped the disk, and was running up to Jax. The man swung the young girl up in his arms and twirled her around. She giggled, kicking her legs out and crowing with happiness.

Mali made him sick, Able thought.

Jax set her down, and she ran toward the back of the house to retrieve the disk. Able stood up slowly, careful not to make any noise. He cocked his arm back and took careful aim with the nut. It was sharp and pointed on one end; if he got it just right he might really hurt the man. Maybe he'd leave, then.

With every bit of his strength, Able launched the nut at the side of Jax's head. It hit him against one temple. He gave a cry, and turned toward Able, eyes searching for his attacker. Bright red blood ran down his face. Able froze. He'd done it, now, he realized. Jax was going to kill him. Mali screamed in the background and took off toward the hostel.

Ignoring the blood running down his face and dripping on to his shoulder, Jax strode through the brush toward Able. It didn't even occur to the boy to flee. He'd run from his father a hundred times, and he always got caught. Jax reached him, and grasped the front of his shirt, pulling him out of the brush. He knelt down and looked him straight in the eyes.

"Why did you do that, Able?" he asked quietly, his face sober. Able gaped at him in surprise. Of all the things he could have imagined Jax might do to him, he hadn't considered being questioned.

"I, uh, I don't know," he said, trying to keep his voice strong. To his disgust, his words came out soft and trembling.

"Did you throw it at me because you thought I was hurting Mali?" Jax asked, searching his face.

"No," Able said. To his horror, he could feel tears building up in his eyes. He sniffed his nose fiercely, bracing himself. He wasn't going to break down and cry, no matter what Jax did to him. He wasn't.

"Did you throw it at me because you think I might hurt your mother?"

"Yes," Able whispered. He couldn't look into Jax's eyes anymore. He could feel more moisture welling up, and his lower lip started trembling. It was so hard not to cry when you knew you were going to get hit, he thought. Too hard. He sniffed again. Jax stood up, surprising him.

"Why don't we go sit down over here and talk about this," Jax said, gesturing to the table where mom sometimes let them have picnic lunches. Jax reached a hand down, touching his shoulder. Able flinched. Jax pulled his hand back, and walked ahead of Able to the table. The boy eyed the distance to the hostel door speculatively, wondering if he could make it that far before Jax caught him. Not a chance...He followed Jax to the table, sitting down across from him. At least this way the table was between them; it might offer some protection.

"Able, I think I understand how you feel," Jax said, looking down at him. Able sniffed again, but this time it came out as more of a snort. This man had no idea how he felt. He wiped a hand across his face, removing the treacherous moisture. Jax was silent, as if he expected a reply. Able just glared at him.

"Able, it's a good thing for a young man to protect his mother," Jax said. "I'm proud of the fact that you take such good care of Mali and Sarai. But I think you need to consider whether attacking me is really going to accomplish anything here. I don't want to hurt your mother, and I don't want to hurt your sister. I like them."

"So?" Able mumbled. He looked up at Jax, then took a deep breath and spoke defiantly. "We don't need you. We had a father, and we don't need a new one. And mom doesn't need you, either. She has us for her family."

He braced himself for the blow he knew had to be coming, his eyes closing.

Nothing happened.

"I'm not going to hit you, Able," Jax said, his voice sounding strange. Almost sad, but that couldn't be right. Why would Jax be sad? "I just want you to understand that it isn't a very good idea to throw things at me, or anyone else, for that matter. Using physical force against someone should always be the last thing you try, when there aren't any other choices left. It's a good way for you to get hurt, and if you get hurt there won't be anyone around to take care of your mother and sister. Do you understand that?"

Able glared at him, hating him. He wanted Jax to go away; he threatened the family. The fact that he was being nice right now was probably just a trick.

"Well, I'm not upset at you this time, Able," Jax said, fingering the cut on his head for the first time. "You sure got me, though," he added with a chuckle. "I knew you were out there, but this was the last thing I was expecting. It just goes to show you should never underestimate someone because he's still young. Let's call a truce for now, all right?"

"What's happening out here?" Sarai's voice was high-pitched and frightened as she came running toward them. Mali trailed behind her, eyes wide. "Able, are you all right?"

"It's nothing, Sarai," Jax said, standing up. "Able is fine. Just a little misunderstanding. He and I have been talking about it."

Sarai stopped short, seeing the trail of blood and the spatters on his shirt for the first time.

"What happened?" she asked again, turning to Able. Her eyes searched up and down his form for damage, but he was fine.

"I think that Able and I have come to an understanding," Jax said firmly. "Haven't we?"

Able stared at him a moment longer, then turned to his mother. Her face was twisted in concern, and remorse hit him. He hadn't wanted to make her upset, or to scare Mali. She was terrified, he could see that. She had crept up behind Mom, gripping her around the knees and hiding her head in her skirts.

"It's fine, Mom," he said, trying to make his voice sound grown up. "Jax and I have just been talking about things. Don't worry about it."

"Jax, I need to know what happened here," Sarai said, hands on her hips. Mali squeaked at her harsh tone.

"Sarai, it's really nothing to worry about," Jax said. He shot Able a quick look, and for a second seemed almost friendly. Able realized that they shared a secret now, a secret just for them. "We were just talking about how a man takes care of his family. Able's going to be a good man some day, you should be proud of him."

Able's chest swelled with pride, although he tried to tamp down the emotion. No one had ever said anything like that about him before. Of course, he wasn't interested in anything Jax had to say about him. Not interested at all.

He gave Jax another appraising stare. He would have to keep an eye on the man, he thought. He was pretty sneaky. He looked back at his mom, who was watching every move he made. He smiled at her, but her face just got tighter.

"Well, you need to take care of that cut on your face, Jax," she finally said. "It doesn't look serious, but I've got some disinfectant inside. You'd better come with me."

Jax nodded, and she turned to walk toward the kitchen, dragging Mali along with her.

Jax gave Able another measuring look, and the boy straightened. He understood what Jax had been saying. There were smarter ways to protect Mom and Mali. Now he just needed to figure out what they were...

* * * * *

Sarai tried to control the trembling of her hands as she washed the blood off Jax's face. Her heart was still racing; the adrenaline had hit her with the force of an ore transport when Mali had come tearing into the kitchen, screaming that Jax and Able were trying to kill each other.

She'd halfway expected to find her son dead. She had no doubt he'd attacked Jax, a man who was trained to kill. After all, soldiers killed for a living.

She still didn't understand what had really happened out there, but Jax wasn't talking. She was willing to bet Able wouldn't, either. The boy was young, but he had a mind of his own. She might never know what had taken place between them...

"Sarai, this really isn't that serious a cut," Jax said, looking up at her with amusement. "I've lived through much worse than this. You don't need to fuss over it."

"Oh, be quiet," Sarai said, pinching her lips. He was right, of course. The cut did seem to be small, and the bleeding had stopped. She wiped away the last of the dried blood carefully, then placed a small healing patch over the cut, pressing against it to activate it. Within seconds it had bound itself against the skin, and its tiny computer chip was analyzing the wound and medicating it. She was still amazed by these little patches that everyone around her seemed to take for granted. They could heal a cut in a day. Back home, this cut would have left a scar. She still couldn't understand why her people refused to accept such simple pieces of technology to make their lives better.

"There, it's done," she said in satisfaction. "You'll be fine."

"Thanks," he said, giving her a wry smile. There was a tenderness in his eyes that made her think he wanted to kiss her, but then his gaze darted across the table to Mali, who was watching them intently. Jax stood, then reached out one finger to touch Sarai's lips. It sent a tingle of awareness through her. She wanted to kiss it.

"Later," he whispered. He turned and left the room. Sarai stared at the empty doorway, touching her lips where his finger had been. *How did he do things like that?* she wondered. He was going to drive her crazy.

Chapter Four

It was maddening, Sarai thought to herself, as she got ready for bed that night. Where the hell was he? He'd been gone all day, not a word about where he was going or when he'd be back. She hadn't seen him since she'd patched up his temple that morning.

She'd been looking for him, expecting him to appear in his annoying way. He didn't show up begging for lunch. She'd even cooked a bit of extra dinner for him, figuring she owed him after his patience with her son's attack. Nothing. No stolen kisses. No wildflowers on the table. Nothing.

And he wasn't in his room, either. Not that she'd been checking up on him, of course. It was just that she'd realized it had been several days since she'd put new soaps in the fresher for him. Lazy on her part, she thought. She usually checked on the soaps every day.

She pulled off her dress and stood before the mirror in her shift, staring at her reflection. She was still attractive, she told herself. Her long, blonde hair had lightened in Hector Prime's sun. It was beautiful now, and she knew he liked to touch it. Her breasts were high and firm. Well, at least as high and firm as they could be after nursing two children. Her body was slim, and her stomach was tight. Sure, she had some stretch marks, but they hadn't bothered him before. Why wasn't he here? The night was halfway over!

She sat down at her dressing table with a thump, making a disgusted face at herself in the mirror. Why should she care where he was, anyway? It was nice to get rid of him for the night. Only two and a half more weeks, then he'd be gone. Well, two weeks and five days. And then he'd be gone forever…suddenly it didn't seem like that much time.

She attacked her hair with the brush, willing herself not to think of him. She was glad he wasn't there. She needed to get some good sleep — last night he'd kept her awake until all hours.

But thinking of him last night sent a wave of heat through her. He'd been so strong, held her so close. He had been hard against her, too. She clenched her legs together, feeling herself grow moist. He could slide right into her; he wouldn't even have to touch her first, she thought. What was *wrong* with her? It was like she had completely lost control over her own body. Disgusting.

She finished combing her hair, and moved toward her bed. It was stuffy. She might as well open the sliding door. It hadn't proven much of a barrier to him last night, and he wasn't even around this evening so there was no point in suffering in the heat.

A sudden thought stopped her dead in her tracks. What if something had happened to him? What if he'd been injured? Was that why he hadn't come home? Her heart raced, her mind running through a thousand different scenarios, each worse than the last.

He could have been attacked, robbed. He could have gone for a walk in the rainforest, and been set upon by predators. It was dangerous out there, everyone had told her to watch her children carefully. Maybe his head wound was more serious that either of them had realized. Maybe he had collapsed somewhere, was in a coma and couldn't tell anyone who he was.

You're being ridiculous, she told herself firmly. Settle down. He's probably just in town at a bar. Maybe he had met a woman there, a beautiful woman who didn't have children. For all she knew, he was boffing some floozy at that very minute!

Sure, he told her he wasn't going away, but he was gone already.

She was so caught up in her thoughts that she didn't even hear the knock on her door. Then the knob turned slowly, and he slipped into the room.

"Sarai, are you still awake?" he whispered into the darkness. She whirled to face him, livid.

"Where the hell have you been?" she asked, keeping her voice low. "I thought you were dead! You've been gone all day!"

"Glad to hear you noticed," he replied in an amused voice. She could only see his outline in the darkness. He paced over to her chair and sat down, pulling off his boots. "I took a transport over to the space station for the day. I needed to send some messages to my family on Saurellia, and it seemed like it might be a good idea to give you and the kids a break from me. I hope you don't mind, but I picked up a doll for Mali, and a game for Able. They just sort of jumped out at me. We can say they're from you, if you don't want them to know I've gotten them a present. I got you something, too."

"Oh," she said, feeling deflated. It seemed so mundane, so normal. "Well, that was nice of you. But you should have left a message for us. We didn't know where you were."

"I didn't realize you'd care," Jax said quietly, sounding pleased. He stood and started pulling off his clothes. She gritted her teeth; the man was too damn confident in himself. "Do you want to know what your present is?"

"I had an inquiry about your room," she said, infusing her voice with sweetness. "If you weren't coming back, I wanted to rent it to someone else."

"Fine with me," Jax said, leaning over her and bracing both hands on the bed. "It's not like I plan to sleep up there any more. You might as well rent it out. I'll move my things into your room in the morning."

"No," she said quickly. He laughed in the darkness.

"Yes," he whispered back, his voice low and sexy in the darkness. "I want your business to be a success. If you can rent out another room and earn more money, I'll do whatever I can to make that possible. Oh, and it's a nightgown. To replace the one I ruined last night. Red silk..."

She tried to protest again, but then his lips were closing over hers. They were soft, warm. He smelled so good. She thought about her vision of him lying dead in the forest, and suddenly she was filled with joy that he'd come back to her. There was no floozy. He was here, and she could touch him all she wanted. And he got her a nightgown. No one had ever gotten her anything like that before.

Touching him was a bad idea, of course. But she didn't care. She just reached her arms up around his neck and pulled him closer to her. She could feel the tensed strength in his muscles, but he was tender, carefully resting his weight on his arms to keep her comfortable. He deepened the kiss, and she felt him lift his legs onto the bed, until he was lying on top of her, straddling her. His hips pressed down against hers and she pushed back without thinking. Back and forth, they slowly allowed themselves to touch in a rhythm as old as time.

Then his lifted his head and whispered in her ear, "You're so beautiful, Sarai."

She laughed, and brushed her lips along his jaw. It was rough and stubbly — so masculine it made her ache.

"Thank you," she replied. "You're not so bad yourself."

He laughed, and started kissing her again, this time on the neck. She wondered idly if she should try to stop him, but it felt so good. Could it really hurt to let go of herself for just one night, to enjoy him for the moment without worrying about the future? She had worked so hard for so long; was it really that bad to give herself this one small freedom?

His lips moved lower, nudging aside her shift as he moved until he reached the valley between her breasts. She shivered against him, nipples hardening in anticipation. He moved his head to the side, swirling his tongue in circles around the stiff peak. Then he flicked it before catching it with his mouth. He suckled and rolled it back and forth between his lips, starting a fire in her lower body. The night before he had only touched her with his hands, but tonight she wanted his hard length inside.

He'd thrust into her, stretching her most delicate spot open. The thought made her quiver in anticipation.

She pushed her hips up at him, and tried to spread her legs. She wanted to feel him between her legs, to cradle him with her body. A soft, tickling need was building, and she knew that if she could just capture his length between her legs he could take care of that need for her.

Without pausing in his ministrations to her nipple, he shifted his legs, allowing her to spread hers wide enough for him to rest against her. In doing so, he pushed the covers aside, but her shift still separated them. He was naked, she could feel his penis resting in the groove of her clit, and his hips moved slowly against hers. It slipped along that groove with agonizing slowness, tantalizing her but not doing enough to build toward anything bigger. She bucked up at him, trying to get him to move more quickly, but instead he stopped moving altogether, pushing down and holding her prisoner beneath him.

"What do you want, Sarai?" he whispered, lifting his head from her breast. He stretched himself out, laying his head down beside hers on the pillow. She pushed at him, trying to get him to start moving again.

"Oh, no," he whispered. "Not until you tell me what you want."

She sighed, frustrated. He was so close, so hard and warm against her. Why couldn't he just keep up what he had started?

"I want you to keep going," she whispered, straining up toward him with her hips.

"How far do you want me to go?" he asked, reaching out to delicately stroke her ear with his tongue. She shivered, tingles running through her body.

"I don't want you to stop," she replied, her voice sounding raspy in the darkness. "Not tonight."

"Anything you ask, Sarai. I'd do anything for you," he whispered.

Before she could respond, his mouth had taken hers for the second time. Where he had been soft before, almost wooing, this was a kiss of possession. His tongue thrust into her mouth, and his hips pressed down between hers. Hard. She could feel the wide tip of his cock pushing against her shift, searching for the wet slit between her legs. She twisted against him, clutching him close with her arms. She wanted him in her, wanted to feel like he was hers, at least for now.

His hand reached down between them, grasping the hem and pulling it up to gain access to her body. He lifted his hips and she whimpered, not wanting to lose that tantalizing weight that held her pinned. Then his fingers were slipping into her cunt, feeling for her clit. He lifted his mouth from hers and grunted, "You're hot and wet for me already."

"Yes," she murmured, and arched under his touch. "I need you to fill me, Jax. Please."

He answered by positioning his rigid cock against her opening, then thrust into her with all his strength. She was filled to bursting. His size was unreal. Having this man inside her was amazing, a curious mix of intense pleasure and stretching pain. She would adjust to his presence in a second, but for the moment she simply savored the sensation of him inside her body.

He withdrew partially, then thrust back into her again. This time there was less stretching, and she smiled up at him.

"You feel so good," she whispered.

"You feel pretty damn good yourself," he muttered, kissing her again, hard and quick. He started moving within her, and after a second she reached around him with her legs, locking her ankles behind his back. The new angle let him come into her more fully; they both moaned.

Down he thrust, his cock scraping against her clit with each movement, and the tendrils of sensation and lust within her grew. Again and again, harder with every stroke. The pressure was growing within her, and she squeezed her inner muscles in anticipation. He grunted in response, dropping his head down to her shoulder. His breathing was harsh in her ear, and he moved faster against her. They strained against each other; coordinating their movements so that each time he came down into her flesh it rocked her back into the mattress.

She was getting closer. She could feel the tension winding tight between her legs. He was moving so fast against her that she could hardly keep the pace, each thrust hitting bottom, each motion rubbing her clit harder againsthim. Then he started moving his hips in a circular motion, grinding against her clit and stirring his cock within her. She closed her eyes and threw back her head, every muscle in her body stiffening. He gasped against her neck and she squeezed him, arms, legs and cunt, trying to wring the last bit of sensation out of him that she needed to push her over the edge.

Then her orgasm exploded, and she came with a deep, ragged moan that worked its way from low in her belly out into the night air. She clenched him, spasming, and he thrust against her hard. A sharp pain cut through her, and she realized that he was biting her shoulder, groaning into her flesh as his own orgasm ripped through him. She could feel the hot spurts of his seed hitting her, and she raised her hips to cradle him more closely. She wanted to pull him into her, take possession of him, and bind him to her…

They stayed like that for several minutes, panting in the darkness. Slowly, he allowed his weight to shift off of her, and rolled to her side. She felt his fingers touching her shoulder lightly, then he spoke.

"I bit you," he said, seemingly startled by his own actions. "I have no idea why I did that. I'm sorry, Sarai. I didn't mean to hurt you."

"You didn't," she replied, realizing it was true. His bite had stung, still throbbed a bit, but somehow it had fit in with the moment. Almost as if he had been marking her as his. Her mind shied away from this strange thought—it was too much to think about right now. He would be gone in a few weeks, so she needed to take pleasure in the moment.

"Well, I'm still sorry," he said, kissing the injured spot with soft warmth.

"That's all right," she whispered, nuzzling into his shoulder. She was suddenly very tired. Time to go to sleep...Jax cuddled her against his body, then pulled the covers over them. In the darkness outside the sliding door, she could hear the insects and small night creatures chittering and scurrying about. She drifted off to sleep, content in her decision. Having a man around, however temporarily, was going to be all right.

* * * * *

She awoke early in the morning, hearing a muffled snoring next to her ear. For a moment she couldn't move, and panic filled her. Something was pinning her down, something heavy. She realized it was Jax, who had sprawled out on the bed, draping his arm and leg across her. She pushed at him with one arm, and he obediently rolled over on his back, still sleeping.

She was free.

She sat up a little, looking at him in the early-morning light. It was amazing to her that this man, so handsome and strong, seemed to want her, of all people. She leaned over him, examining his face closely. There was dark stubble along his jaw, and he was all sharp angles. There was no softness, even in his sleep, yet he had bought her daughter a doll at the spaceport, and a nightgown for her. He certainly seemed to have some softness inside of him.

She tried to sit up a little more, and realized that her unbuttoned shift was pinning her down. She slipped it off her shoulders, then moved closer to him. She let one hand touch the line of his collarbone, then slowly traced it down his body. He was a soldier, she had always known that. But this was the first time she'd really taken the time to look at his body.

There were several scars, small ones that were little more than white lines, and one large one on his side. She touched it in wonder, amazed that he had survived. It was as if someone had melted the skin there, superheating it and twisting it. *Blaster fire?* she wondered. She had never seen a wound like this, but it had to have been terrible.

She trailed her hand a bit lower, pushing the blanket that covered him down with it. She touched the planes of his stomach, taut with muscle. There was no extra flesh on him, only hardness. He seemed so relaxed around her and the children that at times it was hard to imagine what his life must really be like. He said he wanted to stay with her, but he was a soldier. There was no way he'd be content living and working in a hostel on a backwater planet.

A twinge of sadness came over her, and for the first time she allowed herself to consider how nice it would be to have a man like Jax around. Someone to hold her, to teach Able how to be a man. Someone to show Mali that not all men were like her father had been. Someone who would love them not hurt them.

That couldn't happen, of course.

She trailed her fingers along his stomach, watching the tiny black hairs trailing down from his navel stand up under her touch. That wasn't the only thing that was standing, she realized. Directly below her hand, under the covers, his cock was coming to life. She stole a look up at his face, but he was still sound asleep. She wondered if he was dreaming of being touched; if he was dreaming of her. She stifled a giggle, feeling silly and happy all of a sudden. She had been denying herself any joy for so long. It felt good to relax, to enjoy another person's company.

Keeping as quiet as possible, she lifted the covers and pushed them lower, revealing his partially erect penis. It was flushed, hardening before her eyes, lolling to one side. The head was a darker red than the rest, a mushroom-shaped helmet that seemed almost to be watching her, waiting for her touch. She touched one finger to it delicately. His skin there was so soft. She rubbed her finger back and forth along the edge, mesmerized by its silky smoothness.

He was definitely growing harder. Where his cock had lolled to one side before, now it was straightening. The head grew more flushed as she continued her gentle stroking, and a tiny bit of fluid beaded up on the tip. It gleamed in the early-morning sunlight, and she was struck with a sudden curiosity about what it tasted like.

The thought shocked her.

She'd never imagined such a thing, tasting a man's seed. But why not, she wondered? There was no reason she couldn't taste him. After all, he had tasted her. He certainly liked being touched there; why wouldn't he like the touch of her mouth? A shiver ran through her. It would be so daring to lick him. What would he think as he woke up? She had to find out.

Scooting down on the bed, she made herself comfortable and stole one more quick glance up at him. Still asleep. Good. She moved her head in closer to him, then reached out with the tip of her tongue to touch that small drop of liquid. It was salty, strange. Not unpleasant, but strange. She licked him again, and the length of his penis jumped under her touch. It was much redder now, and very hard. She ran her tongue around the edge of the helmet-like head, enjoying the smooth touch on her tongue. Then she was struck with another idea. What if she sucked the head into her mouth?

She opened her mouth wide; careful to keep her teeth covered by her lips, and slowly sucked his cock in. It was big, bigger than she'd imagined, and hot. She could taste a little more of the salty fluid, and his body shifted slightly under her. She pulled her head back up, and his cock came out of her mouth with a popping sound. She looked up at him suspiciously. Was he awake?

But his breathing was slow and steady, and his eyes were closed. She turned her attention back to his erection, then opened her mouth over it again. She sucked it in smoothly this time, exploring the surface with her tongue. She probed the little hole right at the tip, then swirled her tongue around it. He shifted again, but this time she ignored it. She wanted to see how much of him she could fit in her mouth, and started slowly lowering her head down on him. She made it about a third of the way before her mouth was full, so she pulled back up, sucking on it as she went. It was rock hard now.

He twitched again, and she started to lift her head up to look at him. The movement was stopped when his hand gripped the back of her head, holding her still on his hard length.

"Please don't stop," he whispered, his voice sounding strained in her ears. "You have no idea how much it would mean to me if you didn't stop."

He pressed her down, firmly enough to show her what he wanted, but not so hard she couldn't have gotten away. She didn't feel trapped at all, she thought. She felt powerful; Jax was completely at her mercy. She lowered her head again, reveling in the gasp he gave as she did so. He was hers to play with.

She moved her head up and down along his length, keeping a steady suction. She could feel the tension under her hands. His thighs were tight, and as she kept moving she realized they were actually quivering under her touch. This powerful man was hers.

His hands pushed her down against cock urgently. She took the hint, bobbing her head up and down more quickly. More liquid was seeping out of him now. She could taste the salty warmth in her mouth. His breathing was harsh in the morning air. She sucked him in time and again. Her jaw was starting to ache a bit, but the slight discomfort was nothing compared to the pleasure she knew she was giving him. She felt strong and powerful, completely in control of the warrior who lay before her. It made her feel almost giddy.

His hands gripped her head more tightly, and he gave a long, low moan. He was close to coming. She could tell every muscle in his body was rock hard. She sucked against him as hard as she dared, and he pushed her face down into his cock again, fingers tightly wound in her hair. She gripped him with her mouth, sucking and massaging him with her tongue, and then he exploded with a groan.

The wave of hot seed hit her and she swallowed, gulping each time he shot into her. His orgasm seemed to last forever. Finally his hands released their tight grip on her head, and she slowly pulled away from him. She sat up, looking over his relaxed, spent body lying on her bed. He smiled up at her, his face softer than she'd ever seen it.

"Thank you," he said quietly.

"You're welcome," she answered, blushing hotly. "I'm not quite sure why I did that…"

"Well, I appreciated it a great deal," he said, a touch of humor on his face. "I'm not really worried about the analysis."

She laughed, then cuddled up next to him. He tucked her into the crook of his arm, hugging her to him.

"So what now?" he asked finally. She stilled, unsure of what to tell him. Then she spoke.

"I still don't think you have a place in my life permanently," she said softly. He grew still against her. "I don't need or want a man, Jax. I know you're not like Calvin was, but I still don't plan to open myself up like that again. But we have a deal, and it's pretty silly to pretend that I don't enjoy sharing a bed with you. Let's just enjoy ourselves for the next two and a half weeks. I don't want to think beyond that."

Jax stayed silent for a moment.

"All right," he said finally. "If that's what you want."

"It is," she said firmly. "I don't think I can handle anything more than that."

Chapter Five

"Jax," Mali asked, delicately licking a bit of porridge off her finger. "How long are you going to stay with us?"

Jax and Sarai shot each other a glance across the kitchen table. Sarai started to speak, but to her surprise, Able cut her off.

"He's going to be here another week, and then he's leaving," the boy replied firmly, a hint of satisfaction in his voice. "Isn't that right, Jax?"

"Yes," Sarai said. She met his gaze and held it. "Jax will be leaving in another week. We've had a very good visit with him, but he can't stay forever."

"Why not?" Mali asked, looking at her mother in confusion. "Don't you like it here, Jax? I thought you liked us."

"I do like it here," Jax said, thinking his answer through carefully. "And I would very much like to stay with you. But I don't think your mother is quite ready for that, and I don't want her to be unhappy. Making your mother happy is very important to me."

"But if you leave I'm going to be unhappy," Mali said, lower lip quivering.

"Sweetheart, this is a grown-up thing," Sarai said quietly. "Just because Jax came to visit us doesn't mean he can stay and live with us. He has his own life. He's a soldier, you know. He has to go and fight the empire with his people."

"Soldiers die sometimes," Able said, a smug note in his voice. Mali burst into tears.

"I don't want Jax to die!" she wailed

"I'm not going to die—" Jax said, but he was cut off by Sarai's tight voice.

"Able, go to your room!" Able stomped out, glaring at all of them. Sarai sighed, then got up and moved over to Mali. She picked the little girl up and held her close. "Sweetheart, you don't need to worry about Jax. He's a very good soldier, and nobody is going to hurt him."

"I'm not a soldier anymore," Jax added, reaching over to touch Mali's hand. She twisted in her mother's arms, sliding to the floor and throwing herself into the man's arms. "I decided to quit being a soldier after I met your mother."

Sarai froze.

"What are you talking about?" she asked. He looked back at her, a funny expression on his face. Mali had quieted, watching both of them intently.

"Well, in Saurellia only men who don't have a lifemate are soldiers. I have a lifemate now, Sarai."

"What is that supposed to mean?" Sarai asked. Against her will, hatred boiled up in her for the woman. She'd kill the bitch! "What's a lifemate? Who is she? How long have you had this woman in your life?"

Jax looked startled, then he began to laugh.

"Sarai, you're my lifemate, whether you want to admit it or not," he said finally, smiling broadly at her. "What do you think all this is about? Do you think I just move in with women wherever I go?"

She didn't say anything, having thought just that. He sighed, then set Mali down on the floor.

"Sweetheart, can you run outside to play for a while?" he asked the child. "I need to talk to your mother for a while. Just grown ups."

"All right," Mali said. She headed toward the door, then turned to look at him one more time. "Promise you're not going to be a soldier and die?"

"Promise."

She skipped outside, slamming the door behind her.

"Now what is this all about?" Sarai asked. She looked at him, trying to understand. He leaned forward across the table, and took her hands into his.

"In Saurellia, most men never find a lifemate," he said quietly. "For every woman born, we have at least four or five men. The Goddess only creates one lifemate for each of those women, and they share a unique bond that goes deeper than any other relationship. They can only have children together. Only those men who have a lifemate can inherit property or serve in the local government. Most of us leave by the time we're in our early twenties, because staying there is just too painful."

"Well, that's a stupid system," Sarai said tartly. Jax looked startled, then burst out laughing. He sat back, apparently overcome by some private joke. Finally he gained control, wiping a tear of mirth from one of his eyes. She sat amazed, having never seen him like this.

"Only you, Sarai," he said, shaking his head. "Only you would look through the most sacred traditions of our people and judge them like that."

"Well, it is stupid," she said, feeling self-conscious. "To kick out such a huge part of your population because they don't have a wife. Why don't you just bring more women in?"

"I'm afraid it's not quite that easy," he said, smiling sadly. "You see, it's not like we can just choose any woman as our lifemate. She has to be a Saurellian woman, and she has to be the right one. Otherwise the relationship isn't stable."

Sarai grew quiet, allowing his words to sink in. She hadn't realized until that second that somewhere, deep inside her heart, she had allowed herself to hope things could work out between them. His words cut through her like a knife, severing that hope. It hurt. She kept her face impassive, unwilling to give him the satisfaction of knowing he fooled her. She was about as far from being Saurellian as a woman could be.

"I see," she said casually. "So what happens to all of you who don't have a lifemate?"

"Well," he said. "Most of us become soldiers. During peacetime, we tended to hire ourselves out as mercenaries to different nobles throughout the empire. Of course, now that the Saurellian Federation is at war with the empire, we've all come back. None of us would consider fighting against our own people."

"Wait a second," Sarai asked, holding up a hand. "Seth took Calla away from here claiming they were going to be married on Saurellia. How is that possible? Was the bastard lying to her?"

"Oh, no," Jax said quickly. "You didn't let me finish. Just in the past year or so, we've discovered that more and more Saurellian men are finding lifemates outside of Saurellia. They've discovered that a large group of people within the empire actually have Saurellian DNA. Nobody knows quite why, but it's happening. Perhaps the Goddess has a new plan for us, but that's something for the priestesses to figure out. All I care about is that I've found you. You're my life mate, Sarai."

"How can you say that?" she asked, gaping at him in surprise. "You hardly know me! We only met two weeks ago. That's ridiculous."

"Sarai, a Saurellian man knows his lifemate when he meets her," Jax said, smiling gently. "They don't always know right away, but usually pretty quickly. I knew the instant I saw you. You're mine, Sarai, and I'm yours. The Goddess created us for each other."

"I don't believe that for one second," she said, anger welling up in her. He was lying to her. "I don't know what you're up to, but I don't want to play your twisted little game, Jax. You have no right to just come in here and play with our emotions like this. You saw my daughter—she's afraid that you're going to die because you're a soldier. You can't tell me you plan to just give up your whole life and stay here with us, because I know that's not true."

"Sarai, it is true," Jax said. "You are my lifemate. No Saurellian man would leave his lifemate to serve as a soldier, not unless her life was in danger. And your life is not in danger; you and your family are safe. I'll protect you."

"Okay, suppose what you say is true," Sarai said, thinking desperately. "Why would I be your lifemate? I'm a Pilgrim; we don't mix with people from the empire. How would I have this 'DNA' stuff that you're talking about?"

"Well, everyone has DNA," Jax replied quietly. Sarai blushed, realizing this was probably another piece of common knowledge she'd never learned. Her lack of education was so embarrassing some times...

"But not everyone has Saurellian DNA, right?" she asked quickly, trying to cover her ignorance. "How would I have Saurellian DNA?"

"I have no idea," Jax said. She looked at him, startled. "No one has any idea. As far as we knew, our gene pool had never been mixed. But they've found it in imperial slaves. Why not Pilgrims?"

"None of this makes sense to me," she said finally. "I don't understand all these thing you're telling me. But I do understand one thing. You don't have the right to come in here and tell me what to do. I don't have to be your lifemate if I don't want to."

"There's nothing you can do to stop it, Sarai," Jax said. "The Goddess made us for each other. We can't help that. By Saurellian law, we're already married."

"What?" Sarai stood abruptly, sliding the bench back across the floor with a screeching sound. "I'm not married to you! I'm not married to anyone, never again. Being married was the worst thing that ever happened to me. I won't go back to that."

Jax stood too, and leaned his face down close to hers.

"All I meant was that according to Saurellian law, a mated pair is considered married as soon as they first have sex," he said in low tones. "The marriage is usually confirmed at the temple after the birth of their first child."

"Child?" Sarai replied, her voice growing louder. "What the hell are you talking about? I already have two children, there's no way I'm going to have another one. It's all I can to do take care of Mali and Able. I may be ignorant, but I'm not stupid. One of the first things I did after I got away from Calvin was get a birth control implant. I'm not taking any chances, and I don't owe you a damn thing. Like I'm going to go through another pregnancy? I don't think so."

"Why the hell would you do that?" Jax asked harshly. "Do you have any idea how hard it is for a man of my people to find a woman he can mate with? I've been praying to the Goddess this entire time that you were already pregnant. Are you telling me this is just about sex to you?"

"Of course it's just about sex!" she screeched. "We had a deal. You were going to stay three weeks, and then you're leaving. I realized we could have some fun during that time, but nothing more. Do you understand me, Jax? This is *only* about sex. I don't need or want a husband, and I never will. You might as well get used to the idea, because I'm not changing my mind. We have no future together. Nothing. I don't even like you. I just like fucking you."

Jax just looked at her, saying nothing. Then he stood so quickly the bench tipped over behind him as he stomped out of the room. The door slammed behind him, and Sarai sat down heavily. Her heart was racing, and she felt hot. She couldn't believe she'd yelled at him like that. What would Calvin have done to her if she'd raised her voice to him? She couldn't even begin to imagine…

A part of her almost felt bad for saying something so cruel to him. She'd hurt him; she could see the pain in his face as he'd turned to leave. But she couldn't afford to show any weakness. She didn't want to give control of her life back over to a man, even a good man. The sooner Jax realized that, the sooner he would leave them alone. She tamped down the pain the thought of his leaving gave her. A woman in her situation couldn't afford to have feelings like that. She had already let him way too far into her heart.

Joanna Wylde

Chapter Six

I don't even like you. I just like fucking you.

Jax took a long pull on his drink, trying not to let the words play themselves over and over in his head. He couldn't believe she'd said that; couldn't believe she meant it. She cared about him. He knew it—it was in every caress she gave him, all the little things she did for him.

If she was just using him for sex, why did she take the time to cook his favorite meals? Why did she wait up for him at night, take him into her arms and hold him even when they didn't *fuck* as she so crudely put it? Just holding her, standing next to her was the most beautiful thing he'd ever experienced in his life. She made him happy, content, for the first time. There was no way he believed what she'd said.

I just like fucking you.

Bitch. She was trying to hurt him; he realized that. And she had done a damn good job of it. What had he done to deserve this kind of treatment? He'd been kind and caring, he adored her children. He would give anything to make her happy, and all she seemed to want to give in return was her body. And even that was on a limited basis. He couldn't kiss her in public; touch her where the children could see them.

She wouldn't even let him move into her room, insisting that he keep his own even though he'd told her to rent it out a hundred times. A clanking noise caught his attention. The bartender, a pretty woman in her early twenties, stood before him, polishing a glass.

"Want another drink, handsome?" she said, giving him a broad smile. Her look was appraising, an open invitation. He squinted at her, trying to focus on her face. But all he could see were her large, impressive breasts. Something was on them, a nametag. Giselle. She gave a throaty laugh and leaned forward on her elbows, giving him a better view. He realized he could have her if he wanted her, and she'd probably be a hell of a lot more open to him than Sarai.

"Sure, I'll take another," he said, smiling at her. But the gesture felt hollow; he wasn't interested in this woman. He'd spent so much of his life chasing after so many women; he'd never dreamed he could be satisfied with just one. But now that he'd met Sarai, the thought of touching anyone else left him cold.

There was no doubt she was his lifemate.

Who was she to deny that? By Saurellian law, he could take her. He could just take her in his ship to Saurellia, and not a man or woman in the entire system would blame him for his actions. She was *his*, and only his. She had no right to turn him away.

He took another drink, warming to the idea. That's what he would do. He'd just take her. He threw down some change on the bar to cover his bill and a little extra for Giselle, and stood unsteadily. His vision blurred, and he wondered for a minute just how long he had been there. He walked slowly and carefully to the door, then opened it.

Someone had turned off the sun.

Wait. No. It was dark outside. He must have been in the bar far longer than he realized. Not that it mattered. He would go collect Sarai and the children and they would go to Saurellia. The people there would explain everything to her, and she'd realize she didn't have any choice but to stay with him. The thought made him smile, and he started humming a little song as he walked down the street. Everything was going to be fine.

It took him a long time to get home. For some reason he kept turning down the wrong street, and after a while he started getting angry with himself. He had had far too much to drink, he realized. He would have to be careful of that, because Seth had told him that Calvin, Sarai's first husband, had been a drinker. She probably didn't like men who drank.

Calvin.

Now there was a man he'd like to kill, he mused. A part of him almost regretted he was already dead. Sarai had killed him herself, though. To save her children. Seth had been there, and told him all about it. She was such a strong, spunky woman. He loved that about her. She was like a wild feline, willing to do anything to protect her young ones. She might not be a Saurellian woman, but she was definitely as fierce as any daughter of the Goddess. She hadn't given Calvin any mercy when it counted.

An hour later, he arrived at the hostel, and let himself in the side gate. Moving as quietly as he could, he made his way along the side of the building until he reached the little clearing outside Sarai's bedroom. The door was open just a crack to let in the fresh night air, although the light was off. He looked up at the moon, realizing it was quite late. She'd probably been asleep for hours.

He sat on the bench, staring up into the night sky and thinking. Calvin. Damn he hated that man. He had beaten Sarai, terrorized her and the children. He had controlled their every move on that little asteroid mining station. She hadn't seen anyone else for months at a time.

Realization hit him.

If he took Sarai to Saurellia against her will he'd lose any chance of ever winning her love. It was so obvious, he felt like hitting himself in the head. How could he have missed it?

Sarai was afraid to lose her independence, and she was using their sexual relationship to protect her from any kind of emotional dependence on him. As long as it was just sex, her independence wasn't in jeopardy.

He was a dolt, a complete idiot. Pushing her for sex had given her the excuse she needed to keep him distant. With a clenching feeling in his stomach, Jax realized he was going to have to put the sex on hold. He only had one week left, and in the time he was going to have to convince her she wanted him for more than just the physical pleasure he could give her.

He had to convince her to take him as her partner, her equal.

"Shit," he murmured into the darkness. It wasn't going to be easy.

* * * * *

Sarai lay alone in the darkness, wishing desperately that Jax had come home. She couldn't believe she'd said such horrible things to him. Of course, it had worked. He was gone. That was what she wanted. But now she was finding it almost impossible to fall asleep without him, and just kept thinking about the look on his face as she'd screamed at him

He really hadn't done anything to deserve that. He wasn't going to steal her away, Saurellian law or not. She knew it instinctively. He cared about her and the children too much to hurt them like that.

So why are you so afraid of him? She asked herself. *He's not Calvin.*

So maybe not all men were like Calvin. She had come to realize that, started to realize it a long time ago. Before she even met Jax. But she still couldn't quite bring herself to let go of that fear, to put herself into a man's power. It was such a gamble, trusting a man. Was she willing to risk her children's future on Jax? For all his talk of being a life mate, she hardly knew the man.

She rolled over in bed, punching at her pillow and trying to find a cool spot. Jax wasn't with her, and as far she could tell, he wasn't up in his room. She'd been listening. He hadn't taken his things, so she knew he'd be back, at least long enough to pack. She didn't expect him to stick around any longer. Sure, he still had another week of their little "bargain," but now that he knew he wasn't going to get anywhere, he'd be leaving.

Against her will, she sniffed. Her nose was getting stuffed up, she thought in disgust. Her eyes were watering, too.

Probably just allergies. One of the bushes outside her window was blooming. She'd have to start sleeping with the door closed. It was a shame, really, because she loved the night air.

She snuffled again, and this time her eyes watered more. She crushed her head down into the pillow and gave in to reality. She missed him already. The thought of him leaving was horrid. Sobs tore through her and she whimpered into the darkness of her room. How was she going to live without him?

Chapter Seven

"Good morning, Sarai," Jax said as he walked into the kitchen. He had a bit of a headache, and the bright light made him want to wince. He wasn't going to show it, though. He already felt stupid about drinking the night before. A lecture was the last thing he needed.

"Good morning, Jax," she replied from her seat at the table, not looking at him. The two children watched them with interest.

"How come you didn't sleep with mommy last night, Jax?" Mali asked brightly. Sarai dropped her spoon with a clatter and Jax coughed.

"What do you mean, sweetheart?" Sarai asked, her voice deceptively soft. Jax could tell the question made her angry.

"We're not stupid, you know," Able said, putting down his own spoon. He looked at them smugly. "Mali and I know all about where Jax has been sleeping. We've been watching you guys. You're caught."

"Well, I won't be sleeping with Sarai any more," Jax said quietly. "Not unless she decides she wants to keep me for good. I love her very much, and I want to marry her."

"Jax—"Sarai tried to say, but Mali cut her off.

"If you marry mommy, will you be our daddy?" she asked, licking her spoon thoughtfully.

"If you'll let me," Jax said, catching Sarai's eyes. She looked livid, but he didn't care. She'd changed the rules last night. She hadn't been fighting fair, and now he was done fighting fair. He'd do whatever he could to wind his way into her life, whether she liked it or not. He only had a week; there wasn't any time to mess around. If that meant using the children against her, he'd do it.

"I would let you," Mali said with a shy smile.

"Well, I won't," Able said. "You may not be as bad as our father was, but we still don't need you here."

Sarai and Jax both looked at the boy in surprise.

"You think Jax is better than your father was?" Sarai asked quietly. "I didn't realize you were comparing them, Able. They're two very different people, you know. Jax would never do the things your father did."

A wave of warmth swept through Jax. No matter what she said, at least Sarai knew he was better than Calvin.

"I know that," Able said, looking at Jax as if taking his measure. It was the same look he had given him in the garden after he'd attacked him, Jax thought. Clearly, their talk had given the boy something to think about. "But what you need to understand is that you don't need him, Mom. You have me. I'll take care of you and Mali."

"I know that," Sarai said, her face flushing. "You've always done a good job of taking care of me, Able."

"And Mali," Able added.

"And Mali," Sarai repeated softly.

"Mommy, I'm done with my cereal," Mali announced. "I want to go outside now. Did you know that we don't have any lessons today, Jax? We just get to play all day long because our teacher has to go to the spaceport. Are you going to come and play with us?"

"Sure," Jax said lightly. "Why don't we go on a picnic? I'm sure that your mother would like to join us, too."

"I don't think—" Sarai tried to break in, glaring at him, but Mali squealed with delight, cutting her off.

"We're going on a picnic! Can we go swimming? Mommy says we can't go swimming unless we have grownups with us, but Kally's daddy takes us swimming sometimes. Will you take us swimming?"

Even Able perked up at this.

"We have to do what mom tells us," he said loyally, but his desire to go swimming was written all over his face. "Can we, mom?"

"There's a lot of work that needs to be done around here," Sarai said. Jax laughed.

"Sarai, there's nothing that can't wait. You don't have any vacancies right now, and none of the rooms need to be cleaned. They were just done yesterday," he said, trying to tempt her. "You haven't taken a day off since I've been here. It won't kill you to take a little break. You have to do fun things in life, too."

"You realize the children can't really swim, don't you?" Sarai said. Her voice was wavering; he could tell she was close to giving in. "They just paddle around in the shallow water. We'll have to keep a close eye on them."

"I'm a good swimmer," he said, smiling broadly at her. "Maybe I can teach them."

"You can teach me how to swim?" Able asked, his face lighting up. "Kally's daddy has been teaching me, but I still don't know how to do it very well. We don't get to go very often to practice. Mom doesn't know how, so she doesn't like to take us by herself."

"There weren't a lot of places to go swimming on the asteroid where I grew up," Sarai said defensively. She stood and started clearing the table.

"Well, it sounds like I'll just have to teach all of you to swim," Jax replied. The thought was appealing... What would Sarai wear to go swimming? He'd never seen her wearing anything but her long dresses. He watched her stack the dishes speculatively, enjoying the sway of her cute little butt as she moved. What would she feel like all wet and naked against him? It was a pleasant thought, and he could feel himself hardening in response...

"I don't want to swim in the deep water, though," Mali said. "I'm scared of the deep water, Jax."

"You don't have to do anything you don't want to," Sarai said reassuringly, turning back toward her daughter and smiling gently. "We'll just pack a little lunch and go play in the shallow places, all right?"

Yep, she was all his, Jax thought smugly. By the end of the day he'd have her hot and ready for him. Now all he had to do was keep reminding himself why he couldn't sleep with her. Not until she acknowledged that she wanted him for more than sex.

His plan was going to be harder to carry out than he'd expected, Jax realized later that day. He stood in water up to his chest, bracing himself again the current.

Sarai knelt in the shallows water of the riverbed with Mali, helping her build a little fort out of sand and sticks. Her white shift clung to every curve of her body, outlining her nipples enticingly and even giving a hint of shadow at the cleft between her legs. She turned away from him, and leaned forward to pull some more sand over for her daughter. The movement pulled the fabric tight against her heart-shaped ass, and he groaned. Even the cold water of the river wasn't enough to keep his erection down. What had started out as his plan to tempt her was turning into his own personal hell.

"Jax, are you ready?" Able called. Jax turned his attention to the boy, who was standing in water up to his waist. His face was pinched and tight with stress, but he insisted on trying to swim out to Jax by himself.

"I'm ready, Able," Jax said, holding out his arms. "I'll catch you, don't worry."

"All right, I'm coming now!" Able shouted, and then threw himself forward into the slowly moving water. He thrashed his arms and legs desperately, slowly inching his way toward Jax. It took all of Jax's willpower not to lean forward and pull the boy to him, but he knew doing it by himself was important to Able. Then the boy was on him, wiry little arms and legs clingy. He twisted in Jax's arms, shouting in triumph.

"Mom, did you see? I swam all the way out here by myself!"

"Oh, no, I missed it!" Sarai called, turning to look at them. "Can you swim back to shore? I'll be sure to watch this time."

"You can do it," Jax said encouragingly. Able twisted to look back at him, scorn on his face.

"Of course I can," he said. Without warning, he pushed himself free of Jax's arms and started paddling back toward the shore. Instead of watching the boy this time, though, Jax watched Sarai's face. Her expression was a mixture of concern and pride. She loved her children so much it was almost painful to watch at times. He felt like an intruder on their intimacy. Could he ever really be a part of the family?

Able had reached the shore, and Sarai wrapped him tightly in her arms. Mali jumped up and down, squealing in delight and clapping her hands.

"I can do it, too!" Mali said suddenly. She leapt forward.

Before either he or Sarai had time to react, the little girl flung herself into the water, flailing her arms and legs.

Chapter Eight

Jax leapt forward, unsure if she had any idea how to swim. She paddled her arms and legs furiously, just managing to keep her head above water. Then the slow current started tugging her away from him, and he leaped forward to catch her.

She squealed in delight as his arms came around her, clinging to him. He slipped and fell, instinctively holding her above him as he let himself relax and float to the surface. She seemed completely unconcerned, trusting him with the complete faith that only a small child can have. He bobbed up, leaning backward and cradling her in his arms. Then he kicked back, pushing himself upright and finding his footing on the slippery rocks.

Sarai was still standing in the shallows, her face white. She clutched Able to her, although he squirmed against her hold.

"Mom, let go!" he said sharply, and she shook her head, as if coming out of a dream.

"Jax, thank you so much," she said as he started wading slowly toward her. Mali had grown quiet, laying her head against his shoulder and wrapping her arms around his neck. "Mali, you can never do that again! Don't you realize that if Jax hadn't caught you, you could have been drowned?"

Mali turned her head and looked at Sarai in confusion.

"Mommy, if Jax hadn't been here, I wouldn't have had the guts to do that," she said slowly and clearly, as if Sarai were the child and she was the adult.

"I see," Sarai said. She abruptly turned and waded out of the water. "I think it's time for us to go home."

"Mom!" Mali and Able wailed simultaneously. "That's not fair," Able added.

"We haven't even had lunch yet, mommy," Mali said. "Do we really have to go home?"

Jax could see the tension in Sarai's face. Watching Mali fling herself into the water without warning had terrified her, although she was trying not to show her fear. He waded over to the beach, and walked up to her, still carrying the little girl.

"Sarai, perhaps we could eat before we go home," he said in a gentle voice, trying to sooth her fear. "I'm sure both the children will promise not to go near the water again without your permission."

"I promise," Mali said quickly, and Able nodded in agreement. Sarai sighed, and ran a hand through her hair. It trembled slightly, and Jax averted his eyes.

"You know, you might find the water less frightening if you knew how to swim," he said. "I could teach you, too."

"I don't think so," she said with a sigh. She looked up at him, her face full of strain; seeing her like that made him ache. He had to do something to relieve her pain. Without pausing to think, he stuck his tongue out at her. Able and Mali burst into laughter. Her mouth twitched for a minute, then she turned away and walked over to the basket she'd packed their lunches in. He set Mali down, and the three of them exchanged a wicked look.

When she turned back, Jax and the children were all sticking their tongues out at her. Her mouth twitched again, and on impulse Jax raised his hands, spread out his fingers and waggled them along the sides of his head. She burst out laughing, and then they were all cackling.

They laughed until tears ran down their cheeks, and by the time they stopped the tension seemed to be gone. Mali got the hiccups, and Sarai gave her a drink to help her get over them. Inevitably, it didn't work, and the next time she hiccupped, bright red juice came out her nose and they were all laughing again.

By the time they had finished lunch, a sumptuous picnic Sarai served on a large blanket, Mali's eyes were starting to droop. Able was also looking tired. Exchanging a knowing look with Jax, Sarai said, "Do you want to lay down for a little while, Mali? I can scoot over on the blanket so there's room?"

"No, I'm not tired," Mali said instantly, sitting up. Able gave her a superior look.

"Young children need regular naps," he said, his voice a perfect imitation of Sarai's. His mother laughed softly, and padded the blanket next to her.

"I'll tell you what, Mali," she said. "All of us can lay down for a little bit, and I'll tell a story. If you fall asleep, that's okay, but if you don't we'll go for a walk before heading home. Sound good?"

"I want Jax to tell the story," she said, lying down. Sarai raised a questioning eyebrow at Jax, and he nodded back at her.

"Do you want to hear a story that my mother used to tell me when I was a little boy?" he asked softly. Mali nodded. Sarai lay down next to her, on her side.

"Able, you have to lie down, too, before I start," Jax said. Able flopped back on the blanket, and Jax lowered himself to his stomach next to the boy. He propped himself up on his elbows, and started speaking softly.

"Once upon a time there was a beautiful planet where every season was wonderful in its own way. In the spring, all kinds of new plants would grow, and there were parties to celebrate new life. In the summer, everyone would take the time to enjoy the beautiful weather. They would go swimming every day and eat yummy fruits that were only ripe for a few weeks every year. In autumn, they would harvest all the grains, makes piles of leaves to jump in and store up lots of wood to keep warm when it got cold. In the winter they would gather in close next to the warm fire and tell stories at night. During the day they would go sledding and ice-skating. They'd even build giant castles made out of snow and ice, and throw balls of snow at each other. Everyone who lived there was very happy.

"Now, the most amazing thing about this planet is that there were four different kinds of people, and each group had their own king or queen. The winter people had very pale skin, so pale that you could just almost see the light blue veins in their arms. They were ruled by a beautiful queen, who had long, straight black hair and eyes like blue diamonds. Her husband was the king of autumn. Like all of his people, he had dark skin, and beautiful hair full of orange, red and brown streaks. The summer people were all golden, from their skin to their hair. They were the most fun loving of the groups, hosting fairs and dancing from morning until night."

"Every day?" Mali asked, popping her head up to look at him. Sarai reached an arm out to gently pull her back down, and Jax nodded.

"Yes, every day," he said solemnly. "Now, the last group was the spring people. They were magical, because they could make things grow. They had a beautiful queen who was all green, even her hair. Everywhere she walked, little plants would sprout out of the ground and flowers would grow. She was married to the king of the summer people.

"Now, every year all of the kings and queens would take turns ruling over the people. For three months every year, they would open their palaces and have parties and feasts. It was a wonderful place to live, and everyone was very happy all the time. But then one day, something bad happened."

"What?" Able asked, enthralled.

"Well, you see, every 20 years or so they would pick new kings and queens."

"Why?" Mali asked, her face twisted in confusion.

"Well, I think it's because being a king or queen if probably very tiring," Jax said, trying not to laugh. He'd never considered the question before. "But this time, the winter queen they picked wasn't a nice queen at all. All the people had gotten together for a special party to honor the new kings and queens. Now, that new winter queen didn't want to take turns ruling, she wanted to rule all the time. So she invited all the other kings and queens to a special party, and served them a special kind of cake that she made herself.

"What they didn't realize, until it was too late, was that she had put poison into the cake. All of them died that night, except for the king of summer, who didn't eat any of the cake."

"Mommy's cake is very good," Mali said solemnly. "No one ever dies from eating it. Not ever."

"That's good," Jax replied. "Now, because the winter queen wasn't able to kill the king of summer, she put a spell on him, freezing him deep down inside. You see, she knew that if she froze the summer king, there wouldn't be any more summers until he woke up. Since all the other kings and queens were dead, she declared that from that day on, it would only be winter. All the summer, autumn and spring people had to work for the winter people. It was very hard for them, because it became cold all the time. They were very unhappy, but they didn't know what to do to fix things.

"A thousand years passed under the rule of the evil queen, and it was winter the whole time. They learned how to grow all their food in greenhouses, and everyone was cold except for the winter people. The poor summer people were the coldest, and the evil queen forced them to work for her in the mines. No one had any idea how to get rid of her, and she used her magic against anyone who tried to stop her.

"One day, a group of summer people were working down in the mines and they found a magical cave full of ice crystals. Inside of one of those crystals was a frozen man. They realized it was the summer king, still being held prisoner by the queen's spell. They tried to wake him up, but nothing worked. So they took him back to their camp and called a council, inviting all the spring people and the autumn people to help them try to figure out what to do.

"When the council opened, all the oldest and wisest people tried to wake the sleeping king. They used spells and blankets to warm him, but he stayed frozen. Everyone was very frustrated, and nobody knew what to do. One morning, a young woman who was there with her family woke up very early to find something very strange had happened in the night. You see, when she had gone to sleep she and her family had been camping on an ice field, but when she got up there was a little patch of grass around their tent."

"Where did it come from?" Mali asked, eyes wide.

"She didn't know," Jax replied. "But right in front of her eyes, it seemed to be getting bigger. She started walking around the camp, and everywhere she went grass started growing. In the grass were little flowers, and she could feel the air getting warmer. It was so exciting that she didn't know what to do. So she kept walking until she got to the biggest tent in the camp, where they had placed the frozen king. She walked right into that tent and right up to the frozen king.

"Now, he was a very handsome man, and she was a very pretty woman. She took one look at him and fell in love. She decided she had to give him a little kiss, so she walked over to him and kissed him right on his lips. They were very cold against her skin, but the longer she kissed him, the warmer they seemed to get.

"Then he started kissing her back, right there. He sat up and wrapped his arms around her."

"This kissing part is getting boring," Able muttered, and Sarai laughed.

"All right, I'll skip the kissing part," Jax replied, grinning. "They heard a loud noise outside the tent, so they stood up and walked out holding hands. All around them the people were cheering and running around. There were flowers everywhere, and the all the snow was gone in the camp. They could hear birds singing and then everyone was dancing, because they knew the evil queen's spell had been broken. The king of summer was awake, and with him was a new queen of spring."

"Didn't the queen try to stop them?" Able asked, his voice skeptical. Mali nodded her head against the blanket, sucking her thumb.

"Yes, she did," Jax continued. "As they started marching toward her palace, all the snow was melting and she knew she was in big trouble. But no matter what she did, her magic wasn't as strong as the new king and queen. They got closer and closer to her, and as the air got warmer something horrible happened to the evil queen. She started getting very old, very fast. All her magic was failing her, and she aged a thousand years right then and there, drying up and turning into dust. Then all the dust blew away, and her whole palace fell down into rubble.

"The king and queen returned to the old ways, and a new king of fall and queen of winter were selected. Just like before, they each ruled for three months of the year, and everyone lived happily ever after."

"That was a good story," Mali murmured sleepily. Sarai smiled at Jax from across the blanket, and reached out a hand to run her fingers over Able's hair. The little boy was still awake, but he didn't seem inclined to move. She lifted a finger to her lips, and Jax nodded in understanding. If they just stayed quiet for a while, both children would drift off to sleep.

Jax closed his eyes, listening to the children's soft breathing and thinking about Mali's plunge into the river. He could understand Sarai's fear. What if he hadn't been able to catch her? She hadn't given him any warning.

He rolled on to his back, flinging one arm across his eyes. The warm sun was making him sleepy, too. Despite the almost constant ache in his loins, he was happy. Just being with her, with her children, brought so much peace into his life. A soft, rustling noise caught his attention. She must have rolled over, too. A twinge of longing wound its way through him. If she were lying beside him, he'd tuck her against his side and bury his face in her hair. It always smelled so wonderful.

They would lay there, watching the children sleep and perhaps even snoozing themselves. Or perhaps they would get up quietly and sneak down to the riverbank, he mused. They would slip out of their clothes, and slide into the cool water in each other's arms. He would let himself float back into the current, and pulled her lissome body across his. She'd cling to him, her legs tangling with his and they would come together for a kiss.

He could imagine the slippery feel of her skin, how her hair would float out behind her in the water, drifting downstream. Then he would wrap both arms around him, pulling her tight against his body. She would slide her legs around his waist. His hard length would be pressed tightly between them, and he'd kiss her again...

He had grown hard thinking about it. Moving quietly, he rolled back on to his stomach on the blanket to hide the evidence of his arousal, and stole a peek at Sarai and the children. All three were sleeping peacefully.

Closing his eyes again, he allowed himself to drift back into the fantasy.

She would clutch his body to hers, laughing softly, and then he'd slide his hard length into her body. They would rock against each other slowly in the water, letting their bodies become one and enjoying the closeness of their touch. He would make only the barest of movements at first, content to revel in the feel of her snug warmth. Then they'd start to move more quickly, squirming against each other urgently. He'd thrust into her harder, their mouths would meet. Their lovemaking would become wild, building to a climax that was as inevitable as it was powerful.

Jax squirmed against the blanket, trying to find a more comfortable position. His cock was like stone. He took several deep breaths, trying to calm himself down. He hadn't intended to allow himself to become aroused this way, but the thought of touching Sarai, making love to her in the water was too much. Staying away from her had turned out to be much harder than he'd dreamed possible, and he hadn't gone into it expecting it to be easy.

Another soft noise caught his attention. She was getting up. Both children were still breathing deeply, but she had stood up. Then he heard the soft padding of her feet as she walked away. Where was she going?

Jax opened his eyes, and silently propped himself up on his elbow. He craned his head around, and saw her graceful form walking back toward the riverbank. She was still wearing her white shift, but it was dry now, and it drifting around her body in a manner that was almost surreal. She looked more forest spirit than woman. The image was broken, though, when one corner caught on a branch. She tugged at it, and the worn fabric ripped. A look of disgust came across her face.

For the first time, Jax realized he'd never seen her wearing more than three or four sets of clothing. Was that all she could afford? The children were always well dressed...He'd assumed that she was doing all right, but he didn't know for sure. He'd have to look into that, he realized. Making a mental note of it, he turned his attention back to Sarai.

Free of the branch, she walked to the river's edge and sat down. He could hardly see her now. He stood quietly, taking care not to wake the children, and reached over to tab on a motion sensor in his pack. If anything larger than a bird came close to Able and Mali as they slept, he and Sarai would know. Then he started walking toward her. She turned to look at him as he approached, and then a smile so lovely it took his breath away came across her face.

"Jax," she said softly. "Come sit by me."

He lowered himself to the beach, stretching his legs out before him. The water lapped at his toes, cool and fresh. She leaned over and kissed his bare shoulder.

"Jax, this is silly," she said. "I'm so sorry for what I said to you. I can't think of anything but how much I miss touching you. Why do we have to do this?"

Her words twisted through him, sweet seduction. He was rock hard for her, filled with a heavy ache of need that had become his constant companion. How easy would it be to simply roll her under him, take her there on the sand? She wanted him; he wanted her. They were both adults. It should be so simple.

"No," he said, pushing down the treacherous thought. "I want more than sex, Sarai. Don't mistake me, I want sex, too. But I want to be a part of your life, and I want to be a father to the children. Hell, I want to have more children with you. I'm not willing to settle for less than that."

She stared into the water for a moment, moisture welling in her eyes. She gave her face and impatient swipe.

"Jax, you know what happened to my first husband, don't you?"

"Yes," Jax said. "Seth told me, and he told me why, too. You killed him in self-defense. You did it to save your children, and you did the right thing, Sarai. I only wish I could have killed him for you."

"But you don't know the whole story, Jax," she said softly. "I enjoyed killing him. I'll never forget the incredible rush that killing him gave me. I felt so free, so powerful! It was disgusting and exhilarating all at once, and I made myself a promise. I decided I'd never let myself get into a situation where a man controlled me again. I never want to face another choice like that."

A wave of compassion swept through him, and he pulled her into his arms. She was crying in earnest now. He pressed her head against his shoulder, and she started sobbing.

She cried for a long time, and he simply held her, marveling at her strength. Despite everything she'd gone through, she still managed to hold herself and her life together. Eventually her sobs quieted down, and she rested against him. He spoke.

"I've told you that on Saurellia only one in five children are female," he said. "We have a legend about that...according to legend, when the Goddess created the world, she made men and women equally strong. But within the first few generations, she discovered that even though men and women had the same strength, the women's lives were so much harder that it wasn't fair. Not only that, society started falling apart. There were wars and famine. Children starved in the streets, and it was an abomination before the Goddess.

"So she started making fewer women, but making them stronger," he continued. "Now there are more men then women, but our women are so strong that they hold our society together. Any Saurellian man lucky enough to be found worthy to be mated to one of those women is blessed a thousand times by the Goddess. Their relationship can be more wonderful than anything in the imagination, but it will never be unequal. There isn't a Saurellian man alive who can control his lifemate. Our society is matriarchal."

She looked up at him, blinking her eyes.

"What does that have to do with us? I'm not Saurellian, Jax. I'm not that strong."

"Sarai, you are that strong," he whispered, lifting his hand and wiping away one of her tears with his thumb. "Don't you understand? You may not have been born a Saurellian, but you are definitely a daughter of the Goddess. I don't want to control you. I want to be your lifemate, your partner. What makes you happy makes me happy. We belong together, and what Calvin did to you has nothing to do with us. He's dead. He can't hurt you, and I won't. You're safe now. You've made it."

She sniffed, and smiled at him tremulously.

"I did, didn't I?" she whispered. "Jax, I don't feel very strong. I don't know this Goddess of yours very well, but I could use some of that strength you talk about."

"It's there, Sarai," he said. Unable to help himself, he leaned his head down and kissed her softly on the lips. Her head fell back and her eyes closed, then she was opening to him. He deepened the kiss, exploring her depths and trying to control himself. He wanted her so badly he thought he might explode, but somehow he managed to keep himself from simply rolling her over and taking her. Finally, shaking from the effort, he pulled away.

"Sarai, will you be my lifemate?" he asked softly, searching her face. She froze for a minute, as if waging some battle within herself, then she spoke.

"I'll be your mate, but on my terms. I don't promise to do as you tell me, and if I ever feel like I need to leave you, I will."

"That's good enough for me," he said, smiling. She looked up at him in surprise.

"So I can leave you any time I want?" she asked.

"If I'm doing my job as a lifemate, you won't want to leave me," he replied quietly. She sniffed, then gave him a coy smile.

"Well, then I guess you'd better keep me happy," she said tartly.

"That's my girl," he said, abruptly rolling her over into the sand and covering her with his body. She was trapped beneath, a startled look on her face. He kissed her, and her arms came around him. She pulled him close, kissing him back. Then her legs were wrapped around his body, and she was writhing against him. He groaned, pressing his cock against her softness.

"It's been too long," he muttered, pulling his head back. She laughed up at him.

"Silly, it's been less than a day," she replied.

"Too long," he repeated, covering her again. He thought he was going to explode from the exquisite pressure of her body pressing up against his. Her hips moved rhythmically, and he groaned. He had to get inside her. If he didn't, he was going to die.

Her other leg came up, and they both clutched his waist. The soft opening between her legs cradled him, and without thinking he thrust against her. But his briefs and her shift blocked his motion, and he groaned in frustration.

"I hate this damn thing," he said, raising his body and pulling her shift up. "Sarai, I'm getting you all new clothing. I never want to see this thing again. It's caused me too much frustration over the past weeks."

She laughed up at him, then reached down to work on his briefs.

"And what about these?" she asked archly. "They seem to be in my way right now. Do I get to throw them away, too?"

"Yes," Jax replied with a grin. "I'll never wear clothing again. We'll just live naked in your bed, happily ever after."

Then her shift was up around her waist, and his briefs were down around his knees. With a sigh, he reached down to position himself against her. She wrapped her arms around his neck again, pulling him down into her softness. The feel of her hot, moist flesh closing around him was almost more than he could take, and after his initial thrust he stopped for a moment. He rested his forehead against hers, breathing deeply and trying to control himself.

She squirmed against him, kneading him with her inner muscles and pulling him down into her body with her legs. He kissed her, then started moving slowly.

Neither spoke as he thrust into her, his strokes hard and steady. There was a purpose, a tension in their mating that he had never felt before. Almost as if the Goddess herself was there, blessing their union. Even if Sarai wasn't ready to fully admit what was happening between them, he knew they would never be separate again. No matter how far they might be physically, they would always share this connection.

Lifemate.

He kissed her again, deeply. He wanted to mark her as his, make her realize that she would never feel another man's lips again, that his body would be hers for the rest of his life. He thrust harder, and she moaned into his mouth. He took the sound deep within, reveling in it.

Her legs gripped him tightly, and he could feel her body stiffening as she approached her climax. He was close to coming himself, but held back. When they went, they would go together.

He wanted to feel her exploding around his cock, to shoot his seed into her body and claim her.

Her nails were digging into his back now, scraping against him and leaving trails of fire in their wake. The slight pain helped him focus. Down, back. Again. Harder. He twisted his hips, deliberately scraping the length of his arousal against her most sensitive spot. She convulsed in response, and he grunted with satisfaction. She needed him every bit as much as he needed her.

He started moving faster, close to the end of his strength. It was time to push her over the edge. He thrust deeper, harder, again and again. She whimpered, and every muscle in her body stiffened. Her face was twisted with the intensity of her feelings, and she whimpered.

Then she exploded around him, clenching him hard inside and out. He stifled her moaning noises with his mouth, taking them inside and allowing her pleasure to wash through his body. Then he slammed down hard into her and exploded himself, pinning her against the sand with his hard cock and emptying his seed into her body. As the joy and release of his orgasm swept through him, he marveled at the gift he'd been given. This woman was his, and she would be for the rest of his life. He collapsed beside her, and together they gasped for breath.

After what seemed like hours, she stirred against him.

"We should get up before the children see us," she whispered. "But don't think you're getting away from me. We'll continue this tonight, after they go to bed."

"I think they should go to be early," he said, deadpan. She nodded sagely.

"I agree," she replied. "It's been a long day for them. They need their sleep."

* * * * *

Sarai felt light and happy as she they walked back toward town. Able and Mali walked between them, Mali hanging on Jax's hand and giggling. She talked the entire way home, and more than once Able rolled his eyes in disgust.

"She talks too much, Mom," he said for the fourth time. Sarai laughed in response, unable to get upset. She started to reply, but before she could a flash of bright, white light blinded them.

Jax dove, pushing all her and the children into the ditch, covering them with his body. Then sound roared around them, and a terrible wind rose. Sarai wrapped her arms around the children, desperately confused. She could feel herself screaming, but couldn't hear anything. Her ears were ringing, and in an instant she wondered if the world was ending.

Then something hit her head and everything stopped abruptly.

Chapter Nine

She came awake slowly.

The air smelled funny, sterile. She opened her eyes, but she couldn't see anything. She took a deep breath, trying not to panic. What had happened? They had been walking home from the river; how did she get here, and what was wrong with her eyes?

"Please lay still," a smooth female voice said. "You have been injured, and are currently lying in a healing cocoon. If you lay still, I will free you."

"Who are you?" she whispered, her throat dry.

"I am the ship's medical unit," the voice replied in calm tones. "You have been injured, but you are now healed."

"I can't see," she whispered. "And I can't move my arms. Am I blind?"

"No, there are med patches covering your eyes," the voice said. "I am now giving you a sedative. Your heart rate is rising in response to the conditions in which you find yourself, making it difficult for me to extricate you from the healing cocoon. Sleep well."

* * * * *

She woke again, but when she opened her eyes this time she could see. The dim light hurt her eyes. She was lying on a cupped, cushioned bed against the wall. Above her was a canopy, covered in blinking lights.

"You are now free to get up and move around the ship," the disembodied voice said. "Please exercise caution, as your muscles may be slightly stiff from inactivity."

"Where am I?" she asked, leaning up experimentally. Her arms felt strange, weak.

"You are on board the *Serendipity*," the voice said. "The *Serendipity* is a class four cruiser. Our current destination world is Saurellia."

"How did I get here?"

"That information is not contained within my database."

"Where is Jax?" she asked, her voice rising. Panic threatened her again. "Where are my children?"

"That information is not contained within my database."

"You're not much help, are you?" she muttered, then stood. The healing unit wisely remained silent. She clutched the wall for balance, feeling slightly dizzy. Then she realized she was completely naked. She shook her head, trying to think. Everything seemed fuzzy and confusing.

"Is there any clothing in here?" she asked.

"Clothing is located in the cabinet to your left," the voice said.

Moving carefully, Sarai opened the cabinet and pulled out a loose, lightweight shirt and pants that tied at her waist with a drawstring. Then she walked slowly and deliberately to the door. Time to find Jax and the children.

It slid open and she stepped out into a corridor. There were several doors along on either side, and she opened each. All she found were empty bunks. The effort was exhausting, but she kept moving down the corridor. The ship was clearly a small one; they couldn't that be far away.

The corridor opened into a largish room, one that reminded her of the main living area in Seth's ship. The lights were dim here, too, and across the room was a couch, which had been converted into a bed. Sprawled across it was Jax, one child cuddled in each arm. She gave a sigh of relief, and almost collapsed. She was exhausted, and she knew where her children were. She could rest again.

She dropped slowly to her knees, then stretched out on the floor. A small part of her mind whispered that she'd be more comfortable if she could make it to the couch, but that was too much work. She drifted out of consciousness, secure in the knowledge that the children were safe. It was enough.

* * * * *

"Mommy," a small hand was shaking her, and Mali's voice rang urgently in her ear. "Mommy, wake up! Jax! I think Mommy's dead!"

She opened her eyes, meeting Mali's gaze and trying to smile at her.

"I'm all right, sweetie," she said. Mali burst into tears.

"I thought you were dead again, Mommy!"

Again? Sarai wondered.

Then Jax was there, lifting her into his arms. She could hear Able's voice in the background, shrilly telling his sister to be quiet.

"What happened?" she whispered, looking up into his face. He was smiling down at her, his expression filled with love and exhaustion.

"Hector Prime was attacked by imperial troops, Sarai," he said, laying her down on the couch with gentle care. Mali bounded up beside her, burrowing against her side. Sarai clutched the child to her, and looked for Able. He stood off to one side, watching her with concern written all over his face. She gestured to him to join Mali, and his face crumpled in tears as he crawled up beside her.

"Oh, Mom, I was so scared," he whispered. "Jax saved us. We thought you were dead, but you weren't. It was really bad, Mom."

She looked back up at Jax, questions in her eyes. He shook his head, then sat down heavily on the couch beside Able.

"The main blast hit the spaceport as we were walking back from our picnic, he said quietly. "Then they started hitting the smaller towns."

"Why?" she whispered, face filled with confusion. "Hector Prime was neutral, and half the people there were imperial citizens. Students!"

"I don't know," he replied, his voice filled with sorrow. "I suspect we'll be able to find out when we reach Saurellia, but I have no idea why they would do such a thing."

"How did we get here?" she asked, looking around the ship's cabin. "How many survivors are there?"

He didn't meet her eyes, and the true horror of what had happened washed over her.

"We can't be the only survivors," she whispered, eyes filling with tears. She thought of the students who had lived with her these past months, and little Kally from down the street. How could they all be dead?

"We're the only ones I know of," he replied, his voice soft. "I scanned for living humans as soon I got you and the children in the ship, but we were attacked by an imperial patrol ship. I had to get us out of there while I still could."

"Wait," she asked, shaking her head. "Wait a minute. How did we get on this ship? Where did it come from?"

"I called it down out of orbit," Jax said, reaching over to touch her face with one finger. "It's pretty standard among my people to keep an escape ship in orbit when you're traveling with family."

"Traveling with family?"

"Well, if you're anywhere other than Saurellia," he replied. "As soon as I realized you were my lifemate, I made arrangements for us to evacuate if we needed to. I did it the day I went into the spaceport."

She jerked away from him, and Mali squawked in protest.

"You knew something like this could happen, and you didn't warn anyone?"

"No, of course not," he replied, looking startled. "It's just a backup. I had no idea this would happen. If I had even dreamt Hector Prime was a target, I would have taken you away weeks ago. I was just being cautious. It's just dumb luck that we survived, you know. I couldn't even fly the ship close enough to see what happened to the hostel. Too much smoke and radiation."

"Mom, if Jax hadn't been there we'd all be dead right now," Able said quietly, breaking in to the conversation. His face was pinched with concern, and she hugged him close. "And he's been taking real good care of me and Mali while you were sick."

"I realize that, sweetheart," she replied. For once, he didn't protest the endearment. "I was just startled, that's all. Thank you, Jax. Thank you so much for saving me and the children."

"You're welcome," he replied with a smile. "We thought we might lose you for a while. You got hit in the head. Fortunately, the *Serendipity* has a pretty high-end medical unit. Otherwise I doubt you'd still be here."

"We thought you were dead, Mommy," Mali whispered.

"Well, I'm not," she replied, squeezing the little girl tightly.

"I know," Mali replied. "Jax took good care of you."

"Yes, he did," she said softly, looking into his eyes. His face was worn, but his eyes were filled with love for her and the children. Realization hit her, and she knew he had been right all along. They were lifemates. Love welled up inside of her. She blinked back tears, unable to speak. He seemed to understand, though, and leaned toward her, kissing her deeply over the children's heads. She closed her eyes, drinking in the sensation of his touch. Despite the horror they had just escaped, life was very good indeed.

Joanna Wylde

Chapter Ten

Saurellia, Three Months Later

She could get used to this, Sarai thought as she lay back in the grass, cradled in Jax's arms. He had arranged for the children to stay with Calla for the day, insisting that he wanted to show her the sights of his boyhood home alone. It had been an excellent idea, she thought with satisfaction.

Once again they were lying on a picnic blanket, only this time they were naked. Jax was asleep beside her, warmed by the sun and the bottle of wine they'd shared over lunch. Perhaps the fact that they'd made love twice had something to do with it, too, she though wryly. The man was strong, but even he needed a break at times. Of course, getting him to that point was very pleasant.

She leaned up, studying him. There were new lines on his face, the legacy of their disastrous escape from Hector Prime. He'd tried to find out what had happened there, but Saurellian intelligence hadn't been able to tell him. Apparently they were still trying to figure out what had gone wrong…

She still couldn't quite believe everyone she'd known there was gone. For the second time in her life, she'd lost everything. It didn't get easier with practice, she mused. Then she shook her head, trying to clear her sadness. This wasn't a day for regrets. Instead, she focused her attention back on Jax.

He was so handsome. She could hardly believe this strong, kind man was hers. And he hadn't pressured her to into anything, hadn't even asked her to remove her birth control implant. She would, though. She wanted a child with him, a little boy who would grow up to be strong and true like his father. Or perhaps another daughter. He was wonderful with

Mali, wonderful with both the children. She couldn't have found a better father for them.

She trailed her fingers down his bare chest, enjoying the feel of the wiry hairs that covered him. He was waking up, she could tell by the way he tensed under her touch. Then he spoke, his voice a low rumble.

"Just can't quite get enough, can you?" he asked, and she grinned at him.

"Never," she said. She swung her bare leg across his body, rolling on top of him. She wiggled her pelvis experimentally, and his body hardened in response. His hands came down to her hips, pulling her tightly against him.

"That's nice," he said, closing his eyes in pleasure. "Sarai, you feel so good."

She giggled, and squirmed against him.

"So, what should we do now?" she asked, kissing him along his jaw line. His hands tightened in her flesh. He was much harder now, and his hips twitched beneath her.

"I think we should fuck," he said bluntly, and she burst out laughing. He was nothing if not predictable. "Unless you had other plans?" He thrust up at her, and she sighed in satisfaction. She loved the feel of him under her.

Instead of answering, she placed both hands flat on his chest and sat up, still straddling his body with her own. She could feel her nipples tightening in anticipation, and a growing wetness between her legs. His cock was like a pillar of steel between them, and she took pleasure in slipping it back and forth along her vulva and clit. Just the anticipation of that hard length inside her body was enough to drive her crazy.

He reached up to grasp her breasts in his strong hands, massaging them and playing with the nipples. A string of sensation wound its way down through her body from them to that sensitive place between her legs, and she threw her head back and sighed. Then she raised her hips, and reached down with one hand to position his hungry cock. This was going to feel good...

As she sat down on him, taking his length into her body, she could hardly breath. He filled her so tightly. Even after spending months with him she gasped a little as his penis came into her completely. She stilled, allowing herself to get used to his presence. She looked down at him, then slowly leaned over to kiss him. She plunged hungrily into his mouth with her tongue, taking as much as he would give her. For the thousandth time, she marveled at her good fortune. How had she found a man such as this?

She began to move slowly, raising her hips and then sliding them slowly back down over his massive erection. She mimicked each motion with her tongue; enjoying the feeling of power it gave her. She was so free with him; nothing she did threatened his masculinity. She truly was his equal, and she loved it.

She raised her head, braced her hands against his chest and started moving faster. She shook out her hair and laughed as his hands clenched her hips, trying to pull her down against him more tightly. She stopped moving for a second, just to tease him, and he bucked his hips up at her.

"Sarai, you're going to kill me if you don't start moving again," he gasped. With a grin, she started moving, deliberately keeping each stroke slow and steady, twisting as she came down and grinding her clit against his body. It was fantastic. His fingers dug into her, but she didn't care. She was going to take this at her own pace.

But all too soon that pace wasn't fast enough. She moved more quickly, riding him as sensation built up in her body. She was starting to sweat now, and she could feel her heart racing as she moved faster and faster. The feel of him beneath her was incredible. How had she ever thought she could resist this man's touch? They had been created for each other; being with him made her complete.

He had closed his eyes and his head was thrown back as he strained beneath her. She could tell he was getting close to his orgasm; she was, too. Just a little bit longer now, a little harder and she would hit it. She slid up and down his cock as quickly as she could make her body move, breasts bobbing with every motion. Her breathing was harsh and fast, and the tension in her was so tight it was a challenge to control her movements. Just a little more and she would have it. Down. Again. Harder.

Then it washed over her with the force of a storm. She ground her clit against him, screaming out her orgasm. Every muscle in her body clenched, and she could feel his seed spurting within her as he came, too. He cried out, and she collapsed against his body, panting. They lay in silence for several moments, then he spoke.

"Sarai, that was pretty good," he murmured. She swatted at him playfully.

"That was more than good, and you know it!" she said with a laugh. He laughed back at her, then pulled her close for a kiss.

"Yes, it was," he replied. "But it's still not everything. I have this fantasy about you…"

"Oh really, and what would that be?" she asked archly.

"Let me show you," he replied. He rolled her off him abruptly, and pulled her to her feet. Then he took her hand and started running. She stumbled after him, laughing but confused.

"What are you doing? You're crazy!"

"Just wait and see," he replied.

Within minutes they reached a shallow river, crystal clear water running over rounded stones.

"This way," he said, slowing to a walk. He took her along a little dirt path through the brush along the riverbank, until it opened into a wide sandbar. To one side was the river. A line of stones had been placed across it, creating a swimming hole.

"My brothers and I built this when we were kids," he said, pointing out toward it. "We used to swim here all summer long. My sister's children do the same thing. They've kept it in good shape even after all these years. Come swimming with me, Sarai."

She stilled, looking up into his face.

"Jax, you know I can't swim," she said, her voice serious.

"It isn't deep here, Sarai," he replied in a reassuring voice. "Only about four feet at the deepest spot. The water's slow, and I'll be with you."

"If I drown, I'm coming back to haunt you," she said darkly, but she followed him down to the water. He wouldn't let anything happen to her. They waded into the cool water holding hands, then he let go, falling backward and swimming away from her. Within seconds he had reached the center of the pool, and stood up.

"See, you'll be able to touch out here," he said encouragingly. She nodded, and started toward him. The rocks were slippery and rounded, hard to walk on, and she stumbled. The cold water closed over her head, but before she could panic he was there, pulling her up against his body.

"I've got you," he whispered into her ear. Then he kissed her, running his hands down along her back. She wiggled against him, arms wrapped around his neck. The water gave her a kind of buoyancy that was new and different. For the first time she realized swimming might be fun.

"I like this," she said, pulling her head away from his. She lifted her legs, effortlessly wrapping them around his waist. Despite the cold water, he was hard for her. Her face twisted in amusement. "Does that thing ever get tired?"

"No," Jax said smugly. "Not when you're around."

Pleased with his answer, she wiggled against him, and he groaned.

"You're trying to kill me, aren't you?" he gasped.

"Nope, just reminding you who's in charge," she replied pertly.

"We'll see who's in charge."

With that, he started striding through the water, carrying her with him as she squealed in protest. Then he was setting her up on a large, smooth rock that almost, but not quite, reached the surface of the water. He pinned her there with his body, legs firmly thrust between hers.

"Now you're at my mercy," he said. He kissed her again, taking her mouth savagely until she could hardly breathe. At the same time, he reached down between them, fingering her aching clit as sensation wound its way through her. She wanted him again—she could never have enough of him. Finally, they pulled away from the kiss, gasping for breath.

"Now that I'm at your mercy," she whispered, squirming against his fingers, "What are you going to do with me?"

"This," he replied, voice tight with tension. The smooth, round head of his penis replaced his fingers, then he was pushing into her with aching slowness. Both of his hands wrapped around her waist, and she leaned back as his mouth came down on her breasts. He kissed her, then pulled one nipple into his warm mouth, sucking in time with the slow, steady movements of his hips. It was exquisite.

But it wasn't enough.

She twisted against him, trying to make him move faster. She wanted to feel his entire length come into her hard, filling her until she couldn't breathe any longer.

"All good things come to those who wait," he said piously, lifting his head to smirk at her.

"To hell with that," she replied. "I don't want to wait anymore. I want you now, Jax."

He grinned fiercely at her, then pulled back and thrust into her with a force that made her gasp. He moved quickly, slamming her back against the rock with every stroke. A part of her realized she'd probably be left with bruises, but she didn't care. All that mattered was the feeling of him pounding into her body.

Each motion brought her a little closer, and the familiar spiral of sensation started closing around her. She clutched him to her with her arms, and tried to wrap her legs around his waist. But the water made everything slippery and she couldn't keep hold of him. Then the sensations built again, and she no longer cared. She went limp in his arms, allowing him to take her as he chose.

The cold water swirled around them, but she hardly noticed its cool kiss on her skin. All she could think about was the tension building in her body. It was urgent, compelling. She had to fix it, to climb over it, to get relief. Otherwise it would crush her.

He angled her hips down slightly, and then his cock was rubbing along her clit in a whole new way. Each stroke pushed her higher, and she could feel her muscles tightening. His erection scraped against her clit again and again, plunging in to hit bottom with every stroke, and her hips started twitching. The sensation was so intense it was painful, but she couldn't allow him to stop. She needed this; she needed him.

"Jax," she gasped, then flew apart in climax, unable to control herself any longer. She broke into a thousand pieces, and sagged against him. He kept moving a moment longer, then joined her. She could feel his hot seed pumping into her body, and for a moment she fantasized about what it would feel like to carry his child.

With any luck, she'd find out before too long.

"I love you," he gasped against her shoulder, and she squeezed him tightly.

"I love you, too," she replied.

They stayed there for several minutes, until the coldness of the water started seeping into her. Startled, she realized she was shivering, and Jax was covered with goose bumps.

"I think we should get out of the water," she said. With a smile, he swung her up in his arms and strode toward the bank.

* * * * *

"All you have to do is sign right here," the beautiful lady told Mali, pointing to a black line on the paper. She looked up at her mother, who smiled encouragingly. Able snorted in disgust. Once again, Mali just couldn't seem to figure out what to do, despite the fact that he'd been practicing with her for days. He looked up at Jax, hoping he wasn't too upset by the delay. The last thing they needed was for him to change his mind now.

Jax just gave him a wink and smiled. Able sighed. If Jax wasn't upset, then things weren't too bad. It would be all right. Mali was now slowly and painfully writing her name, copying the letters that mom had written out for her. Bored, he looked around, trying to remember everyone's names. Jax's whole family was there, along with Aunt Calla. Seth was there too. Able had never liked Seth, but he sure seemed to make Aunt Calla happy. They were even going to have a baby, although Able couldn't understand why. All Mali had ever done as a baby was poop and cry. *Boring.*

The beautiful lady was clapping her hands to catch everyone's attention. Mali was done signing the paper, finally. The lady spoke.

"As Priestess of this temple, I now solemnly declare before the Goddess and these people assembled here that Jax Falconer has asked for and been given legal and spiritual parenthood over these children, Able and Mali. From this day forward, they will be known publicly as Able and Mali Falconer, of the House of Falconer. They will share equally in the rights, privileges and responsibilities of that House, along with their father. Let the Goddess' will be unquestioned."

Everyone started cheering and clapping. Mom was even crying. Then Jax kneeled down, and held out his hand for a solemn handshake. Able responded, trying to keep his grip firm and manly.

"I am so honored to have you for my son," Jax said quietly. "Thank you, Able, for accepting me."

"I'm just doing it for mom and Mali," Able said gruffly. His eyes felt all weird and watery, and his nose was starting to run. For one horrible minute he thought he might start crying. But before that could happen, Jax nodded knowingly.

"I know that," he replied. "You and I have the same job, taking care of them. Good thing we know how to work together."

"Yup," Able said thankfully. He and Jax were the men of the family now. It *was* a good thing they could work together. Mali was flinging herself into Jax's arms, and then mom was kneeling beside him, hugging him close. It felt pretty good, Able thought. He liked being a family.

Jax set Mali down, and she tugged on Able's sleeve.

"It wasn't a stupid wish, you know," she said smugly. He looked down at her blankly.

"What are you talking about?" he asked in confusion, looking around to see if anyone had heard her. No one seemed to have noticed.

"To wish that we had a daddy," Mali said, rolling her eyes impatiently. "Remember, I wished that we had a daddy, and now we have one. What do you think I should wish for next?"

"You just got lucky," Able snorted. "Wishes aren't real."

"Really?" Mali said. "Well, then I'm going to make another wish, just to prove that you're wrong. I wish that you'll meet a girl and fall in love and get all silly. Then you won't be able to make fun of me any more. I'll make fun of you!"

"Mali, that's just stupid," he said.

"We'll see," Mali said smugly. She turned away from him as Aunt Calla swept her up in a hug. Silly girl.

"Able, I want you to come and meet your new cousins," Jax said, pulling him through the crowd. After several moments they broke through the mass of people, and came face to face with a group of five children. They eyed him curiously. They all shared similar features, dark black hair, bright green eyes.

"These are my sister's children," Jax said. "Devon, Julian, Marcus, Luke and Anita, the baby of the family. We call her Nini."

Nini stepped forward, and Able's jaw dropped. She was the prettiest little girl he'd ever seen in his life, and he had the sudden urge to reach forward and pull one of her long, black braids. The largest of the boys, Julian, seemed to read his mind. He stepped forward protectively.

"You can play with us if you like," he said. "But you have to be nice to Nini, or we'll get you."

"You have to be nice to my sister, too," Able said, bristling. Nini laughed, breaking the tension. She stepped forward, put both hands on Able's shoulders and stood on her tiptoes, giving him a quick kiss on the cheek.

"I like you, Able," she said brightly. "We're going to have a lot of fun together."

He couldn't help himself. He didn't think at all, he just reached up and pulled one of those braids as hard as he could. She screeched in protest, and he took off running, dodging through the crowd. All four of those boys would be on him in seconds, and he was pretty sure he was gonna die.

It had been worth it, though. That Nini was pretty cute…

Also by JOANNA WYLDE:

- Price of Pleasure
- Price of Freedom
- Dragon's Mistress
- Aphrodite's Touch anthology with Lanette Curington

About the authors:

Stephanie Burke, Marly Chance, and Joanna Wylde welcome mail from readers. You can write to them c/o Ellora's Cave Publishing at P.O. Box 787, Hudson, Ohio 44236-0787.

Why an electronic book?

We live in the Information Age—an exciting time in the history of human civilization in which technology rules supreme and continues to progress in leaps and bounds every minute of every hour of every day. For a multitude of reasons, more and more avid literary fans are opting to purchase e-books instead of paperbacks. The question to those not yet initiated to the world of electronic reading is simply: *why?*

1. *Price.* An electronic title at Ellora's Cave Publishing runs anywhere from 40-75% less than the cover price of the <u>exact same title</u> in paperback format. Why? Cold mathematics. It is less expensive to publish an e-book than it is to publish a paperback, so the savings are passed along to the consumer.

2. *Space.* Running out of room to house your paperback books? That is one worry you will never have with electronic novels. For a low one-time cost, you can purchase a handheld computer designed specifically for e-reading purposes. Many e-readers are larger than the average handheld, giving you plenty of screen room. Better yet, hundreds of titles can be stored within your new library—a single microchip. (Please note that Ellora's Cave does not endorse any specific brands. You can check our website at www.ellorascave.com for

customer recommendations we make available to new consumers.)

3. *Mobility.* Because your new library now consists of only a microchip, your entire cache of books can be taken with you wherever you go.

4. *Personal preferences are accounted for.* Are the words you are currently reading too small? Too large? Too...**ANNOYING**? Paperback books cannot be modified according to personal preferences, but e-books can.

5. *Innovation.* The way you read a book is not the only advancement the Information Age has gifted the literary community with. There is also the factor of what you can read. Ellora's Cave Publishing will be introducing a new line of interactive titles that are available in e-book format only.

6. *Instant gratification.* Is it the middle of the night and all the bookstores are closed? Are you tired of waiting days — sometimes weeks — for online and offline bookstores to ship the novels you bought? Ellora's Cave Publishing sells instantaneous downloads 24 hours a day, 7 days a week, 365 days a year. Our e-book delivery system is 100% automated, meaning your order is filled as soon as you pay for it.

Those are a few of the top reasons why electronic novels are displacing paperbacks for many an avid reader. As always, Ellora's Cave Publishing welcomes your questions and comments. We invite you to email us at service@ellorascave.com or write to us directly at: P.O. Box 787, Hudson, Ohio 44236-0787.